Denial of Service

By Maddi Davidson

Denial of Service

Outsourcing Murder

Denial of Service

A Miss-Information Technology Mystery

Maddi Davidson

ISBN: 1478273445
ISBN-13: 978-1478273448

Dedication

To Pretzel, the original chesty puller, and to the many friends and family who have encouraged us to write, penned glowing reviews, purchased books, and shamelessly shilled them – in particular, our mother, the woman who knows everybody, and Cheryl Thomas, owner of Chapter One Bookstore in Ketchum, Idaho, for her one-woman marketing campaign. *Mahalo nui loa* to you all!

Acknowledgements

We gratefully acknowledge the wonderful Hawaiian music and talented Hawaiian musicians that we refer to in *Denial of Service* and *Outsourcing Murder*. Hawaiian music has been part of our lives since we were children and it continues to be a source of joy for us.

Our parents, living in Hawai'i during our father's military service, enjoyed the Kalima Brothers (known as "1000 Pounds of Melody"). You can still buy the Kalima Brothers' music on www.amazon.com or www.mele.com.

One of Emma's favorite groups (and one of ours) is Maunalua – Bobby Moderow, Richard Gideon and Kahi Kaonohi. Nobody does "Koke'e" better than they do and they generously have performed it for us upon request. When in Hawai'i, we arrange our schedule so we can hear Maunalua play. You can find more about them and their music at www.maunalua.com.

Special *mahalo nui loa* to 'Ike Pono – Michael Lowe, Bobby Yu, and Stan Oshiro – whose music inspires and delights us, and who are three of the nicest guys and most talented musicians you'll ever meet. We'd drive miles – and have – to listen to them, and it is always so very well worth it. You can find out more about them and buy their music at www.ikeponomusic.com. We strongly recommend their *Deep Waters* CD. If there is a better Hawaiian song than "Ka Ho'olauna," we don't know what it is. Extra special thanks for letting Keoni "sub" for Stan. We love you guys!

PROLOGUE

You can tell a lot about a woman by examining her purse. Anyone looking in mine would see I'm a surfer (the bar of surf wax), on the girly side (lip balm, a pretty shade of lipstick with matching lip gloss and an only slightly clumpy waterproof mascara I should have thrown out last month) who fully expects to be attacked (pepper spray, whistle, can of mace and Shrieker, all courtesy of an overprotective mother). It's clear that I participate in numerous loyalty programs, including racking up miles on United and Hawaiian Airlines and Resuscitation Points from Elixir of Life, my favorite caffeine haunt.

What I do not want but have nonetheless acquired is a Copious Corpse Card, earned for finding three dead bodies in five months. No, I don't own a search and rescue dog and I'm not appending this dubious accomplishment to my résumé.

The first bona fide stiff was my boss Padmanabh (rhymes with what-a-snob). Since I found the body and didn't like him – hardly anybody did – I was a prime suspect for a few weeks until the real perp tried to off me. He was stopped by my cricket bat-wielding rescuer who left the killer dazed just long enough for the cops to arrive. My mother was thrilled that I'd used her gift of pepper spray whilst fleeing the murderer and concluded that I could use more self-defense gizmos, so she bought me a baseball bat, the local sports store having been fresh out of cricket bats. She also gave me a gift certificate for a self-defense class, or was it batting lessons?

The second stiff was a wave hog I'd had a fight with – maybe several fights with – in the lineup at my favorite surf break, who turned up dead under my car. I hadn't helped matters by asking the cops whether they ever watched *CSI*: I had no bruises on my hands, the wave hog outweighed me by seventy-five pounds so, as any idiot could see, it couldn't have been me. The "any idiot" comment did not earn me any brownie points with the police – just a few more Police Potential Perp Points – but, in my defense, I had been surfing for two hours, was as cold as a seal's butt on an ice floe, and I was experiencing severe carbohydrate deficiency. When the police found the baseball bat in my trunk (thanks a lot, Mom), it was enough for them to put my prospective Hawai'i trip on hold, a trip I had planned in order to wind down from my previous murder investigation. Eventually, they determined the bat was clean and Wave Hog had died from a head slam to a concrete parking block.

I should introduce myself before I uncover, so to speak, corpse number three who is, after all, as dead as Ugg boots with miniskirts and not going anywhere. My name is Emma Elizabeth Jones, and I am most definitely not a private investigator, detective, beat cop, sidekick or girlfriend of any of the above. Although with friends and family I make light of being a corpse magnet, I have recurrent nightmares of the freshly dead.

I work for GD Consulting, a group that offers information technology services to Fortune 500 companies and barely-there organizations. When I am not traveling on various consulting gigs or jumping on a plane to Hawai'i for warm water surfing with my recently on-again *'ipo* (sweetie) Keoni, I might be hanging out with my best friend Stacey. I live in a one-bedroom apartment in San Francisco. Though it's not part of the rental agreement, my landlady Magda offers stellar concierge services: she waters plants, takes in packages and floral deliveries, and keeps the cops from messing up tenants' underwear drawers while executing a search warrant. She has also been known to drop off homemade goodies for tenants who have had a hard week, or throw an extra jigger of booze in the drink she makes for gin and sympathy sessions on her couch. After the number of stiffs I've tripped over recently, I've needed a fair bit of both.

If Magda sounds like a saint, she isn't. She has a temper like Kīlauea erupting, and it is never more on display than when someone is disrespecting the military. Since both of her husbands and two sons served in the military, I figure she's got the right to get hot under her elegant mandarin collar if someone trashes the troops.

Which brings me to corpse number three, a card-carrying, protest-leading, anti-military agitator named Laguna Butterfield. I discovered her body three days after Magda threatened to kill her.

ONE

"Argument is the worst
sort of conversation."
– Jonathan Swift

NOBODY CAN DELIVER THE GOODS like Aretha. "All I'm askin', woo, is for a little respect, woo." I bopped and sang along as I searched for a parking spot in which to stash my 1995 Honda CRX, always an elusive commodity in the Cow Hollow neighborhood I lived in. It was hard for me not to sing and sway with the music when Aretha got hold of a tune and wrapped her vocal cords around it. I'm sure I looked like an idiot to the other drivers – and scary when I'd pump my arms at the chorus – but I didn't give a darn. There are more than a few village idiots who've migrated to what one of the old-time columnists for the *San Francisco Chronicle* called "Baghdad-by-the-Bay," so I am in good company if I want to act like a loony. Here, almost everybody not only marches to her own drummer, but a distinctly offbeat one at that.

I'd left work on that mid-November Friday in a pretty good mood. Earlier in the week I had started a new assignment at Zuckers Confectionaries, a global candy company that had hired Grant and Denholm Consulting (GD), my employer, to help convert Carson, a recently acquired boutique candy company, to Zuckers' technology systems. My GPS system had assured me that my apartment in San Francisco was a mere forty minutes away from Zuckers' headquarters, except during Critical Mass, the once-a-month mayhem when bicyclists whiz through populous SF neighborhoods ignoring all the stop signs and jamming up traffic for an hour or more while commuters are returning home at the end of the work week.

As usual upon leaving work, I'd plugged my iPod into the car FM stereo to listen to Hawaiian music, whose soothing harmonies cooled me off like the fabled trade winds so that I could endure the centipede-like crawl in the East Bay. I was *da kine* until one too many SUV's cut me off and my iPod shuffle selected "Ka Māmakakaua," a war-like chant written by Palani Vaughan. Sudden Onset Road Rage made me want to channel King Kamehameha's warriors and shove the SUVs off the road. As I moved into aggressive driving mode, I switched my playlist to Vent and began to sing along with the likes of Kelly Clarkson ("Since U Been Gone"), Carrie Underwood ("Before He Cheats") and Aretha ("Respect").

The City was fogged in, as is so often the case, and the frowning skies and damp-drenched air soon chilled my anger. As I neared home, a black BMW pulled out of a space just in front of me – hallelujah! – and I swooped in with my Honda. I sat for a moment or two, as Aretha and I powered down while three people drove by with desperate expressions and raised eyebrows, the universally-recognized distress signal for "Are you vacating that space anytime soon?"

Still pumped about getting Respect, I made a quick two-block walk to my apartment located in an unprepossessing three-story building largely indistinguishable from the bank of decades-old stucco structures that comprised the area, unless you spotted on the uppermost floor the large Fresnel lens one of my fellow tenants had mounted in his window.

In a city with as many drivers and as few parking spaces as San Francisco, guerilla rules parking is the norm. Fed-up residents take matters into their own hands – or brushes – and paint red areas on the curb gray so they can park there "legally." Or they cut a hole in the bottom of a trash bin and drop it over the nearest fire hydrant. I opt for driving a small car that just fits into the teeny spaces between garages – the ones that Urban Assault Vehicles can't fit their bumpers in.

I opened the front door, grabbed my mail from the ancient, creaking iron mail slot, then proceeded through the door to the front hallway, stepping into the middle of a war – or at least, verbal salvos – between my landlady and another tenant standing at the bottom of the staircase.

"Your brother fought and died for your freedoms. You're dishonoring his memory and his service," my landlady Magda proclaimed, her hands clenched on her hips. Her back towards me, I imagined rather than saw her jutting chin and narrowed eyes, a visage I'd seen before when Magda was up in arms. A shade over five feet, impeccably dressed in a city where dressing up usually meant designer blue jeans, Magda Basilone is a combination of aging cover girl and drill sergeant.

"Stop talking about my brother," said the woman a scant three feet from Magda. "You didn't even know him. I loved my brother but invading other countries is wrong, wrong, wrong." Magda's opponent was a stocky woman – about my height, five foot seven, but easily forty pounds heavier than my size six ... okay, size eight frame. She had curly red hair and more metal in her face than could successfully pass through airport security. Her voice rose several decibels as she spit out the "wrongs." She held a peace symbol-emblazoned sign affixed to a sharp metal pole, which she pounded on the polished wooden floor with each "wrong," prompting a metallic ringing to echo in the hallway.

So intent were the combatants on their exchange that neither noticed when I flitted across the hallway to the sturdy wooden table strewn with magazines, packages and fliers – everything too big to fit in our miniscule mailboxes. If only I had a grappling hook, I could hop on the table, throw the hook to the next floor and climb my way to peace and quiet: anything to avoid walking by the escalating altercation.

While pretending to sort through the items on the table, I peered at Magda's opponent. This must be Laguna Butterfield, the new tenant. For her sake, I hoped gold body rings were cheaper by the dozen: she sported a lip ring, a hoop through her right eyebrow, assorted sizes of rings in her ears and a diamond nose stud. Laguna had a good seven inches and three pounds of jewelry on Magda, but Magda trumped Laguna on decibels.

Chesty, Magda's miniature dachshund puppy, strained at his leash and barked loudly at Laguna. He made a huge racket for such a little dog and showed plenty of teeth, though I knew from experience that he'd be more likely to lick an intruder to death than bite one.

"You have the freedom," Magda said, emphasizing the last word, "to express your opinions, however wrong, wrong, wrong they may be. And I will not be quiet in the face of disregard for our military. Nor will I allow you to mess up the courtyard with your sign painting. And stop banging that sign and scratching up my floors," she added, her voice becoming louder. Typical Magda: escalation through full frontal verbal assault until she was an exclamation point away from fixed bayonets.

"Fine," Laguna threw back. "But you can't stop me from walking wherever I want with my sign: in the courtyard, in front of this building or up and down these stairs if I want to."

Chesty had fallen strangely silent. He sniffed intently at the metal pole holding Laguna's placard. Then, coming to an enigmatic doggy conclusion, he lifted his leg.

Laguna, staring at Magda, almost missed it. At the last moment, she noticed the movement at her feet. She snatched her sign away from Chesty and simultaneously pushed him with her foot – a push that turned into an off-balance kick.

Chesty's yip of pain was a clarion call to Magda. Racing forward, she knelt down, grabbed Chesty and enfolded him in her arms before turning her wrath upon Laguna. "What the hell do you think you're doing?" she bellowed. "Lay a hand on my dog and I'll ..."

"You'll what? There's no law against kicking vicious dogs."

"You touch my dog again and you're a dead woman."

"Then keep your damned dog away from me!" Laguna lifted her sign to her shoulder, waggled her placard and flashed a peace sign before flouncing up the stairs. She paused at the landing, turned her head and stuck out her tongue before resuming her swagger up the stairs. With her red face, red hair and stocky body encased in a red tracksuit, she reminded me of a saucy fire hydrant. No wonder Chesty had lifted his leg.

Magda murmured endearments to Chesty and stroked his silky red ears, but far from calming down at her ministrations, he squirmed vigorously in her embrace until she was forced to put him down. He raced toward the stairs and slid to a halt, almost banging into the first step as he barked at Laguna's retreating figure, his faux ferocity well short of rabid dog. Eventually, he ceased barking and flopped down, his short legs splayed out on the wood, as if the effort had worn him out.

"Good doggy," said Magda, walking over to scratch his head. "You tell her. Did the mean old wacko hurt you, precious? You have mommy's permission to anoint her shoes next time."

I cleared my throat. "Well, that was entertaining."

Magda turned on me with a glower that immediately vanished when she recognized me.

"Emma! Oh dear. I'm so sorry you had to see that. And hear it. I tried to hold it together but really, the nicest thing I can say about Laguna is … I wouldn't waste a bullet, of any caliber." She scooped up Chesty, nestled him in the crook of her arm and started toward her half-opened door. She paused for a moment with her hand on the polished brass knob. "Join me in a drink? I could really use one."

Magda's apartment reflected her peripatetic life as a military wife. She'd collected furniture and *objets d'art* from the many places she'd been stationed as a Marine wife (her first husband, a sergeant, had been killed in Vietnam) and an Air Force officer's wife. Her second husband had retired as a lieutenant colonel and shortly thereafter dropped dead of a heart attack on the eighteenth hole of the best round of golf he'd ever played. "Which," Magda often said, "is all many men aspire to in retirement." Pictures of her husbands in uniform at various ages, ranks and duty stations and of her children and grandchildren covered her end tables and bookcase shelves. The room was full of colors and textures: the jewel tones of her Oriental rugs, the golden glow of her highly polished brass coffee table, and the dark lacquer of her Chinese Coromandel screen. The refined ambiance of most of her furnishings contrasted with what Magda referred to as her "bloody box" – a display case with multiple unsheathed knives including her first husband's father's Ka-Bar knife with which he had, according to Magda, "efficiently dispatched four Japanese in hand-to-hand fighting on Peleliu." Wherever that was.

"What'll you have?" Magda asked as she put Chesty in a wing chair with a last loving pat after which his long pink tongue lapped at her face. "I'm having a TKE." Magda had introduced me to the TKE – Ted Kennedy Express – last summer. It was a G and T with just enough tonic that it wasn't technically a GAG, gin and gin, or GWTL, gin with token lime. It came with a "do not drive, operate heavy equipment, balance your checkbook or do much of anything for the next several hours" admonition from Magda. That assumed you could focus your eyes to find your keys, much less put the correct key in the ignition. Also assuming you remembered where you parked your car and what city you were in.

I wasn't in the mood for heavy drinking. "Do you have any white wine open?" A small glass appealed as I wasn't planning on going anywhere tonight, except to my door when the delivery guy showed up with an Amici's extra large Philadelphia pizza with mushrooms.

"Of course." Magda hummed "The Marines' Hymn" as she milled about the kitchen, poured me a glass of Riesling and fixed herself a TKE in a tall cut-glass tumbler with crushed ice, fresh lime, diet tonic and Junipero, a locally-made gin.

Five minutes later I was sitting on the couch with drink in hand. Magda offered me St. Andre cheese, artisanal crackers and kibble from a Chinese lacquer tray. I took the cheese and crackers but passed on the kibble. Chesty had vacated the wing chair to sit at Magda's feet. His little red paws splayed out carelessly as he intently watched the proceedings, woofing from time to time for someone to throw him a piece of kibble. Edson, Magda's Maine Coon cat, reclined in splendor on the back of the coral camelback sofa, radiating boredom until Magda brought out shrimp for him, at which point he meowed "peel me a shrimp" in kitty-ese.

"So," I began, "what's going on?"

Magda picked up a cracker and spread cheese on it so hard the cracker broke. "I didn't just go to Defcon 3 overnight. You haven't been here much over the past two months, so you've missed the build-up."

I nodded. "I've been in San Diego and Phoenix on consulting projects. But even when I am home, I rarely hear anything through the walls." Occasionally, I heard Calvin Shaw playing jazz piano on top of me, but the noise only penetrated the floor when he played "It Ain't Necessarily So," so I couldn't complain.

"I'm glad for that, because we've recently escalated to yelling. Laguna moved in nearly three months ago. I didn't find out until she'd been here a couple of weeks that she was a leftwing lunatic Lime-O."

"S'cuse me?"

"You know, a Lime-O. One of those crazies who hate the military."

I'd heard of them – the Lime Organization or Lime-O for short. "I get them mixed up with the Code Pink group," I said. "Both seem fixated on colors that scream golf course or Easter Sunday."

"All of the same ilk," Magda responded. "I found out while chatting with Laguna one day that she works full time for Lime-O in accounting. But it isn't just a job for her – she protests whenever she can. And if there is anything worse than having an antimilitary crackpot as a tenant, it's having one that brings in her leftwing lunatic friends for antiwar activities. They had the nerve to stick their antiwar literature in my tenants' mailboxes and on cars in the neighborhood. One of them even put a 'Peace Now' bumper sticker over the 'U.S. Marine Corps' decal on my car!" Magda broke another cracker as she roughly plopped St. Andre on it.

Some things can't be done well while in a bad mood. I grabbed the second spreader and gently eased the cheese onto a cracker, handing it to Magda before making one for myself. Four full moon eyes gazed at me in waiflike fixation, so I peeled a shrimp for Edson and threw a couple of pieces of kibble into Chesty's open mouth.

"I would think protesting was a condition of employment at Lime-O," I said. "Just like you can't work at Baskin Robbins and be anti-dairy."

Magda gave a slight shrug as if acknowledging my point. "What really galls me about Laguna is that her brother was an Army Ranger."

"Is he also a Lime-O member?"

"He was killed in Afghanistan."

"Ah. Laguna told you all this?"

Magda nodded. "I asked her if she even knew anyone in the military. So many of these wackos haven't a clue about our soldiers and sailors."

"Obviously, Laguna does."

"Her brother fought for this country, and now Laguna is protesting against everything he stood for ..." Magda's voice rose.

"Maybe she doesn't know how else to deal with his death," I said as I tried not to imagine my older brother Virgil or younger sister Ariadne returning from overseas in a flag-draped coffin. My grandfather had served in Korea, but that was my family's only association with the military. That, and the West Point washout Ariadne had briefly dated: one of a trail of boyfriends she had left in her wake during her freshman year at UC San Diego.

"Goodness knows there was a lot of anti-war anger during the Vietnam War based on the loss of life. Back then many young men were drafted into the military. But Laguna's brother was a volunteer: he knew he could go to war, and he knew the potential consequences. Her actions in protesting against the military dishonor everything he stood for."

She stuffed an entire cracker in her mouth and her eyes bulged. Whether she was beginning to choke on the cracker or with anger, I couldn't tell. She took a large swig of her TKE.

"I think Chesty would like another treat." I hoped that focusing on the dog would distract Magda. Hearing his name and the 'T'-word, Chesty wagged his tail and started yo-yoing: jumping up and down and twirling in anticipation of a handout. I'd had the same reaction to a new caffeinated concoction at Elixir of Life. Though I'd stopped just short of pawing Shaun the Barista and barking at him for more sprinkles. Only just.

"Oh, right. Poor little tyke. You need more kibble to keep your strength up so you can bark at all those crazy Lime-Os." Magda tossed a few nuggets to Chesty. He tried to catch them in his mouth and I laughed as one hit his nose and flew over his head. Sniffing around Magda's feet, he finally located his treat and gobbled it gratefully. He raced back to her feet and yipped insistently, the doggie equivalent of "more, more, more." Edson, doubtless feeling left out, yowled for another shrimp. I peeled a couple and put one between his neatly aligned paws, which he began daintily nibbling.

"I take it that Chesty doesn't like Laguna, either."

"Not at all. Perceptive little fellow. His aggressiveness towards her comes from his namesake."

"Chesty Puller," Magda added at my raised eyebrows.

I reached for another cheese and cracker, trying to think. "Uh, I don't get it. I've heard you call him that, but I thought it was because he has a deep chest and he pulls on his leash."

"Good heavens, no," she laughed. "He's named for Lieutenant General Lewis Burwell 'Chesty' Puller: the most decorated U.S. Marine in history, including five Navy Crosses. Chesty outranks Edson," she said, nodding to the cat.

"Sorry?" I said, now totally confused.

"Edson is named after Major General Merritt Austin Edson, also of the U.S. Marine Corps and a recipient of the Medal of Honor."

"I didn't realize I was in such august company. I'll treat these two with more respect from now on." I threw each one a mock salute. Edson twitched his tail and narrowed his eyes, deeply focused on the second peeled shrimp, which I placed at his feet. If he were channeling his namesake, I expected nothing less than an imminent frontal assault on the shrimp. Chesty sat on my foot and wagged his tail for more kibble.

"See that you do." Magda held up a bit of kibble and said to Chesty, "Semper fi!" in response to which he woofed enthusiastically. She dropped a nugget in his open mouth. He swallowed the kibble without chewing and sat at attention. With his short hair, muscular forearms and perfect posture, he was the very picture of a Marine, albeit a short one.

"So, how have you been, Emma? I haven't seen much of you lately. You always seem to be on your way to or from the airport."

"Good," I replied as I grabbed another cracker. "I started this week on a new assignment in Oakland. We're doing a project for Zuckers, so I'll be around a lot more. I might also be a lot more round – they have big bowls of candy in all their conference rooms. It will be constant 'get thee behind me, Satan' working there, especially if Satan is offering dark chocolate."

"I'm a sucker for their Shock-o-lade bars with almonds," Magda said. "Sounds like a sweet assignment, but I detect a lack of enthusiasm in your voice."

"No, just tired," I replied.

"And how's your love life?"

"Oh, that. Keoni is coming for Christmas," I said, smiling. I couldn't help it. I could feel my smile widen and my face burn.

"Hmm. Serious, is it?"

"Well," I said, hesitating. Keoni and I had been serious when we were attending the University of Hawai'i and for a year afterward when we maintained a long distance, San Francisco-Honolulu relationship. We broke it off when it was clear he would never leave Hawai'i.

"Are you or aren't you?" asked Magda.

"I don't know," I confessed. "Getting back together this summer, well, it was almost like old times. But Hawai'i is still his home and I still want to have a career."

"And yet, whenever we chat, you seem ambivalent about your work."

I remained silent. Consulting wasn't turning out to be what I expected when I joined GD. I'd been under the impression that I'd be "designing, building and implementing innovative solutions for market-leading companies." That's what GD's recruiting brochure stated. And to be fair, I had worked on interesting issues for a variety of well-run companies in consumer product and service industries. Rather than tech work, however, all too often I'd find myself up to my neck in calculating metrics and costs, or discussing font choices for customer presentations. Nobody except a typesetter wants a career pushing Palatino 12-point.

"What about that other guy you surf with: tall, handsome and never without a cup of coffee?" Magda said, interrupting my musings about the critical differences between Calibri and Verdana fonts.

"Huw? He's just a friend. I've been giving him surfing lessons. In fact, we're going surfing tomorrow."

Magda nodded. "One can't be too rich or have too many boyfriends, particularly ones who enjoy vigorous physical exercise," she said, with a twinkle in her eye. She picked up the Chinese lacquer tray, now empty except for cracker crumbs and two pieces of kibble, and placed it on the ground for Chesty to lick.

"Or be too thin," I added, hooking my thumb into my waistband to ease the pressure on my now full stomach. Zuckers not only made great chocolate, but they had an assortment of tasty candies. I'd been liberally sampling their Z's: sweet and sour candy balls in a variety of fruit flavors including lick-em lemon, outrageous orange, cheerful cherry, and great grape. I had a vision of myself surfing with Keoni, twenty pounds heavier and resembling a baby orca in my wetsuit. I'd better rein in my sweet tooth, at least until Christmas. Hawaiian culture of old might value an *'ōpū nui* (big stomach) but that didn't mean I wanted Keoni to see me with one.

"By the way," Magda said, "I hope you found a parking space close by."

"I did. Why?"

"There have been disturbing incidents in the neighborhood lately. Aggressive panhandlers have moved in and two weeks ago a young couple was robbed at gunpoint a block away. I worry about tenants leaving early in the morning or coming in late at night. Particularly at this time of year, when it gets dark early."

"Thanks for telling me. I'll be careful. Just don't tell my mother about the uptick in the crime rate. I don't have room in my purse for any more self-defense gizmos. She'd give me my own personal ninja warrior if she could figure out how to fit him in my backpack." Mother's obsessive arming of me with self-defense gizmos was a result of her near rape as a young woman. She'd used a can of mace to escape and ever since had been a proponent of women carrying personal protection devices.

"It is a good idea to have something for self-defense." Magda advised. "My personal favorite is a Smith & Wesson 9mm: a bit large, but packs a nice punch. Although, it's next to impossible to get a concealed carry permit in California unless you know the sheriff. Maybe your best deterrent is to carry the baseball bat – it'll ward off everything except a well-thrown curve ball."

TWO

"The best surfer out there is the
one having the most fun."
– Henry David Thoreau

"'*ŌKOLE PUKA!*" I SPAT under my breath at an Urban Assault Vehicle as it zoomed into the small space in front of Huw's late model Acura before immediately decelerating, causing Huw to slam on his brakes. Driving down the northern California coast in hopes of finding surf-based stress relief, we'd encountered a monumental back-up just before Half Moon Bay. Drivers frustrated by the glacial pace of traffic were changing lanes the way politicians change positions.

"I didn't quite catch that," Huw said.

"She compared him to an anal cavity," Stacey said from the back seat.

"I thought you didn't swear," Huw said.

"I don't. Mostly. I was just practicing my Hawaiian." I've never been comfortable using expletives as they were not used in our home. My close friends swore rarely, but found amusement in my lexicon of substitutes: "darn," "gosh darn," "gol darn," "by-our-lady" and courtesy of studying Hawaiian for four years at the University of Hawai'i, the aforementioned "*'ōkole puka.*"

"It's still swearing, hon," said Stacey. "God knows Hawaiian as well as your thoughts."

"Which means He knows very well that the SUV driver really is a ..."

Before I could voice what I was thinking, Huw spoke. "I don't need a running commentary on the traffic, cursing or not."

Just then, a Saab cut in front of us.

Huw grit his teeth as he again hit his brakes and I swear – figuratively, that is – he was going to swear. He stole a glance at me as if he sensed what I was thinking.

"I didn't say a thing," I said.

"As the driver, I reserve the sole right to cuss out other drivers," he responded. "Or not. So, *silens*."

I could take a hint, especially one I recognized as expressed in the vocative case in Latin, thanks to my father, a Classics professor at the University of California Berkeley, who had tried (unsuccessfully) to teach his children the virtue of dead languages.

Huw was one of my father's PhD students in the Classics department. He was currently stuck on one of the finer points of his dissertation, the subject of which was beyond me despite my childhood dalliances with Greek and Latin and the occasional head-banging encounter with Biblical Hebrew. As eager as Huw was to learn to surf, he initially begged off the surfari invitation to work on his thesis. I convinced him that pounding surf was more pleasurable than pounding one's head against the wall. Now faced with mind-numbing traffic, I wondered if he regretted his acquiescence.

Persuading Stacey to go surfing had been easy; she and I regularly surfed together on weekends. Stacey had been a surfer dudette from her days growing up near Houston surfing ankle-high – okay, they can reach a couple feet – swells along the seaweed-covered beaches near Galveston and the occasional bow wave from a big oil tanker transiting the Gulf of Mexico. We had met on a cold day surfing near Santa Cruz two years ago and quickly became surf pals and good friends.

Huw and Stacey arrived early that morning with Stacey's surf rack and board already mounted on Huw's car, and with coffee for me. Grande mocha. Yum. While they loaded my new long board, a present from Keoni, I went inside to retrieve another board.

I grabbed my eight foot six "egg" – a good board for a beginner like Huw – from behind my piano and wrangled it out of my apartment without knocking anything over or whacking the board into the walls, ceiling or door. On the way down the stairs, I found myself trailing Laguna, who sported a lime green sweater over too-tight puce jeans. She carried protest signs on her shoulder, which she banged into the wall as she made the turn at the landing. I was maneuvering my board around the landing when I heard Magda's voice from below.

"Off to dishonor your brother, I see."

I navigated the turn and saw Magda standing in the front hallway with Chesty at her feet, both of them staring up at Laguna, who had paused on the steps.

"No, I'm off to prevent the lives of young men being squandered by warmongering generals who will do anything to justify their ridiculously wasteful defense budgets," Laguna said haughtily as she strode down the last few stairs.

Here it comes. Magda is going to throw another zinger and the battle will ensue. Nope, don't want to see that. I cleared my throat loudly and started down behind Laguna. Not wanting a public fight, Magda threw Laguna a hostile glare and stalked into her apartment, pulling Chesty after her. If looks could kill – to borrow that old phrase – Laguna would have been vaporized on the spot. Laguna's stare at Magda's retreat appeared equally venomous. Both women seemed to know how to launch verbal salvoes designed to create maximum anger: mutually assured destructive dialogue.

I reached the front door as Laguna, encumbered by her signs, was struggling to get it open. We assisted each other through the double doors and out of the building, mumbled our 'thanks' and went our separate ways.

"What was that hideous green apparition?" asked Stacey, watching Laguna march off confidently.

"Tell you in the car," I said and I did.

"My money's on Magda," Stacey said. "She'll find a way to send Laguna packing."

"The sooner the better," I replied. "I'd rather not be caught up in any more of their battles, particularly if they are about to escalate to flame throwers."

WE HAD DECIDED TO SURF Half Moon Bay – a crescent about five miles in length with numerous surf breaks – because of favorable surf reports. The downside of the good forecast (why is there always a downside?) was that, like us, others from the Bay Area would forego the longer trek to Santa Cruz and the waves were bound to be crowded. We drove south past Linda Mar (a favorite spot for beginners and surf camps), through the twisty-turny section of the Coast Highway (known as the Devil's Slide), and by Mavericks (a mecca for crazies who like thirty-foot waves) before pulling off the highway into a bumpy parking lot just beginning to fill up.

We were immediately enveloped by the inviting scent of salt water and eau de kelp, that lovely odor of decaying seaweed (with accompanying sand flies). Huw wrinkled his nose in disgust.

"Kelp straightens the waves out, dude," I said. "Kelp is your buddy, kelp is your friend ..."

"But you hit it on takeoff, you go head over end," Stacey finished.

The sun pierced the dark clouds and illuminated the ocean, which resembled a boundless cauldron of copper. The beach held its fair share of non-surfers: dog walkers, families and young girls wearing hoodies and waiting for the surfer boyfriends to come out of the water.

"Are you going to get ready or what?" Stacey asked. She and Huw had pulled out their wetsuits while I admired the view.

With water temperatures in the fifties, wetsuits were a must. As we suited up, I was glad to see my suit wasn't too tight and I hadn't turned into a Godzilla-sized chocolate bunny despite my colossal consumption of chocolate candy. Stacey, as always, looked fabulous. When you're tall, with gorgeous blonde hair, perfect skin and curves in all the right places, you can wear anything – even black neoprene. Don't get me wrong, I'm not jealous of Stacey.

Mostly. I've got a decent figure – although I'd rather be a size six – with nice features and sorta blonde/light brown hair that had been distinctly blond when I was younger. I manage to attract my fair share of attention from the opposite sex, except when Stacey is around. She's a guy magnet, and all the XY chromosome pairs in the room just naturally glom onto her like *'opihi* with a death grip on rocks in Hawaiian tide pools.

Huw is also easy on the eyes; not as dashing as Keoni, he's still on the upper end of the hottie scale. Tall, slim, with curly brown hair and pale blue eyes, he reminds me of a young Indiana Jones: a professor at heart, but up for any adventure. Huw caught me staring at him and gave me a quick wink. I blushed and turned away.

My father was Huw's PhD advisor and this past summer had invited him over for dinner. Mother thought Huw needed to know more "nice young people" in the area, like me, her elder, unmarried daughter, and I thus received a dinner invitation. For most of my friends, an introduction like that would be the kiss of death for any potential relationship. Who wants to be fixed up by her mother?

I was confident that my mother was not engaged in matchmaking. Married right out of college, she dearly loved my father, but had mentioned numerous times that she wished she'd had three or four years on her own with no responsibilities. Consequently, she encouraged her children to not rush into marriage. Still single at twenty-six, I'd seen a number of my friends take the plunge while others were in serious relationships – a commitment conga line all headed towards happily ever after. At times I wondered if I would be left without a dance partner. On the other hand, one friend had started divorce proceedings before she'd even finished writing the thank-you notes from her wedding. I wasn't in any hurry to better her record.

As for Huw, I wasn't sure if I was grateful or upset that he'd never made a serious move on me. Even if he didn't roll my socks, a girl wants to know that she's attractive and a man is thinking about her as more than just another guy pal or, in Huw's case, as a surf instructor.

I found an open spot on the beach and placed my board in the sand to wax it. Not for the first time, I admired the rich red wood shining through the oiled finish and the curly pattern of the grain, giving it a depth not found in other woods. With help from his cousin, a master surfboard shaper, Keoni had made the board himself, shaping it, installing and finishing the koa wood veneer and inlaying the shell *honu* – sea turtle – and finally inscribing his name, Keoni Kalaniwai, on the tail.

Throwing our boards in the water, we paddled out until we reached the lineup where about fifteen other surfers were parked. We bobbed up and down as we scanned the incoming waves. Stacey and Huw chatted while I tried to focus on the rhythm of the waves and clear my mind. Calls of "ick, ick," broke across the waves and I watched the terns swooping and calling to one another in excitement as they executed kamikaze dives into the water.

"Incoming," yelled Stacey, breaking my reverie.

I glanced over my shoulder, spotted a wave with three madly-paddling surfers almost upon me and did a quick turn into the wave to avoid being rolled. The following wave looked equally promising, so I rapidly turned my board towards shore and paddled hard, just managing to catch it. As I felt the wave begin to break, I popped up. I was on it. Sheer exhilaration. The rail bit into the wave and the board moved fast and true across the face.

"Yee haw!"

Gradually the force of the wave abated. I stepped on the back of the board to turn out, catching it and dropping into the prone position to paddle back out. Woo hoo! That felt great.

As I approached the lineup I noticed Huw striving to catch a wave. He started to push up on the board and purled: the nose of his board caught in the water, he fell in front of it and then bodysurfed, his board trailing behind until he ran out of leash and his board boomeranged back at him. An enthusiastic beginner, Huw didn't yet have the skills to stay up more than a few seconds. It never dampened his stoke, though – he was as happy with a three-second ride on junky beach break waves as many surfers were on much longer and better waves.

Huw and I reached Stacey's position in the lineup about the same time.

"Nice try, Huw," said Stacey. "Don't worry about the fall. Happens to the best of us, darlin.' Angle the board when you take off, or move your weight back a bit."

We resumed our bobbing vigil. The sets were spotty – small, waist-high waves coming in groups of three or four every ten minutes. Surfing can be like that: long spells of not-a-pop-on-the-horizon interrupted by a handful of good waves in succession.

I drifted away from Stacy and Huw, and contemplated the clearing skies and God's decorative talents. My musings were interrupted by a fellow surfer murmuring something I didn't catch, doubtless because my mind was on neither the lineup nor the incoming waves.

"S'cuse me?" I said.

"That's some board. Koa wood?" said the deep voice.

"Veneer only. All koa would be too heavy. My boyfriend made it for me."

"Excellent! Name's Harrison, and you are …?"

"Emma."

With dark hair pulled back in a short ponytail, a long thin face and sharp cheekbones, Harrison appeared to be in his mid-thirties. He was small and wiry, the type of person whose idea of dieting was skipping the whipped cream on his ice cream sundae (three scoops, hot fudge, and lots of peanuts). Why did men get those genes? And the good eyelashes, too?

"Hey, Spaffy," he said, greeting another surfer just arriving. "Nice to see you out here. Ribs must be better. How's Roberta?" Harrison launched into an interrogation of the younger surfer. Through his near monologue, I learned that Spaffy had cracked his ribs wiping out at Steamer Lane a couple of weeks ago and his wife Roberta, also a surfer, was eight months pregnant with their first, which was the sole reason she wasn't out in the lineup, maternity wetsuits being a non-existent item. Also, Spaffy was – uncharacteristically for him – on a long board instead of the fish he usually rode and was trying a new wax made by friends in Santa Cruz. Harrison turned towards me and started telling me all about the "Life and Times of Spaffy and Roberta" – punctuated with "Right, Spaf?" and confirming "uh-huhs" from Spaf.

I broke away from Harrison's incessant talking to catch a small left, and then another. Nothing inspiring, but being on the waves was enough for me to feel happy all over. I paddled back out to see Harrison engaged in an earnest conversation with a young woman I'd noticed during previous surf sessions in Half Moon Bay. She was distinctive: crew cut, three earrings in one ear and a big nose ring. I wondered if the conductive property of metal made her nose and ears freeze.

Harrison asked about her future body-piercing plans. Having tapped out both ears and a nostril, she was contemplating moving south and putting a ring through her lip. I was amazed that he could ask a question like that and receive such a matter-of-fact response from her. My Midwestern upbringing inhibited my prying into such personal matters. One could walk into church with three heads and we Midwesterners would still nod and say "good morning" to each of them without uttering another word. Not a one.

I turned my board towards shore and began paddling, checking over my shoulder to see how the next wave was forming. It was just starting to break when I caught it. I heard yelling behind me as I dropped down the face. *Nice.* I kicked out and dropped back on my board. *Definitely nice.*

I paddled back to the break and found Harrison waiting for me. "Way to go," he said. "Nice ride."

"Thanks. Felt good."

"You've got nice form."

He seemed to mean it as a genuine compliment and not as a pick-up line. Turning to a middle-aged surfer just entering the lineup, Harrison made positive comments about his last ride. Then he told a grommet surfing with her dad was that she "totally ripped." An older lady who was clearly a newbie got a pointer on how to paddle more effectively. Harrison knew and greeted almost everyone and complimented or coached those he didn't know. Occasionally, he'd focus on catching a wave, expertly riding it towards shore as he did the cross step cha-cha-cha on his long board, dancing on the wave. He wasn't showing off. He was just that good.

I caught a couple more small waves, sharing the last one with Stacey and the grommet, a little tow-headed, gap-toothed girl in a pink wetsuit who was all of seven and whose board was more than twice as long as she was. Stacy paddled over to me and we parked next to Harrison.

"You were there when Shamu was killed," he said in a sudden departure from surf banter.

"Shamu?" I said in confusion.

"The guy who was killed at San Mateo Beach last summer. Someone offed him in the parking lot. We all called him Shamu, like the killer whale, cuz the dude thought he owned the place, could take all the waves and bully the crap out of everyone else. His real name was Richard Johnson."

My sense of calm fled like flying fish as the name rang a bell. After discovering his body, I'd checked the papers news on the investigation but found only one article mentioning his death and another regarding the identification of the body. "Wave Hog."

"Right," Harrison said, bobbing his head. "Johnson was that, a primo wave hog and a moron."

Huw joined us, but sat just inside the lineup. I don't think he could hear Harrison. Stacey had edged away as she paddled to maintain position.

Harrison didn't need any prodding to continue his monologue to an audience of one. "The cops interviewed every surfer who was out that day. Who's watching the shore when the waves are primo? No one. They should have checked out his workplace instead of vibing all of us. Shamu was a financial guy. Remember how shitty the market was last year? He had a lot of angry clients.

Way angrier than the people he surfed with." Harrison continued to talk about Shamu and deals he had done that didn't pan out.

"Did you tell the police all this?" I couldn't help myself. He'd captured my attention.

Harrison looked startled as if he wasn't used to people interrupting his soliloquies. "Yeah," he said, matter of factly. "Morons wouldn't listen to me."

Suddenly, he spun his board around, threw himself on top of it and started paddling.

I twisted around to see what had startled Harrison. A rogue wave. "Dang." The swells had been between two and four feet. This one was overhead. I had to make a quick choice: turn into it or try to catch it. I chose the latter and started paddling like mad.

I was too late. The wave sucked me up the face and then broke right on top of me, pushing me off the end of my board and into the spin cycle. I didn't panic, but calmly flutter kicked my way to the surface, only to have another wave break and hammer me. I uttered my mental mantra – don't panic, just relax – and I emerged from the washing machine of a two-wave hold-down breathless, but none the worse for wear. Surfacing, I caught a glimpse of Pillar Point in the distance. A two-wave hold-down at Maverick's would be a death sentence for all but the hardiest big wave surfers.

I grabbed my board and eyed the next wave to ensure I wasn't going to get pounded again while I considered what I'd just heard. Harrison's information might hold the key to Wave Hog's – er, Johnson's – murder. If I could talk to two or three of Johnson's investors ... but how would I find out their names? I could start by checking whether anybody had filed a lawsuit against him. Wait, what was I thinking? Get real, Emma; you're not the police. One murder investigation was enough for anybody, and I literally had already given at the office.

I pulled myself onto the board, looked around for Huw and Stacey and paddled over to where they were bobbing, hoping Harrison wouldn't join us. I liked him but I'd had enough of reliving last summer and my close encounters with two dead bodies.

Stacey caught a few more waves before announcing that she was going in and would pick up coffee for everyone. Huw followed her, and after two more good rides, I called it quits, too.

By the time I reached shore, Stacey was walking towards the rolling coffee stand at the other end of the parking lot. My numb fingers were incapable of grasping the pull on my wetsuit, so Huw did the honor of unzipping me. He stood by smirking as I skillfully peeled off my wet suit, donned a fleece hoody and extracted my bikini top from under the hoody, all without exceeding a 'G' rating.

"So, when are you coming snowboarding with me?" he asked.

"I don't recall your offering."

"I'm offering now. You told me once that you'd never been on a snowboard. Since you're teaching me to surf, the least I can do is give you snowboarding lessons. A surfer like you should find it easy. Besides, I'd like to see you flailing for a change. That's my evil agenda. Other than having a great time, I mean."

"I've always wanted to try it. Where and when were you thinking?"

"My cousins have a place at Tahoe and they've invited me to use the place whenever. I thought the weekend of the thirteenth would be good. We could go up Friday night, board on Saturday, and come back Saturday night. What do you think?"

Ah, an overnight. Was this a random "let's try sleeping together" invite, or "let's be practical and not spend the whole day in the car" invite? I tended towards the latter based on Huw's prior behavior.

He saw my hesitation and guessed the reason for it. "Hey, give me some credit. I can do better than a five-hour drive as a means of seduction."

I smiled. "I'd love to come. Thanks."

Huw responded with a smug look.

We had just finished racking the surfboards when Stacey returned with three large coffees. "Ready to go? I'm starving!"

"Almost ready," I said, taking my coffee from Stacey. I wrapped my fingers around the cup, hoping the feeling would soon return to my frozen appendages. Stacey knows my coffee preferences and had picked out a concoction with whipped cream, but alas, no sprinkles. I took a large gulp, replaced the lid, and then squatted down to peer under the car.

"What are you doing?" Huw said.

"Checking for stiffs."

"Beg pardon?"

"You know, 'stiffs.' Dead bodies, corpses, ex-people, *cadavera innumera, nā kino make.* I check to make sure the heat, the coffee, and stove are all off before I leave the house, and I check under the car for stiffs when I leave the beach. I don't want a repeat of Wave Hog, ever." I straightened up and walked to the back of the car where I squatted down to get a different viewpoint.

"This is part of her routine now," explained Stacey. "Drives me crazy. Honestly, hon, what are the odds of finding another dead surfer under a car?"

"What were the odds of finding two bodies in two months?" I countered as I stood up.

"Aren't you being a bit paranoid? I mean, this is my car and I'll be driving," Huw said. "You're the one who's the stiff magnet, not me."

"Not I," I said, automatically correcting his grammar. "If you want to become a murder suspect because you've run over someone, that's your business. But it's no fun having your life dissected and cops search your apartment."

"Especially your underwear drawer," Stacey added.

"That, too."

"Even if it was a really cute cop, although probably not Huw's type."

Stacey and I dissolved into giggles.

"Enough," Huw said disgustedly. "Let's go." And with that and one more glance under the car just to be sure the only stiffening corpses were those of dead sand flies, we headed into downtown Half Moon Bay to Flip-Flop Heaven for mega-carbs.

THREE

"I've always felt that the best place to hide a body is in the trunk of a cop car, with a note affixed to the body that reads, 'I'm sorry.'"
– Jaron Kintz

MONDAY DAWNED COOL AND FOGGY, in contrast to my mood. I was excited about being on-site at Carson's headquarters for most of the week. With a cult-like foodie following, Carson had won numerous awards for its candy and even more awards for its corporate culture, worker-friendly environment and all around group hugginess. In contrast to Zuckers, a behemoth in the candy world, Carson was a boutique company and their product ads were infused with serial eco-friendly adjectives like "organic," "artisanal" and "local and sustainable" – as local and sustainable as they could be given that cacao beans didn't grow in even the prodigiously fertile soil of the Central Valley. I was hopeful that Carson, like Zuckers, might stock their conference rooms with their own high-calorie offerings. Since Carson was so eco-friendly, eating their candy would support the environment and our client's business through personal involvement. Yum.

After a quick shower, followed by moisturizer, a splash of lipstick and blush, I searched for a suitable outfit to throw on. Ah, dark pants I hadn't worn in awhile because they were a bit tight. Perfect for keeping my sweet tooth in check. I struggled into the pants and added a soft gray tunic sweater that hung a bit long; if things got too uncomfortable, I could always unbutton the pants, move the zipper down just a tad, and no one would notice. Silver hoop earrings and a triple-stranded silver necklace, a pair of flat, dark shoes and I was out the door and ready for work. Or I would be after swinging by Elixir of Life for a double espresso and an IV.

When I reached the lobby, Magda was just emerging from her apartment with Chesty for his morning walk. Chesty's nostrils quivered, he wagged his tail in rapid tempo and strained at the leash, awaiting the morning appointment with His Tree, the one just outside the apartment building that was the neighborhood doggie pit stop and post office.

"Mornin' Magda. Looks like Chesty is raring to go."

"He's been up for hours and out already," she replied. "I just fed him so it's time for another walk." She no sooner finished the "W" word than Chesty began to shimmy. Whining and wagging his entire body, Chesty was bucking like my Honda CRX on a bad tank of gas when, through contortions of his tiny body, he slipped his collar. Magda and I both made a grab for him as he raced not for the door, but up the stairs, letting out tiny barks of excitement as he proclaimed his freedom. For a tiny dog with short legs, he moved like a weasel on a turbocharged skateboard.

"At least we have him trapped," I said. "You guard the bottom of the stairs and I'll get him, or herd him down."

I took the stairs two at a time, laughing under my breath at the little tyke's escape. I didn't spot him when I reached the top of the stairs, but I heard his excited barking from the other end of the corridor. As I walked down the hall, the barks increased in intensity, interspersed with plaintive whining. Reaching the end, I discovered the door to Laguna's apartment ajar, a constant buzzing coming from within augmented with Chesty's sharp barks.

"Chesty! Come here, boy!" I knocked lightly on the door. "Laguna, you there?"

The buzzing continued. A clock-radio alarm? Maybe Laguna was too tired to get up. Or was that an oven buzzer? Not that I would know – it had been so long since I used my oven that a moth was likely to fly out the next time I opened the door. Again

I knocked and called out, louder this time. No answer, except for Chesty's insistent barking and whimpering.

Laguna must have left and forgotten to close her door all the way. No one could sleep through all that noise.

In retrospect, it was obvious that I should have had coffee before heading out that morning. If I'd taken the time to drink even a small cup, I might have had a few neurons firing. Those neurons would have told me to call Magda upstairs. It was her dog to retrieve and as the landlady, it was her job to worry about why a tenant's door was open with her alarm blaring and annoying the local dachshund door warden.

Instead, calling Chesty's name loudly, I slowly pushed the door open and eased into the apartment. Two Japanese wood block prints graced Laguna's narrow entry hall, flanking a gold-framed mirror above a small, cherry Queen Anne side table, topped with a vase of dried flowers. An oriental runner led back into the living area. Laguna and Magda might be worlds apart on politics, but they were kindred spirits in decorating styles.

"Chesty, come here, you silly boy," I called again, following the runner to the main living area. The apartment layout was identical to mine with the kitchen opening off the hallway to the living/dining area. A small door off the living room led to the bedroom, which fronted the street for me, the courtyard for Laguna. I poked my head into the kitchen. It was as neat and picked up as mine was cluttered but the buzzing sound was not emanating from there. It must be the alarm clock.

Two more strides brought me to the edge of the living room. Chesty sat on the floor and turned his head when he heard me approach. Giving me a pitiful look, he turned away again and whimpered. My eyes followed his, across the pristine rug toward …

No, not again. No way. This is a dream, a nightmare.

A body lay sprawled between a butler's table and a pale peach settee. Laguna. Her unseeing eyes stared at the ceiling and a pale white hand festooned with silver rings gripped a long, metal pole emerging from her chest.

I closed my eyes and the vision of my dead boss, Padmanabh, appeared as I'd seen him five months earlier, lying on the floor of his office. I shook my head to remove the image from my mind and reluctantly opened my eyes. The scene hadn't changed, but I noticed more details. The pole sticking out of Laguna's chest was still attached to a peace symbol emblazoned sign. Below Laguna's rigid hands, a large dark stain spread across her soft green sweater and onto the richly dark hardwood floor. *God!* I began to feel nauseous and light headed as darkness crept around the edges of my vision.

Don't faint. Not here. Breathe, Emma, breathe.

I fled the room and stumbled down the hallway. When I reached the stairs I stood well back from the edge, afraid my growing dizziness would impel a fall. Surprisingly, I found I had a squirming dachshund in my arms. I put Chesty on the floor and he gamboled down the stairs to Magda, who was calling him. My legs were too weak to do the same, so I just sat on the carpet and put my head between my knees.

"Police," I yelled.

"Emma, what's the matter? Are you all right?" I heard Magda call, from the end of a foggy gray tunnel.

"Call police," I replied, my eyes still closed, hands holding my head. "Laguna's dead. Murdered."

I half-expected Magda to come pounding up the stairs. Instead I heard the click of her heels as she moved rapidly across the wood floors toward her apartment. The waves of nausea were winning; it was only a matter of time before I lost what little was in my stomach. I reached under my sweater, unbuttoned my too-tight pants and moved the zipper down slightly. The pressure on my abdomen eased and I crawled to my apartment door, let myself in and lurched for the bathroom.

After my little hurl session, I felt better. Not great, just better. Still too shaky to move, I sat on the cold tile floor while visions of dead bodies danced behind my closed eyelids. Another dead body. It was too much to believe. At least this time, unlike my previous dead body experiences, there would be no grilling by the police and no fear of body cavity searches. I'd held the door for Laguna precisely once and listened to her scream at Magda exactly twice. Hardly a first name basis, even in "can't we all be friends" San Francisco, and certainly not enough to put me on the PP – potential perps – list.

The nausea subsided and I pulled myself up by the edge of the sink, easing into a standing position. A quick teeth brushing, reapplication of blusher and lip gloss and hair comb made me presentable again, at least on the exterior. Moving gingerly, I located my messenger bag in the hallway where I had dropped it and made my way downstairs just as the police entered. Magda directed them towards the second floor and herded me into her kitchen where she poured a fresh cup of coffee, doctored it with cream and two packets of sweetener and stuck it into my outstretched hands.

I drained half the cup immediately. Coffee probably isn't the best thing to calm one's stomach, but I needed the caffeine to deal with what I'd seen.

"Do you want toast with that?"

I shook my head and sipped my drug of choice while she popped a slice of bread in the toaster. Was that Acme Fred Bread: pecans, cranberries, and currants? At any other time I'd be all over it and asking for peanut butter and dried figs on the toast. Not today.

Magda sat down with her coffee. "Well?"

"You didn't go up and see her?" It was unlike Magda to be incurious, or to avoid an unpleasant sight.

"No, I thought it best that I stay here to let the police into the building."

In as few words as possible, I told her what I'd found. She didn't say anything, but got up to get her toast and refill my coffee. Before she could sit down again, there was a buzz at the front door.

While Magda answered the door (more police officers) I rooted around for my phone in the dark depths of my messenger bag – why can't manufacturers make the inside of bags and purses in bright colors so women can more easily find their stuff? After unloading half my bag on Magda's kitchen table, I found the phone and called Laura, the project manager on my current assignment, to tell her I'd encountered a minor emergency and I'd be late for work.

Laura wasn't an overbearing boss, so she didn't pry as to details of my emergency or the exact time I'd be in. Instead, she asked if I was okay. I lied and said I was fine, by which I meant "better off than Laguna," and that I'd see her later.

Grateful that explanations could wait, I put my phone away just as a plain-clothes officer stepped into the kitchen with Magda. He gave his name as Jose Torres and asked – no, told us – not to leave the premises until we'd been questioned. A tad on the short side, but with thick, dark hair and broad shoulders, he was definitely attractive. And he had a deep "bedroom" baritone voice. Hey, I might have had a shock, but I wasn't totally out of it. I still appreciated nice scenery. And as if to confirm my assessment, Chesty leaped up and down at Officer Torres' feet to get his attention.

"How long do you think this will take?" I asked.

"I can't promise anything, ma'am, but I expect 'bout an hour."

'Ma'am'? How old do I look? I'm at least two decades from being a ma'am.

Torres turned to Magda. "About that list of tenants?" With Chesty dogging his steps, he followed Magda into the living room, where she withdrew the list from her block front desk and handed it to him. He left with the list and Magda returned to the kitchen to zap her coffee in the microwave. Before returning to her seat at the table, she took a large bottle from an upper cabinet and poured a generous slug into her coffee. "For medicinal purposes," she said. I could smell the single malt "medicine" from across the kitchen.

She took a long sip of coffee, put her cup down and sighed. "All I can think about are her poor parents," she said, after a moment. "Losing a son in Afghanistan, now a daughter to murder. I can't imagine how they'll feel when they hear the news. And I hope I don't ever have that experience."

Magda's two sons were in the Marines, although I didn't know where they were posted. She had a daughter on her own in Dallas and a married daughter in Los Angeles.

"Who could have killed her?" I said.

"Not me, dearie."

I mentally corrected her grammar – "not I" – but said nothing. We sat awkwardly for a moment. I'd meant it as a rhetorical question, not an accusation. I'd no doubt Magda could kill to protect life or property, but could she be a murderer? No way. Not her style. I'd heard her say often that our Constitutional rights were secured by the U.S. military, including the rights of "rabble-rousers."

"Do you think it could it have been a random killer off the streets? You said there'd been an increase in crime in the area."

Magda shrugged and took another swig of coffee. She put her cup down with both hands and began circling the top of the cup with her index finger.

I knew virtually nothing about Laguna, so I couldn't speculate on any more possibilities. It occurred to me that I was going to have to tell my parents for the third time in five months that I'd discovered a dead body. I could just imagine how that would go.

What's new, Emma?

Not much, mom. Paid bills, went to work, stumbled over a stiff. Another day, another decedent.

Terrif. I wasn't sure what the prospect of another corpse would do for my mother's habit of pushing self-defense gizmos on me. What was there left for her to buy me, except a pocket H-bomb?

The next hour dragged by as the police rousted the tenants who hadn't yet left for work and quizzed each one of us in turn. Lucky me, I was interviewed twice. First, Jose Torres questioned me about finding the body. It was the high point of my day. Under the spell of his soothing baritone, I felt as if I were being seduced, rather than interrogated about a murder. It would be so easy to be lured into confessing while under the spell of his thick lips, deep voice and graceful hand gestures.

Why had I gone to Laguna's apartment? Why did I enter? Did I touch anything? What did I do after finding the body? Is there anything you are not telling me?

I'm not telling you how hot you are. Oh, and I'm definitely not giving you the details about throwing up.

After my date – er, session – with Jose, I returned to Magda's kitchen to wait for the second detective who was questioning Magda. Chesty, overwhelmed by the commotion, came over to the table and sat on my feet.

"Poor fella. Are you upset by the body, or all the people coming in and out of your building and not scratching you?"

He stared up at me with mournful eyes and I felt compelled to take the larger crumbs from Magda's plate of toast and toss them to him.

Magda entered the kitchen. She appeared beat, evincing only a small smile when Chesty greeted her with turns and twirls at her feet. "You're next," she said.

"You okay?"

"I'll live." She sat down heavily, picked up her empty coffee cup, sniffed it, and sipped the dregs. She then got up and put the kettle on the stove to heat more water, opened the freezer, took out a small plastic container of ground coffee, and deposited four coffee measures into a French press.

"Some days, only dark roast will do," she said.

"More medicine with that?" I asked. "Second cabinet to the left of the sink, upper shelf."

"I know where I keep my hootch."

Before I could inquire further, the second detective appeared and gestured for me to follow him. Jim Johnson was nothing if not forgettable: middle aged, middling height and middling weight. He'd taken over a maintenance closet on the first floor and conducted his interview surrounded by mops, half empty cans of paint and varnish, sections of PVC pipe and an assortment of tools. The one naked bulb hanging from the ceiling completed the ambiance. I half expected him to threaten to strip me

– paint strip me, that is – if I didn't talk. I made myself at home on a slightly broken chair that normally resided in the front hall. The uneven legs caused me to teeter as I was being interrogated, as if finding Yet Another Body hadn't already thrown me off balance. I felt guilty thinking of Laguna that way. I hadn't know her, hadn't necessarily wanted to, but she didn't deserve a pole in the chest and I knew I shouldn't think of her as an inconvenience or as merely another on my ever increasing tally of stiffs. The only way I was holding it together was thinking about the macabre humor of it all – "Emma Jones, you've just earned ten copious corpse points!" – because humor was the only way I could block out the gruesomeness of her death.

When Johnson asked if I had ever heard Laguna and Magda argue, I figured someone had already spilled the beans on the feud – maybe even Magda – so I admitted I had been witness to a couple fights, although I tried to be vague on what was said by whom to whom and at what decibel and proximity to sharp instruments or untraceable poison. That wasn't too hard. Really, how many people remember conversations word for word? I didn't lie to Johnson, but I saw no reason to volunteer absolutely everything I knew, either.

As expected – and quite unlike when I found my dead boss, Padmanabh – Johnson indicated no interest in me as a suspect. I guessed that meant the police wouldn't be searching my underwear drawer again as they had when they were searching for proof that I'd offed Pad. As if unmentionables were ever a factor. (Colonel Mustard in the library with the rope and wearing a thong?) Too bad, really. After the last search, I'd upgraded my lingerie to include some slinky bikinis (nothing says "rrrowr" like leopard print undies). Not that I cared what Johnson thought but I wouldn't mind impressing Detective Torres.

By the time Johnson was done with me, I had an incipient headache and my stomach was churgling like Halema'uma'u, the fire pit of Kīlauea, either from my earlier shock or from lack of food. Johnson told me I was free to go. Even though I was already way late for work, I took a small detour to heaven: Elixir of Life, my favorite house of java worship. Okay, I actually have four or five favorites, but Elixir is one of the top two, definitely. Just the smell of their coffee makes me perk up. The dark, well-worn wooden tables and chairs at Elixir speak of a coffee shop that has been around for a while – going on seven years. In a city where restaurants have a half-life of six months, Elixir of Life qualifies as an institution.

I especially enjoy Elixir between Halloween and the Ides of March, when they add beignets to their breakfast menu. Fried dough isn't generally a big seller in a city so self-righteously health conscious as San Francisco. However, Elixir started beignets-for-breakfast thing as a tribute to Mardi Gras and over the years, they expanded the season. It was unfortunate for my waistline that the beignet season now overlapped the eggnog latte season and had backed up all the way to the pumpkin spice cappuccino season.

I decided to go for a healthy breakfast and only ordered a short pumpkin spice cappuccino – which clearly counts as a vegetable – and a lemon croissant, which counts as a serving of vitamin C. A beignet was tempting but totally impossible to consume in the car without coating my pants with powdered sugar.

I hadn't been by for a few days and was surprised to see that Shaun the Barista appeared almost corporate. He'd removed his eyebrow jewelry, his nose stud, and only had one small, tasteful earring, a silver feather, in his right ear instead of the usual two or three earrings per ear.

"My new girlfriend doesn't want me to wear more jewelry than she does," he said in response to my inquiry about his unusual dearth of metallic accessories.

"What about buying her a gift certificate for more piercings? You could both wear more jewelry and you'd never lack for gift ideas."

Shaun brightened at the suggestion and threw extra sprinkles on my coffee. At least I'd improved up someone's day.

Nearly nine-thirty when I drove out of the city, the fog monster was already retreating. It had crept in overnight from the Farallons and swallowed the Golden Gate Bridge and the normally breath-taking views of the ocean and the bay. The lateness of the hour also meant that the rage-inducing traffic had dissipated. Light traffic, caffeine, and a croissant; I felt a lot better by the time I arrived at Carson's offices. Not great, mind you. I knew nightmares would follow, as they had following the murders of Pad and Wave Hog. But for now, the sun was shining brightly over the rolling hills of Marin County and I was hopeful that after my horrendous morning, the rest of the day would be better.

FOUR

"A consultant is someone who takes a subject
you understand and
makes it sound confusing."
– Anonymous

ZUCKERS AND CARSON WERE a mere thirty miles apart geographically but worlds apart architecturally. Zuckers' corporate headquarters and plant facilities squatted in an industrial park in Oakland behind one of the freeway cloverleafs. The buildings – tall, concrete, and only missing the high intensity lights of the nearby minimum security prison with which they were often confused – were surrounded by acres of parking resembling a car dealership for SUVs; acre upon acre of big black trucks blanketed the asphalt. The only color was the occasional bright yellow dandelion forcing its way through a crack in the pavement before being ruthlessly poisoned with weed killer. The sweet smell of cocoa – which might have relieved the bleakness – had been eliminated several years ago when Zuckers installed a filter system at the behest of the EPA due to concerns about the health risks of cocoa dust. Now, the odors of vehicle exhaust and heavy industry settled on Zucker's buildings, completing the charm.

In contrast, Carson's offices were tucked away in a small valley off Highway 101 in Marin. Slouching eucalyptus trees whose pungent fragrance perfumed the campus enveloped the low-rise buildings. In the tree-canopied parking lot, compact cars, hybrid automobiles, and smart cars played hide and seek among the greenery.

Electric vehicles nuzzled charging stations like lambs nursing from a benevolent ewe.

I drove through the wrought iron main gate covered by an arch of Bougainvillea, parked the car and strolled through a series of small buildings laid out upon terraces, each connected by flagstone steps wandering through meditation gardens planted with native California flora. I half expected to see chipmunks tidying up the occasional fallen leaf and chirping birds making a dress for an employee.

A rustic bridge spanned a small stream that meandered amidst the buildings and rippled down the terraces, joining other streams that eventually became one big happy estuary of San Francisco Bay. I'd visited cemeteries that weren't as peaceful as Carson's headquarters, but the only bereaved here were employees mourning the Zuckers takeover.

GD's clients typically provide us with unused office space or cramped conference rooms with which to work our IT magic spells. Carson had given the GD team a small conference room that overlooked a meditation garden. As if the name of the conference room, Namaste, didn't send a strong enough message, the hammock slung between two old eucalyptus trees and the yoga class in progress in the courtyard reiterated that Carson took relaxing at work seriously. Maybe they had been so relaxed they didn't noticed Zuckers gunning for them until it was too late to do anything except embrace their inner mass marketer.

"What's up?" Maria Guardino said when I walked in. She was a twenty-youngish consultant with high cheekbones, high heels and a high metabolism that kept her a perennial size six. "Laura said you had a small emergency. What happened?"

"Found another dead body, threw up and was quizzed by the police," I responded. I had found from my alarmingly frequent experience that, when announcing you've stumbled over a stiff, blurting it out is better than a lot of preamble. It's like your credit card bill after serious shopping; best to rip it open and see the *Titanic* hit the iceberg as fast as possible.

Holly Conway, a fortyish brunette and a Silicon Valley start-up's ex-trophy wife (she had recently reentered the workforce after the prenup proved not enough to live on) sputtered "Oh my God," and spilled her coffee. Shafiq Rahman, a thirtyish, slightly pudgy guy with thinning jet black hair, stopped in mid-chew of a glazed donut.

"Bummerang," Maria said, as she blinked her eyes a couple of times.

I blanked at this latest Maria-ism. Although I was only a few years older than Maria, we seemed to be from different generations regarding speech and fashion. Today she wore leopard print stiletto boots, a short black leather skirt and a cowl-neck lavender sweater, which said "fashion fiend" more than "competent, slightly nerdy but with enough management skills not to geek you into oblivion consultant." My idea of daring work attire was peep-toe shoes. With kitten heels, woo hoo.

"A good friend?" Holly asked, interrupting my thoughts.

"Huh?"

"The dead person. Was he, or she, a good friend?"

"She lived in my apartment building. I barely knew her. But still, really … awful."

I was pressured for more information, but said as little as I could; I had no interest in reliving or recounting the gory details. The room fell silent when I made it clear there would be no more "up close and personal with Emma and the expired."

Except for Maria, who always had something to say. "Totally insane. Hey, I forgot to mention we have fresh coffee and Shafiq brought in donuts – a bit stale now, but they're all yours. The maple bars are seriously scrumptious."

I mentally shook my head at Maria's seamless transition from corpses to crullers. Holly frowned before turning back to the computer.

"I'll take a pass. I've had enough caffeine and sugar," I said. Discussing Laguna's *corpus delicti* had started my stomach churning again; I wouldn't be snarfing any more empty calories for awhile.

I pulled out my laptop and seated myself at a small, narrow table next to Shafiq, a senior consultant on the project as well as our resident donut expert. He'd staked out the food table as his workspace, which gave him more elbow room and first crack at the fat pills. Holly, responsible for transferring the Carson human resources information into Zuckers' HR system, huddled at the end of the conference room table softly humming old show tunes and a few choruses of "I Will Survive." Maria had taken over a third of the table to sort through reams of paper related to Carson's financial and procurement systems.

Wendell Taylor, a tall, clean-shaven African-American whose triathlete-on-the-weekends frame almost burst out of his dark tailored suit, popped in to ask Anwar Ibrahim a quick question. Wendell was charged with overseeing the consolidation of the infrastructure (the hardware used to interconnect computers and users) with the help of Anwar, whose contrasting short, rotund body, full beard, longish hair and café latte skin made the pair of them a visual oddity. Anwar had parked himself in a corner with three stale donuts not already claimed by Shafiq and was busy constructing a spreadsheet on his computer, totally oblivious to his surroundings, courtesy of massive earphones. I wondered if he could pick up Mars with them.

Consolidation of the sales and marketing systems had fallen to Shafiq, whose artistic hands – long, tapered fingers and clean, neatly-clipped nails – raced across the keyboard. When Maria briefly left the room, I surreptitiously asked him if he knew what "bummerang" meant. He shrugged his thin shoulders. "I speak and read four languages, not including programming languages, but not extraterrestrial ones."

"Beg pardon?"

"Maria is from another planet."

My primary role on the project was to catalog and quantify the cost savings from consolidating Zuckers' and Carson's systems: work far removed from cutting-edge technology and only exciting for those who possessed an accounting gene. You know, the ones who experience rapture at the sight of a well-ordered spreadsheet. Laura also had enlisted my help with the financial systems consolidation. Not a great fit with my interests, but better than spending all my time on spreadsheets.

"Laura has set up a bunch of meetings over the next three days with the finance app group," Maria informed me, using the shorthand for applications group. "She'd like you to attend whichever ones you can."

"Not a problem."

"And you should bring your self-defense weapons; we're not exactly welcome here."

"Laura said that?"

"No, but in the meeting you missed this morning, the Carson Chief Information Officer called us Gee Dee several times," Maria said, using the unmistakable emphasis of the expletive that so readily came to mind when using Grant's and Denholm's initials. "He didn't leave any doubt about what he meant by it, either."

"Are you sure that was us? I thought he said Gee Dee Zuckers," Holly said.

"I don't think that's quite accurate, but we were definitely the 'goddamn Gee Dee consultants.' Is that redundant, do you think?" Maria said. "It's certainly alliterative."

I'd worked with clients that didn't like us, but was astonished that the CIO would be so openly hostile and unprofessional as to speak that way in front of an audience.

Shafiq spoke up. "Carson's CIO and Laura had just come from a meeting with Grundy. According to Laura, Grundy baldly stated that Carson might be a quality brand but they sure as hell didn't know how to run a business."

I nodded my head in understanding. "I can see as how the CIO might not have been in a great mood." Grundy was the Zuckers Senior Vice President with oversight responsibility for the merger. Over six feet tall and equally wide – probably from intensive product sampling – he was brusque, biting and unyielding in his demands, including the requirement that GD's part in effecting the IT part of the merger "be completed on time, period." Laura would have her hands full trying to satisfy Grumpy, er, Grundy.

"And I heard that Zuckers told Carson management over the weekend that they plan to close this facility and move all operations to Zuckers' Oakland plant by early next year," added Maria.

"A rumor?" I asked.

"Fact," Maria responded.

Outside, birds flitted along the grounds practicing population control on errant worms. A couple of bunnies hopped into the kitchen garden and nibbled on deep green leaves. I couldn't imagine anybody being happy at giving up "the lion will lie down with the lambs" for "lions and lambs have been killed, buried and paved over with asphalt." Zuckers' Oakland plant had already been nicknamed "Mordor" by the Carson employees. I can't say I disagreed with the analogy.

"I'd slit my wrists if I had to move from this place to Zuckers," I said.

"Don't assume these people will have a choice. Zuckers may fire them," Shafiq said.

"Has anyone heard anything definite about layoffs?" I asked.

"Not yet. Just rumors," Maria said. "But Laura should know for sure since she's been working with Zuckers' corptocracy." Another Maria-ism to decode that sounded too close for comfort to corpse-ocracy.

Since there didn't seem to be any more information or credible rumors, we hunkered down to work. For once, I was happy to be creating the world's largest spreadsheet; the mental effort kept my mind from returning to the horrific scene of that morning.

FIVE

"He that would live in peace and at ease must
not speak all he knows or all he sees."
– Benjamin Franklin

ALCOHOL WOULDN'T MAKE my day any better, but it might dull the edges. On the other hand, I needed a clear head while divulging the latest news to my parents.

I decided on a nice Pinot Grigio and took both bottle and glass to the living room. Maybe I should have gone for a bottle and a straw, but in my family, we believe in observing the niceties. Settling into a large overstuffed chair with a matching ottoman, a hand-me-down from my parents, I considered my approach.

Last summer, I'd kept the news of finding my murdered boss Padmanabh from my parents for a week, finally telling them over dinner. Virgil, oft in trouble during his childhood, advised breaking the news gradually; let Mother and Dad draw it out of me.

"My boss was found dead in his office. No, it wasn't a heart attack. We're not sure what happened. He appears to have been killed. He was hit on the head. The police haven't arrested anyone yet and seem to believe that it wasn't a thief but someone who knew him. Oh, and they apparently have me down on their list of potential suspects, which sucks."

My mother was only slightly more upset that I was a murder suspect than the fact I'd used "sucks" at the dinner table. Only the presence of Huw – it was our first meeting – tempered Mother's ballistic tendencies as she struggled to be the perfect hostess and remain calm in the face of any and all calamities. After Huw left, she let loose and her voice reached G above high C with the power of a three-hundred pound operatic soprano delivering her signature aria. I hadn't known she could hold the note that long.

When I told my parents about finding Wave Hog's body, Mother's response was more muted. I think she was out of emotional juice, still recovering from my encounter and lucky escape from Pad's killer, who thought I was getting too close to discovering his crime.

Unexpectedly, my father took the news of each discovery in stride, or at least appeared to. The last time he and Mother came over, he brought his knife sharpener and gave every sharp object in my kitchen a lethal edge. I was good to go, whether tomatoes or criminal crania were on the chopping block.

It was absurd to think my parents would be unfazed by the announcement of a third body. I thought for 6.9 nanoseconds of holding off the news until next Thursday, Thanksgiving. Stalling would give me a few days free of mother's worry and of her obsessive search for more self-defense gizmos like a Pocket Homicidal Murderer Detector. On the other hand, my parents could accuse me of ruining Thanksgiving – "Dear Lord, we are thankful that our beloved Emma discovered Yet Another Body" – and if my niece Rebecca overheard the news, I'd get yelled at for corrupting her. Nope. Better to do the deed now. I took a big swallow of my wine, then a deep breath, and called home.

"Hi, Mom."

"Hello, sweetie. I was just thinking about you. Your father and I were cleaning the basement and found your old Barbie dolls. Would you like to pass them along to Rebecca? They are more attractive than the trolls she is currently fixated on. Barbie's hair is better conditioned, too."

"Sure, Mom. It'd be nice if you would box them up so I could give them to her." I'd have to pass them on with appropriate warnings about Barbie being misshapen: nobody really had legs that long or wore high heels all the time. Except for maybe extremely tall trannies in the Castro, but I wasn't going to explain that to Rebecca.

"And did you find the Barbie weapons, too?" I asked. As a child, my brother Virgil had a collection of G.I. Joes and had almost as many helmets, backpacks and weapons as Barbie had shoes. I was fascinated by the weapons – assault rifles, lasers, crossbows, flamethrowers – and had convinced my parents that I needed toys like Virgil had. They obliged and bought me a few G.I. Joes.

"Yes dear, her guns are there. Are you sure you want to pass those on?" she said, no doubt wondering about how Virgil and his wife Ashley would react to their daughter Rebecca receiving a gift of firearms.

I couldn't guess Ashley's response, but I was hoping Virgil would be reminded of the times my Barbies bested him in battle. Three times the size of his action figures and carrying an arsenal appropriated from my new G.I. Joes, my Barbies not only won every skirmish, but looked good doing it, too.

"Definitely," I said. "Guns and Barbies. You should approve. You're always saying that women needing to know how to defend themselves. It's not too early for Rebecca to learn that."

Mother sighed. "Okay. I'll pack up everything and have it for you next Thursday. You are still coming for Thanksgiving?"

"Of course I'm still coming. Maybe I'll give the dolls to Rebecca then and not wait for Christmas. I'm just dying to see the expression on Virgil's face when I give them to her."

"Emma," Mother warned.

"I'm sure he'll be thrilled; he likes empowered women," I added hastily.

Another sigh from Mother. "Anything else new with you, dear?"

"Uh huh, but really, it's hardly worth mentioning," I paused, hoping Mom was tired and would opt for a quick "good night, dear."

"Emma?"

Lights, camera, direct approach, take one. "Well, ah, a woman in my apartment building was murdered. But don't worry; I don't think I'm a suspect this time. I mean, I found the body and all, but I didn't know her. I think Magda might be a suspect. She fought a lot with the dead woman. When she was alive, of course. The victim of course – Magda is still alive. The woman was stabbed. She'd been dead for a while, I think."

Good God, I was babbling. Shut up, Emma. Keep cool. It's just your Mom, not the police. Although my mother could be more intimidating than the police. Her "I'm so disappointed in you," was the worst punishment I'd ever received. Being grounded only went on for a week or two; maternal disappointment was the guilt trip that kept on traveling.

I waited for the explosion. Nothing. Nothing at all.

"Mom? Are you still there? Did I lose you?" I took another sip of my wine and starting humming the *Jeopardy* theme song while I waited for a response.

"Yes, I'm still here. And I certainly hope you're joking." The disapproval in her voice came through clearly. "You know how frightened we were when you found your boss murdered. And then that poor man under your car who, fortunately, seems to have been killed by someone you don't know."

"Fortunately seems to have been killed"? Now Mother is babbling.

"But, Mom. I'm not joking. There was a woman murdered in my apartment building and I found the body. For real."

Silence. Then, "Are you sure?"

Sure? Sure of what? That there was body, or that it was dead? Or that it was a woman? Yes, yes, and yes. That I wasn't a suspect? Well, pretty sure. That I wanted to tell my parents about this? No. I'd rather skip the entire conversation, but better they hear it from me than from the evening news.

"Yes, Mother. I'm sorry, but it's true." I'd be even sorrier if I pulled this on Mother and it weren't true.

"Bruce? Bruce! You have to come to the phone. Yes, now. Hold on, Emma, I'm going to get your father."

In no time, both my parents were on the line and I was recounting the death of Laguna Butterfield for what I was sure was not going to be the last time. If it weren't in colossally bad taste, I had half a thought to post the information online. It would be a digression from opining on Bay Bridge traffic, the latest abysmal San Francisco 49ers score and the surf report.

By the time I hung up, I was worn out from the tension of trying to remain upbeat about a downer subject, but pleasantly surprised at how cool my mother had remained. Was she becoming inured to my corpse-finding habit? Mother's calm was in stark contrast to my father's reaction. Was there a parental principle that in the face of disastrous news, one parent must remain calm while the other was allowed to erupt?

My father had let loose a torrent about crime in San Francisco and declared that he'd immediately buy me a handgun and arrange for shooting lessons. He also planned to talk to Magda about building security. I wouldn't be surprised if he called her as soon as I hung up and demanded she change out the door lock, install security cameras and hire ex-commandos with bad-tempered Rottweilers as security guards. I just hoped he didn't propose that I move home until Laguna's killer was caught or until I got married, whichever came first. Neither one would be measurable on a stopwatch – heck, even a regular watch. Maybe a calendar. A multi-year one.

Next on the list were my siblings.

"You need to stay out of it," Virgil said.

"It's a little late for that," I replied. "I can't put the body back."

"Very funny. I say again, stay out of the investigation, Emma."

"Who said anything about investigating? I've no intention of getting involved."

"Even if Magda is a suspect?"

Hmm, good point. If Magda were in trouble, I'd have to help.

"That's what I thought," said Virgil at my silence.

"She's my friend."

"Don't. Just don't. Remember the last time? You almost became the second victim."

I had confronted my coworker Brian about the murder of my boss Padmanabh, and he'd pulled a gun on me: the next best thing to his signing a confession. When I told my family and friends about the episode, I'd said I'd pepper-sprayed Brian (true, though I missed everything but his ear) and run toward Sanjay, who felled Brian with a cricket bat. I didn't tell them that Brian had a gun or that I didn't actually know Sanjay was in the building until I heard the thump as Brian's body went down and turned to see a triumphant Sanjay. Only Virgil knew the whole story – I had to tell someone – and now he was raking it up, rubbing my face in it, and engaging in every hackneyed guilt trip he could muster. I knew it was because he loved me but I still resented being told what risks I could take.

"I don't need your advice. I can make my own decisions," I said.

"Generally, I would agree, but not this time. Stay out of it, Sis."

I dearly love my brother. We had passed the stage, or so I thought, when one of us would be contrary just to get a rise out of the other. A calm, adult response to Virgil would have been to acknowledge his concern and agree with him. In my defense, I was tired and stressed.

"I don't know. Maybe I should get involved. Magda's concerned she's going to end up in the clink and I have experience now, having solved one murder." Once Brian's gun was pointed at me, it all became clear who the perp was.

The conversation quickly deteriorated. Virgil reminded me of all the times I had been overconfident and ended up in trouble while I countered with my successful and imaginative extrications from such dilemmas. I had managed to bring the car to a stop against a tree (my five-year-old self) and I had made it down the mogul field (my eight-year-old self), albeit walking after sending my skis flying. I soon tired of point / counter-point and pleaded exhaustion as an excuse for hanging up on him.

The call to my younger sister went slightly better. Ariadne was in her senior year at San Diego State University. As the baby of the family, she gets more than her fair share of advice from my parents;

they seem more reluctant for her to grow up than they had been with Virgil and me. Her coping mechanism is to rebel, early and often. I think she and my parents were both relieved when she went away to college.

"This is great news," she said. "As long as you keep getting into trouble, Mom and Dad won't worry about me. I expect your murder will be the main topic at Thanksgiving dinner. If it isn't, I'll introduce it and no one will even think to ask what I've been up to."

"What do you mean, 'getting into trouble'? How is my inadvertently finding a dead body my fault? Not like your dating choices, such as that forgettable toad, who thought *The 300* was a better treatment of Thermopylae than Herodotus's. You knew toad-boy and Dad were going to get into it ..."

"His name was 'Tobias.'"

"Whatever. Oh, and you also knew Dad was going to want to – what's that Greek verb for 'waste utterly' – oh yes, *ἐκπέρθω* him. Why do you bring losers like that home? Just feed them to the sharks, Arie. Or the harpies."

Since she'd left home, Mother and Dad rarely knew what Ariadne was doing. She would use the excuse that she was running off to class to avoid mentioning that she'd taken up hang-gliding at Torrey Pines, or was dating a man fifteen years her senior, or committing other indiscretions. She'd taken a cue from Virgil and decided that non-disclosure beat spilling the beans as a legal strategy. Consequently, Mother and Dad now exercise most of their parenting on their ugly but ever-so-sweet dog, Gorgon, who, like Arie, ignores all their over-solicitous ministrations. And, like Arie, he occasionally brings home a rodent.

I reminded Ariadne that Rebecca would be at the dinner table, and if she brought up the topic of murder Mother would come down on her like a Category 5 hurricane on Florida. I could hear Mother saying "Santa Claus will not come," her ultimate threat when we were growing up.

After I got off the phone with my sister, I poured another half glass of wine – hey, it had been a rough day – and cut up cheddar cheese chunks in hopes that they would absorb the alcohol that I was consuming all too quickly.

My last call was to Stacey. Before I could tell her about Laguna, she started ranting about the "stupid-ass" assignment she'd been tasked with at work. Strong words for her.

As a corporate fixer, a cross between an executive assistant and a faith healer, Stacey had often been tasked with the impossible, such as arranging for high-tech gear to make it through customs in less than an hour, or ensuring a visiting international businessman got an invitation to the Governor of California's garden party. That morning, her boss, Tyler, had given her an assignment that he thought would be a cinch. Stacey didn't see it that way.

"He wants me to ask Darrell to attend a scheduled corporate golf outing at the Sequoia Club. I explained that Darrell and I had split up, but he didn't care; he'd promised his bosses that Darrell would attend and it was my job to deliver."

Darrell Jackson, a cornerback for the San Francisco 49ers, had dated Stacey for a few months at the beginning of the football season. Although Darrell initially ranked very high on Stacey's personal Key Dating Factors or KDF system (and Stacey said I over-analyzed things), they'd parted ways when Stacey got tired of Darrell blaming his poor on-field performance on referees and field conditions. Stacey told him to "man up" and dumped him.

"Maybe they'd be happy if I delivered just part of Darrell, like his head on a platter. The last thing I want to do is ask him for a favor," Stacy fretted. "He's on bimbo number three since me. I mean, he's on his third girl that I know of since dating me."

I resisted the temptation to laugh at her verbal slip. Stacey just wanted to vent, so I also refrained from mentioning that within three weeks of splitting with Darrell, Stacey had found herself a new boyfriend, Jake. I'd yet to meet him but had heard all about his business career (entrepreneur), his looks (totally hot), his house (in the Marina), his record-setting KDF score (152) and the great places he took her (impossible-to-get-reservations restaurants).

"I think I can take your mind off Darrell for a minute," I said as Stacey paused for breath. I told her about my day.

Like Virgil, Stacey assumed I was planning to investigate. Unlike my brother, she was all for it and even offered to call in a favor from George. A private investigator and friend of Stacey's, George had helped me a bit on my last case. That is, "last case" as in what I had thought would be "first, last and only case." Really. Who aspires to the Corpse-of-the-Month Club to the point where she gets good at finding whodunit? I don't. I assured Stacey that I was through playing detective. Or would be through once I found out who offed Laguna.

By the time I'd concluded the call with Stacey, it was nearly ten-thirty. As much as I wanted to hear Keoni's voice, I was wiped and in no mood to provide yet another recitation of my 'interesting' day. I picked up my empty wine glass and cheddar cheese plate in preparation for heading to bed.

My cell phone chose that moment to break into "Henehene Kou Aka." I glanced at it. Keoni. He liked to sing that song to me: "Your Laughter is So Contagious." As tired as I was, the song and the thought of him made me smile.

"*Aloha pumehana. Pehea 'oe?* Howzit, Keoni?"

"*Aloha*, Emma. *E kala mai iā'u nō ka hola.* I am sorry to call so late but I had that feeling that you needed to talk to me. *Pehea 'oe?* Is everything okay?"

Keoni and I had always had an ESP thing going. We seemed to know when the other was upset or worried or about to call.

"I'm good, but a woman was killed in my building. I found the body. They don't know who did it, yet, but my landlady may be a suspect."

"*Ei nei*, was the woman a good friend of yours?"

"No, I barely knew her."

My phone beeped, announcing a text message. Curiosity compelled me to check. Virgil. I might have known.

"Darnit. *Auwē, ku'u kaikaina.* Sorry, Keoni. Virgil is texting me. I'll try to get rid of him."

Virgil: Must talk. Concerned about you.

Me: Thanks kaka head. Didn't say I'd get involved.

Virgil: Buffalo butt. Know you. Impetuous.

Me: Eel enema. Can't talk now. On phone.

"I'm back. It was just Virgil pushing me to stay out of investigating Laguna's murder."

"He worries about you. So do I. We know you often jump into trouble when you try to help others."

"I do not jump. I'm more a stick-a-toe-in-the-water-ever-so-gingerly type. Besides, my purse is registered as a deadly weapon, it's got so much anti-mugger equipment in it."

Everyone seemed overly concerned about my safety. What did I need to do? Carry a pocket Doberman?

"*Auwē.* I do not want to upset you, but we all love you and would be heartbroken if anything happened to you, *ku'u pua.*"

There was nothing I could say to that.

At Keoni's urging, I recounted my discovery of Laguna's body, interview with the police, questioning at work and the atmosphere at Carson as we settled into a comfortable rhythm. Soon Keoni was speaking about his family and I found myself sitting on the couch, feet tucked underneath and clutching a pillow while Keoni chatted about his recent work with his *'onokola* – his uncle. I'd never heard him so excited about anything that didn't include surfing or Hawaiian music. Uncle Kimo was working with Hawaiian activist groups to obtain the return of ceded lands – those taken from the Hawaiian monarchy when it was overthrown in the 1890s – to native Hawaiians. Keoni was doing research for his uncle and helping him to draft position papers.

Keoni's earnest tone surprised me; the Keoni I knew had been interested in preserving the Hawaiian culture through his music and work with Hawaiian woods like *koa* and *'ohi'a lehua.* But he'd never been involved in the Hawaiian sovereignty movement.

"Why this sudden interest in politics?" I asked.

"It's not sudden." I could hear the defensiveness in Keoni's tone. "I've been helping Uncle Kimo for over a year now. It's clear that our real Hawaiian culture is being lost in the Aloha Industry and will not survive without the return of our lands and our sovereignty."

The tourism industry presentation of the Hawaiian culture may be warped, but at least the aloha spirit it embraced included everyone. The Hawaiian sovereignty movement was all about those that could lay claim to the land through native blood.

Keoni's voice softened. "*Ei nei*, this is very important to me and I want it to be important to you, too. It is very difficult to explain my feelings over the phone."

"I understand," I said. But I didn't. Not really.

Perhaps sensing my uncertainty, Keoni changed the topic to *Kalikimaka* and his visit. He'd been teasing me for weeks that he had "big news" to tell me at Christmas. My playful guesses so far (he was going pro in surfing, he had a new tattoo, he dyed his hair red) had been wide of the mark. Claiming that the long day and fatigue were getting the better of me, I declined to even guess this time. By now, not even Keoni could ignore my mood and we ended the call, rather abruptly.

My phone had beeped again while I saying goodnight to Keoni. Expecting the worst, I checked my messages. From Virgil, of course.

Virgil: Rebecca needs her Auntie Emma. Already bought your Xmas gift☺

I considered what Keoni had said. I should feel lucky I had a loving family that cared.

Me: I promise not to go looking for trouble.

Virgil: Thx, little Buffalo Butt.

Me: Aloha, gopher guts.

I had written "aloha" unconsciously but it gave me pause. It was a word that covered a multiplicity of occasions and feelings, among them, "hello," "goodbye," and "love." Whatever my issues were with Virgil, or with Keoni, the answer was and always would be *aloha.*

SIX

"How sweet are your words to my taste,
sweeter than honey to my mouth!"
– Psalms 119:103

I'M NOT ONE WHO likes to live in a rut, encountering sameness day after day. But when one area of my life is exciting, say discovering a dead person in my apartment building, having the other areas continue in a boring routine is a good thing. I'd realized last night that it was not going to happen; the rest of my life was, if not headed over a cliff, at least generally headed towards a precipice. My uncertainty about Keoni was shaken by our recent conversation and I even wondered if I'd made a mistake inviting him for Christmas. Also, the tension at work was palpable and, as I was soon to discover, potentially dangerous.

DADB (day after dead body) found me again working at Carson headquarters. I'd attended a meeting with some of the finance professionals in the morning. They were clearly not happy to be there, but Laura managed to secure a large amount of information about their systems costs, which I was now loading into my spreadsheet. Around one o'clock, several of us took a break to grab lunch at Carson's cafeteria.

The Sweet Life Café bordered one of the meditation gardens. Wrought iron tables with umbrellas provided shade from the sun, and a small oval koi pond nestled in the curve of the terrace. What a company. Even lunch was designed to be restful instead of hurried and frenzied. Fresh, organic and sustainably-grown greens graced the salad bar and the daily special highlighted local suppliers by name. Not that I wanted to get to know my lunch before eating it ("the bacon in this BLT graciously provided by Wilbur"), but all things being equal, I liked the idea that the chicken in my sandwich had a nice life before it was snuffed out for my benefit. As one would expect, most desserts featured Carson's chocolate: ice cream, chocolate mousse and death-by-chocolate brownies.

Not up to an entire brownie, I nevertheless helped myself to one of the small samples. Really, how many calories can one square inch of chocolate, butter, nuts and more chocolate have? Dark chocolate has flavonoids in it, so a brownie is really health food. Everybody knows that.

The indoor seating area offered a plethora of empty tables. Since GD corporate culture promoted 'aggressive friendliness' with clients, the four of us – Wendell, Maria, Shafiq and I – eschewed the open tables and seated ourselves at the end of a long rattan table occupied by a half-dozen Carson employees wearing sports jerseys in honor of "Wear Your Favorite Team Day." If our corporate attire hadn't given us away, the visitor badges with "Consultant" in large print centered on them like a bulls-eye clearly identified us as The Enemy.

Two questions into the "How are you? Nice to meet you" dance with the others at the table, you'd have thought someone just said, "Waiter, there is a fly in my chocolate." I tried several opening gambits, including "How 'bout them 49ers," with no takers, not even from the two occupants wearing San Francisco 49ers jerseys

With nothing to lose – hey, they already disliked us – I took a big swig of my fruit smoothie, made sure there were no sharp instruments within reach, and addressed myself to the woman sitting next to me with the New York Yankee earrings.

"I know we are *personae non gratae* here, but for the record, none of us had anything to do with Zuckers buying out Carson, nor are we participants in any manpower allocation decisions," I said, effortlessly dropping the corporate code words for layoffs.

I detected a slight softening in her expression and one of the 'Niners fans shifted slightly in her seat. "Fair enough. I'm Sonia – Sonia Sackett. I work in HR."

"Emma Jones, and these are my colleagues Maria Guardino, Wendell Taylor and Shafiq Rahman." The Carsonians around the table introduced themselves. They seemed nice enough, if still wary, except for two men who shot cold stares as if we had just espoused the torment of small mammals in satanic rituals. Or even worse, hated chocolate.

One of the men, Tony, was a fiftyish silver-haired fireplug with dark chocolate brown eyes and an obvious 'Niners fan. He put down his silverware with a pronounced clang and a glower. "If you really want to know why you are about as welcome as a St. Louis Rams fan, it's not just the layoffs – yes, 'layoffs,' not 'rightsizing' or 'corporate consolidation' or 'rethinking our core mission' or whatever corporate crap terminology you use now. Carson is a great company: state-of-the-art manufacturing, dedicated associates, sustainable, high quality ingredients and artisanal care."

Geez, I didn't know people actually talked like their marketing brochures.

Tony continued. "And, we've been acquired by an uncaring global behemoth that sells third-rate chocolate using ingredients they buy in bulk from other corporate behemoths who don't care where the ingredients come from as long as they are cheap. To buy, that is; they don't count the cost of despoiling the environment and putting the local farmer out of business. Chemical crap, that's all it is."

He had worked in everything causal except protecting endangered species, unless you counted the endangered species known as Carson employees. Nevertheless, he seemed to truly care about producing a quality product, and not just a cheap chocolate thrill.

Tony wasn't the only Carson employee to speak his mind. Gareth, a thirtyish man with boyish features and a closely-cropped head contrasted by thick, dark eyebrows, told us not to expect him or other Carsonians to help us do our "dirty work." He didn't stick around for a discussion, but tugged his San Francisco Giants hat down on his head, grabbed a chocolate from one of the ubiquitous bowls perched on the table and stalked off with his tray. Tony followed.

Sonia and another woman, the one who'd been doing yoga in the courtyard earlier, murmured half apologies for their colleagues' behavior but were interrupted by another man at the table who suddenly claimed he knew me.

"Really?" I replied, not recognizing him.

"I've seen you near my apartment. On Greenwich."

"Yeah, my apartment's on Greenwich." I returned his stare, hoping for a sense of recognition. I'd already forgotten his name. He was in his thirties, I'd guess, with light brown hair two weeks past a good cut, hazel eyes under heavy lids, and a build about six months past the last gym visit. He'd make a forgettable murder suspect: no tics, tattoos or tells. Now why was I thinking that? I couldn't recall ever having seen him before.

"It's a nice area, isn't it?" I said. "Except for being right in the middle of the land-of-hardly-any-parking, especially in the evening after seven."

He didn't say anything, but stood up, grabbed his tray and left. The remaining Carson people at the table did the same. Sonia lingered just long enough to give me an apologetic smile. "It's not personal." She picked up one of the chocolates, unwrapped it and stared at it for an extra second before she bit into it with a frisson of pleasure. "This," she said, waving the half-eaten chocolate to make her point, "is worth preserving. But Zuckers ... well, they just don't care."

"I did warn you," said Maria after Sonia was out of earshot.

"Who knew that artisanal chocolate is a religious cult? I mean, I love chocolate, but it's all kind of the same, except dark chocolate is tons better than milk chocolate."

"Carson employees don't see it that way," said Wendell, who had remained quiet throughout the exchange. "So now you know that, and you might not want to confront them again, particularly in a dark alley."

Six months ago I would have dismissed Wendell's comment as hyperbole. I'd been on multiple projects where GD consultants were the focus of loathing by disgruntled employees. It was part of the job, especially if our work threatened their jobs and I'd learned to shrug it off. But Padmanabh's death last summer changed that. For a time, it had appeared that his killer could be one of Tahiti Tacos' technology employees unhappy about GD's outsourcing project. And indeed, although he hadn't murdered Padmanabh, one of the TT staff had sent ugly and threatening notes. I still had mine.

The guy who knew where I lived hadn't made any threats, but ... I shivered and made a mental note to start carrying my Shrieker again, a device that fits in the side of a purse or a pocket. Hitting it hard activates a siren so intense, it sounds like the early warning system for Armageddon, as I discovered once when my purse fell over in the car at a stop sign and three pedestrians came up to the car to see if I was okay. I might put the baseball bat back in my trunk, too. Just in case.

SINCE I'D ARRIVED AT WORK particularly early that day (nightmares had awakened me before dawn), by four that afternoon I was oh-so-ready to get out of there and go surfing. I'd reached a stopping point in my analysis so I saved all my files, packed up my laptop and slipped out when everyone else went to get a late afternoon 'chocolateine' fix, as Maria called it: a latte and two or three of Carson's prototype chocolates. I was happy to forego the calories for a concoction of a quite different nature: eau-de-kelp finished by a spritz of salt water.

I beat the traffic odds crossing the Golden Gate, out Nineteenth Avenue and down the coast highway to San Mateo Beach. By the time I reached San Mateo, there wasn't much light but I knew I could surf the afterglow of the sun going down. I whipped into a slot in front of the restroom/shower stalls and suited up as fast as I could strip publicly without exposing one more square inch than I had to on account of my regard for public decency. That, and the fact the temperature was in the fifties with a gusting wind.

The surf report had said it was "two to four feet and crumbling, with a few workable corners." The surf wasn't any better than the report, no thanks to the onshore winds, that pushed "crumbling" right into "pulverized." There was a smattering of cars in the lot – populated by dog walkers, only one other surfer appeared to still be out in the lineup – and I was surprised to see a large van for one of the local news channels parked in front of the sea wall. Maybe it was a slow news day and the news crew wanted to watch the waves in between reports of Girl Scout cookie pushers hitting up the elderly to buy boxes of thin mints. Or there might be a report of an arch-criminal smuggling plastic bags into town, in obvious defiance of the ban on them enacted by San Francisco. The horror.

Despite the eminently forgettable waves – I caught a few and far more caught and rolled me – I nevertheless felt great. Pelicans glided overhead in great lazy circles, occasionally folding their wings and spearing the water in pursuit of a fish. A seal surfaced a few feet away from me and surfed a couple of waves before wandering off in pursuit of dinner.

By the time I got out, the news van hadn't moved, but the sun had slid under the ocean and the early evening stars were beginning to party. I did a quick rinse under the shower, hitting the button every four to five seconds to keep the water flowing (Pacifica took water conservation to an annoying degree of anality), peeled the key from the pocket on my left ankle and unlocked the car. I stripped the top of my wetsuit from my shivering limbs, threw an extra large fleece hoody over my head and peeled my bathing suit top from under it. I finished the wetsuit mambo, peeling the suit off like a neoprene banana peel, and added fleece pants and fleece-lined sheepskin footgear to my outfit. Surfing in northern California in November – well, even Donner and Blitzen would avoid such cold climes. When I read about surfers traveling to Norway and Greenland in pursuit of never-ridden waves, I had to ask, "Why?"

As I drove home, I turned on the radio and searched for some good music but instead found seventies, heavy metal, more seventies, easy listening, classical, mores seventies, sixties, and so forth. I gave up and tuned into one of the news stations.

"... shark attack at San Mateo Beach ..."

What the?

"... eviscerated a seal in front of onlookers at three ..."

A couple hours earlier and I could have been sashimi.

"... warning signs posted on the beach ..."

Signs? What signs? I didn't see any signs.

"San Mateo Beach was largely deserted except for a few hardy surfers ..."

Foolhardy, you mean.

"Experts from the Monterey Bay Aquarium believe it was a Great White."

Of course. The Bolinas-Farallons-Santa Cruz triangle is the Great White Shark capital of the world.

When the pounding in my heart slowed, it occurred to me there was a bright side to this, other than my not being eaten, that is: the beach wouldn't be crowded for days.

On the other hand, wherever I went lately, predators lurked.

SEVEN

"The Puritan's idea of hell is a place where
everybody has to mind his own business."
– Attributed to Wendell Phillips

"Oh, it's you," Magda said, her expression of exasperation replaced by a small smile. Chesty whined and nudged Magda's ankles from behind as he tried to wiggle his way towards the open door. As Magda moved aside, Chesty leaped up and yipped until I bent down and consented to multiple enthusiastic doggy kisses.

"I came by to pick up your apartment key," I said. Magda was leaving the following morning, Friday, to drive to Los Angeles to spend Thanksgiving week with her family. She'd asked me to bring in her mail while she was gone, and keep an eye on the building.

"Just the apartment key?" Magda said, eyebrows raised.

"Well, I did wonder how things were going, with the police and investigation and all. And whether your underwear drawer had been strip searched. I mean, why should I have all the fun?"

Magda smiled and gestured to me to enter so I did, careful to avoid stepping on the whirling dachsie dervish. Edson strolled by, avoiding eye contact and flicking his tail in my direction. That passed for an enthusiastic greeting in Edson-speak.

We assumed our usual positions in the living room; Magda and I relaxed on the wing chair and couch, respectively, while Edson draped across the back of the couch and Chesty perched expectantly at Magda's feet in case a piece of dog food fell out of her pocket. Magda, ever the accomplished hostess, had prepared a tray with drinks – ice water for me as I'd been overdosing on chocolate and a vodka tonic for herself – and hors d'oeuvres.

"I don't mind telling you it's been a stressful few days," Magda began. "Calls from Laguna's family about clearing out her apartment, another visit by the police to interview the tenants they missed in the first sweep, friends and neighbors phoning or stopping by to see how I am," Magda said, her voiced laced with sarcasm, "but really just wanting to get more details on Laguna's murder and the police investigation. I've barely been able to find time to get Chesty out to do his business. Even Edson is acting a bit rattled. He only ate four shrimp today. I'll be glad to get away."

I visibly squirmed. "I confess I've been kinda worried about you. I, uh, haven't had a chance to tell you that the police knew about your relationship with Laguna and your, ah, disagreements."

"Fights, Emma. Viet Nam was a war, not a police action. September 11th was an act of terrorism, not a 'man-caused disaster.' Laguna and I had fights, not disagreements. Call things what they are. And before you ask, I was very clear with the police about when and why we had fights and that yes, I did lose my temper and threaten her but only after she'd kicked my dog. But that's all it was: multiple skirmishes, no prisoners and no casualties."

Except that Laguna was dead.

While I selected the smallest piece of cheese off the hors d'oeuvres tray, Magda stared at Chesty, whose expression clearly communicated that he was neglected and probably hadn't eaten in five years. Tossing a piece of cracker in his direction, Magda continued in a high sing-song voice, "Well, we have to protect the ones we love, don't we, little fellow?" He wagged his tail vigorously and issued two short barks in acknowledgment.

"When the police came by to interview tenants they missed, they questioned me again," Magda said. "I think they've latched onto me as their prime suspect. The ski pole had no fingerprints."

"The what?"

"The ski pole. The metal rod Laguna used for mounting her protest sign was an old ski pole: strong, lightweight and unfortunately for Laguna, a pointed end. Now, where was I?"

"Fingerprints."

"Right, no fingerprints and I've deduced, from what the police are not saying, that Laguna doesn't have the skin cells of the murderer underneath her nails nor are there fingerprints of the killer on the ski pole. Unlike one of your TV crime dramas," she finished.

Chesty was nosing around the chairs and under the coffee table searching for anything he might have missed. I dropped the last piece of my roll on the floor. "What about epithelials in the apartment?"

Magda gave me a blank look. Obviously, she wasn't a *CSI* aficionado. "Skin cells, from whence you can get DNA," I added.

"The police didn't say. Laguna had a lot of friends over to her apartment, so I'm hopeful they'll find other suspects to pursue."

"But they won't find your fingerprints, right?"

"Wrong. I've already told them that I was in Laguna's apartment last Saturday. We had a heated discussion about her kicking Chesty."

"Fight, you mean," I said. "How about time of death? Do you have an alibi?"

"The police wouldn't say when she'd been killed, but they were interested in my whereabouts late Sunday afternoon and evening. Edson and Chesty are the only ones who can testify that I was home," she said, tossing Chesty a piece of kibble.

An unbidden vision of Laguna's impaled body flashed into my mind and my stomach churned. "I've been thinking," I said, "that since Laguna died in her own living room, she probably let the killer into the apartment. Not that I really checked out the doorjamb, but it didn't look kicked open or anything. Then there was a fight, Laguna was killed, and the murderer raced out, leaving the door ajar in his panic. Either that or it was a cold, calculated kill and the murderer left the door ajar in an attempt to lower the ambient temperature and fudge the time of death. Except that leaving the refrigerator door open would have worked better."

"A simpler explanation is a break-in gone wrong," Magda countered. "And how was last weekend's *Law and Order* marathon?"

I ignored her *Law and Order* crack and I didn't believe Laguna's murder was a result of a break-in. Why her apartment instead of any other apartment in the neighborhood, preferably one on the first floor? Plus, I'd read – or heard on *Law and Order*, I admit it – that most victims know their killers, though I wondered how that statistic was compiled. "Mr. Smith, you readily admit to killing Ms. Jones. Would you say you were close?"

We both fell silent. If this were a TV series, the local CSI team would swoop in and pick up a few fibers that could only be from a fabric used in a limited edition Wilkes Bashford men's sports jacket, one of which had been sold to a man who'd threatened Laguna ten days ago and who had used a credit card, the same one he'd just used five minutes ago to check into a hotel a block and a half from the police station. With commercials, that would wrap up the murder in less than an hour, prime-time style.

"I'm beginning to understand how you felt last summer," Magda said.

After Padmanabh's death, I'd been one of the prime suspects and the police had gone so far as to search my apartment. The experience had so unnerved me that I'd been close to tears – okay, in tears – on Magda's couch feeling sorry for myself.

I noticed the slumping shoulders. "Unsettling, isn't it?"

She nodded.

We sat quietly again, sipping our drinks. When I'd fallen apart on her couch, Magda had given me a drink, a tissue and two minutes of sympathy followed by a kick in the butt to stop playing victim and start hunting for the real killer.

Magda hadn't asked for my help but …

I cleared my throat. "I have experience, you know, in finding murderers." There, Virgil couldn't say I was looking for trouble; I was just talking over old times with a friend. Yes, indeedy, that's all I was doing.

Magda hesitated for a moment, sat up straighter on the couch and looked me straight in the eyes. "There's something I haven't told you."

Oh my God! Was she going to change her story and confess?

"Although I've owned this building for a long time, I didn't move in until four years ago. In the intervening years, I rented out this apartment, my apartment, to a series of tenants."

I had no idea where Magda was headed with this story. I merely nodded and she continued.

"When I didn't renew the last tenant because I planned to move in, he pleaded with me for an extension, saying he didn't have another apartment lined up despite the fact I'd given him six months warning on the lease termination. So I let him stay an extra month, and then another, but he still wouldn't move out. When I pointed out that he'd had enough time to find an apartment and no extensions were forthcoming, his language became abusive. Long story short, I started eviction proceedings."

Magda paused and took a sip of her drink before continuing. "I was angry that I now had to wait even longer for the eviction to go through, and then I'd have to pay him thousands in relocation benefits. I went to his apartment, my apartment, to talk with him. I offered a cash settlement if he'd move out within the week. He yelled at me, trying to intimidate me. I yelled back. He grabbed my arm, hauled me out of a chair and pushed me against the wall, towering over me. But I had come prepared in case he got violent. I pulled out my Ka-Bar knife," Magda said as she nodded towards the knife display case.

I didn't hear her next words as I saw an image of Laguna looming over the diminutive Magda, Magda grabbing the ski pole and thrusting it through Laguna and then twisting the pole while Laguna screamed. I shook my head and the vivid picture disappeared as Magda's voice returned.

"... skedaddled out of the building and called the police. I was just defending myself, but the police are aware of that little incident and seem to think I'm a hothead." She sat back in her seat. "I need to get a lawyer."

My eyes fleetingly met Magda's and I glanced away. Could she see what I'd been thinking, that she could have killed Laguna?

But if Magda had killed Laguna, she wouldn't hide from what she had done; she'd call the police, explain the facts and claim self-defense. Magda had to be innocent.

"I can help you with finding a lawyer," I said. "I have a list from when I was under investigation and everyone I knew was giving me the names of lawyers. I think there are ten to twelve names on the list. If those don't suit, go get a latte at Elixir of Life. Shaun, the barista, claims he knows a ton of lawyers. And tattoo artists," I added. "And ask for extra sprinkles on the lawyer, er, latte."

"I'll keep that in mind, although I do know retired JAGs, military lawyers, who are still practicing law. Or I could network through the Navy League."

"When the police investigated me for murder, you said getting a lawyer wasn't enough; I needed to find other suspects the police could focus on."

"That was different. It was clear that someone at your workplace murdered your boss. Anyone could be Laguna's killer."

I coughed lightly. "But it's more likely the killer is someone she knew. And you do have the key to her apartment. We might find clues there."

"We?" Magda said, raising her eyebrows.

"I'm volunteering to help."

"That's sweet of you, Emma, but the police have already been through Laguna's apartment. Besides, no one can go in now: it's a crime scene. And I can't let you in after they release it because her parents have taken responsibility for the lease and they haven't authorized your entrance."

"Oh," I said, disappointed.

"But," she added, giving me a sly smile, "the police said they'd be done with the apartment by Monday. After that, Laguna's boyfriend is going to keep an eye on the place for her family. He's not a full-time live-in, so the apartment will be vacant for long stretches."

"Soooo," I said, wondering what her point was. Did she think I knew how to pick a lock?

Magda tossed Chesty another piece of kibble. He tried to catch it but missed, his nose redirecting it under the couch. He sniffed around, bewildered as to what had become of his treat.

Magda got up, walked over to her slant top desk and pulled down the desktop to reveal a pigeon-holed interior. She removed what appeared to be a solid block of carved wood, revealing a concealed cubby-hole, reached in and pulled out a set of keys, jangled them and then put everything back. "A good landlady is careful with the master keys," she said.

I nodded in understanding. Good ol' Magda. She returned to her seat and I asked her to tell me what she knew about Laguna. Magda didn't have much real information about Laguna, her friends or coworkers. However, she had a lot to say about Laguna and her politics including a few choice words about Laguna's friends painting protest signs in the building's courtyard. She didn't know any of their names, and didn't care to know them. "Just one more group of San Francisco loonies," she said. "As much as I like this area, there are times when I do feel like packing it in."

"Aw, c'mon Magda. If you left, who would take on the city over military recruiting?"

Four months previously, the City had tried to ban military activity of any type, including JROTC in the high schools, recruiting and the United Services Organization (USO) kiosk at the airport. Magda had organized a protest at City Hall and recruited military friends from across the state to attend.

Magda smiled. "That was fun, wasn't it? I loved the look on Tavistock's face when he had to apologize: like he was eating a live toad," she said referring to Mayor Sean Tavistock, whose apology was precipitated by a now-viral video of him being rude to a disabled veteran.

"And you won."

"Well, I helped." When local tourism was threatened by a large and influential veterans' group call for a nationwide boycott of San

Francisco, the City backed down. "You're right, what's life without challenges? Especially when I'm the one doing the challenging."

"I think we can do without challenges that include potential murder charges against friends and family," I said. "Speaking of which, how is your family taking the news?"

"I haven't told them."

I cleared my throat, but before I could say anything, Magda spoke.

"Emma, please stop clearing your throat every time you want to say something important. Just blurt it out. Life's short. Get to the point."

I swallowed in mid-throat clear. "You'll tell your family over Thanksgiving, right?"

"I don't think so, no. It's not anything they need to know."

"What? You were after me when I hadn't told my parents about Pad's death." I was indignant.

"This is different."

"Oh, like, totally," I said with all the sarcasm I could muster.

"A young person like you should tell your parents about serious matters. Parents, however, shouldn't worry their children by foisting their problems on them."

"When will you tell them? At your sentencing?"

Magda gave me a knowing smile. "How could that happen with you as my ace detective? I'm sure you'll discover the real murderer."

And with that, I considered myself hired. But if Virgil should ask, I'd deny I was investigating anything; I was just keeping my eyes and ears open. I'd keep them especially wide open when I snuck into Laguna's apartment.

EIGHT

"It is quite a three pipe problem ..."

– "The Redheaded League," Sir Arthur Conan Doyle

I GOT OUT OF MY APARTMENT early the next morning to swing by Café de la Fog for a double latte. CDLF didn't do sprinkles, but their coffee was stronger than Elixir's, and I needed all the caffeine I could pump into my fuzzy and sluggish veins. They also had delicious walnut-orange scones and between the omega-3s (walnuts) and vitamin C (orange), I'd feel good about eating a healthy breakfast. I admit it; the biggest lies are the ones you tell to yourself.

The prior evening I had ruminated about investigating Laguna's murder. That's ruminated as in pondered, not ruminated as in rechewed partially digested food. Eew. I'd even gone so far as to sit in a hot bath with mountains of bubbles, a large glass of sparkling wine in hand with the sweet aroma of jasmine candles tickling my senses. I'd used the long hot soak method in the past successfully to sort out boyfriend problems. Of course, none of my former boyfriends had been associated with a murder, unless you counted killing a budding romance.

Laguna's case, if I may be so bold as to call it a case, presented more of a challenge than solving Pad's murder. I worked with the suspects in Pad's death, which meant I could interrogate them over the water cooler ever so casually with clever gambits like, "So, off any arrogant, ambitious bosses lately?" or "May I have all the blunt objects in your cubicle so I can luminol them?" I'd learned about luminol, the chemical that reacts with blood to produce a blue glow in a darkened room, in a *Bones* episode.

Laguna's murder was a different kettle of gummy fish. I didn't know any likely perps or even FOLPs, friends of likely perps. Even to help Magda, I couldn't quit my day job, pose as a convert to the cause and bring my vast talents and clever interrogation skills – okay, meager talents and haphazard interrogation skills – to bear on the Lime Organization. My investigation had to take place when I wasn't working, sleeping, surfing or getting ready for Christmas. That added up to about twenty-two seconds per day.

Providing that Lime-O had protests on their agenda, I could meet Laguna's co-workers by joining them in marching, heckling or hoisting a placard. Though I'm apolitical, I have nevertheless had activist adventures across the spectrum supporting my friends in their *causes célèbres*. At one time or another, I'd worked for gay rights, military recruiting, saving the environment, safe sex and butterfly habitat. I mean, safe sex and also butterfly habitat, not a habitat where you could have safe sex and watch butterflies. Not that there's anything wrong with that, particularly in San Francisco, where you'd be a shining example of "make love, not war," and saving the environment, all at once.

A protest might be the perfect gambit to ingratiate myself with Laguna's co-workers, although I drew the line at handcuffing myself to inanimate or animate objects, except maybe that dreamy Detective Torres. Perhaps one of Laguna's co-workers would conveniently divulge who amongst them wanted Laguna dead, or at least lead me to Laguna's other friends, enemies or even frenemies.

With a plan of attack in mind, I went to bed. At three, I awoke with the brilliant idea of taking a leave of absence from GD to go to work for Lime-O. By four I'd dreamed that I impersonated a police officer, dragged the suspects to a large warehouse, and tortured them with bright lights and bad eighties music. The music probably came from the caterwauling cats that lived in the area and were notorious for their night arias (they'd embraced their inner atonal post modernists). I was punished for my evil thoughts when

I tried to get back to sleep while eighties tunes ran through my head; "Wake Me Up Before You Go Go" annoyed me even more than usual. I must have fallen asleep for a few minutes, because when my eyes next sprang open, five-fifteen registered on the clock. I awoke just knowing I had the solution to make the murderer confess, but I couldn't remember what it was. I arose for good at six-thirty after a vague dream about Wave Hog, who was not really dead, but was posing as a lime green spandex-wearing pizza delivery man to get into Laguna's apartment, where he could kill her with the fin of a surfboard.

The barista at Café de la Fog handed me a 16-ounce caramel-laced concoction and I immediately drained half of it and wiped the foam off my lip with the back of my sleeve. I glanced over my shoulder reflexively to ensure my Grandmother Swenson wasn't watching. She was the "pat your upper lip daintily with a linen hanky" type, not the "wipe your sleeve across your mouth and belch contentedly" type. And I couldn't absolutely swear I didn't emit a very small, tasteful belch.

I took another big gulp. Heavenly. Or at least, my idea of heaven, which was, admittedly, not based on sound theology. My heaven included twenty-four hour coffee service with plenty of steamed milk (and sprinkles, of course). My coffee cup runneth over.

I grunted my appreciation for a taste of the divine, put more tangible evidence of it into the tip jar, and headed for work.

WHEN THE CARSON conference room emptied that morning, I took the opportunity to plow through the morning tranche of email – three online newspapers that were barely worth reading (except for the sob sister columns), two "forward this to five friends and in precisely twelve hours you will receive a blessing" and one offer for *Nigeria Oil and Gas Monthly.* (How on earth did I get on that solicitation list?) Then I called Stacey to enlist her help in my investigation.

"I knew you'd get involved in finding Laguna's killer," she said after I broached the subject. "I'm definitely in – anything to help get Magda off the noose. What's the plan?"

I gave her a condensed version of my offer of help to Magda and my desire to infiltrate Lime-O. "I was counting on your natural snoopiness to help me meet Laguna's co-workers. There's a protest on the Saturday after Thanksgiving ..."

"Oh, I'm sorry, hon. I'm spending the weekend with Jake? Remember?"

I'd totally forgotten that Stacey was joining Jake for "The Big Weekend in Napa." She'd been talking about it for weeks, and had even paid extortion to the airlines to rearrange her flight schedule so she could return early from Thanksgiving with her folks in Texas.

"Darnit." What is a sleuthette without her comic-relief sidekick?

"Ahm so sorry I can't make it. Is there anything else I can do to help? You know we can call on George's PI skills whenever you want them."

"I need a list of suspects first."

"Have you thought about going to Laguna's funeral? On TV shows, all the suspects show up to see the body buried."

"That did occur to me. However, Magda told me Laguna's parents are having a small service in L.A. They're not even coming up to San Francisco to clean out her apartment; Laguna's boyfriend volunteered to do it."

"Ah ha! A boyfriend. Suspect numero uno."

"Yup. According to Magda, a Mr. Justin Thyme."

"You're joking."

"Nope. It wouldn't surprise me if he had a brother named Nickov. Honestly, what were his parents thinking?"

"In Texas, we shoot people for less."

"In Texas, you shoot anything that moves that you can eat. Like armadillos – isn't that just possum on the half shell? Anyway, as I was saying ... what was I saying?"

"Cleaning, funeral, protest, armadillos."

"Right, the protest. You're not leaving for Texas until Sunday, right? How about going shopping with me tomorrow? I need to procure a suitable lime green outfit, if the juxtaposition of 'suitable' and 'lime green outfit' isn't an oxymoron. I did a quick search online but couldn't find anything; lime green is apparently not an 'in' color this year."

"And let's thank God for that," she replied. "Lime green makes us natural blondes look like cover girls for *Malaria Monthly*. Fortunately, I know the perfect place to find hideously ugly and coincidentally unfashionable clothes and tomorrow is good for me."

We chatted a few minutes more, mostly about Thanksgiving, and hung up.

"A protest, huh?"

Maria's question jolted me. Engrossed on the phone, I hadn't noticed her entrance.

"I heard you talking to your friend. You're going to spy at an anti-war protest to help your landlady. I'd be glad to help."

"Uh, that's nice of you to offer, but …"

"You're not really good at meeting people. I am. I'm also pretty good at pumping people for information, as you know. You could use my skills. Besides, I've never been involved in a murder investigation. It might be fun."

"I'm not really investigating a murder. I'm just asking around, trying to help my landlady."

"Well, whatever you call it, I can be your snoopsistant."

I didn't know Maria that well, and I still had an image of her running down the hall shrieking that I had offed Pad with a cricket bat. Still, she was more constructively nosier than anybody else I knew, and that had worked in my favor when looking into Pad's death. Well, why the heck not? What could it hurt? I might enlarge my vocabulary, too, given Maria's penchant for inventing new words. What could I say to such a generous offer except "Absogorforit?"

"The protest is being held the Saturday morning after Thanksgiving at the Embarcadero, near the regional headquarters of Towson Peabody."

"The mega contractor for the Department of Defense?"

"That's the one. You'll have to wear lime green."

"Cool. My first protest. Something new to Tweet about."

"Protest? Are Carson employees staging a protest?" Shafiq asked as he entered the room.

"No. At least, not that we know about," I amended.

"After the meeting I just had with them, it wouldn't surprise me if they staged an armed insurrection," Shafiq said as he threw himself into one of the vacant leather chairs. He twirled around in the chair several times and then slouched down.

"Let's hope they don't take hostages," I said.

"Who are your annoyertants?" Maria asked as she got up from her seat and headed for the side table where candy bowls staged a caloric siren call.

Annoyertants?

Clearly, it was a shotgun marriage of "annoy" plus what? Ants? Pants? Mutants? Pollutants? Debutantes?

Maria was shuffling through the bowl of candy. I'd already tried one of everything and was about to recommend the dark chocolate macadamia truffle when Maria snatched, unwrapped and popped a confection into her mouth. She turned around to find Shafiq appearing confused.

"Who's givin' you a hard time?" Maria explained.

"That would be just about everyone connected with the sales systems," Shafiq said. "I'm merely trying to find basic information on sale leads, customers, orders, vendors, and the like. I need to figure out how we can transfer the information to Zuckers' systems and ensure we have a plan for cutover. "

"And?"

"The apps team doesn't want to talk about any of that. Instead they're singing the virtues of a custom application they built that integrates their sales, demand forecasting and procurement systems to reduce purchasing and production costs 'from bean to bar.' They claim they can beat Zuckers on pricing raw materials, deliver a better product and produce higher profit margins on premium chocolate than on the pedestrian confections, as they put it, that Zuckers makes."

"Have they heard the term volume discounts?" Maria said, licking the remnants of a Carson Dark Chocolate Bar from her fingers. "Zuckers is a ginormous global company; I bet their purchasing volume in a day equals Carson's in a month." She reached for another candy bar.

She must be going through three bars a day. How can she do that and not become a blimp?

"I'm not saying I believe it," Shafiq said, "but this one guy, Anthony ... Cato, right, Anthony Cato. He's a zealot about this software. He's positive that once Zuckers sees how it works, they're going to be desperate to use it."

"Is it scalable?" I said. It was a common story to have superneato software run as slow as molasses in January when faced with the information requirements of a large corporation. Imagine a three hundred pound woman trying to fit into a child seat: it will be really slow going and painful and probably won't work at all.

"Scalability is the million dollar question, isn't it? I bet Zuckers won't even be interested in a digital tire kick. But I'll mention it to Laura; I've got a meeting with her in five minutes. I'll also let her know this group is being less than cooperative."

Shafiq rousted himself from his chair, grabbed his laptop and left.

"This is just the beginning," Maria said thoughtfully.

I looked at her in surprise. "What do you mean? Do you know something?"

"Only the obvious," she said. "A number of Carson employees have figured out they have no future in Zuckers, so they're not going to help us drive a stake through the truffle center of Carson's chocolates. So to speak. Several accountants even signed a pledge of non-cooperation. Figuratively of course; no one would actually put his name on something like that."

I wondered what non-cooperation means for accountants; they cook the books to *not* balance? They'd probably get all twitchy. Or start eating their eyeshades. Knowing Maria's ability to insinuate herself into a group, I was confident she'd spoken directly with some of the pledge signers and the information was true. Carson employees were planning to wage guerilla warfare. I just hoped that didn't include removing the candy from the GD conference room. I was pretty sure that would be a violation of the Geneva Convention.

NINE

"Fashion is a form of ugliness so intolerable
that we have to alter it every six months."
– Oscar Wilde

Stacey arrived at my apartment the next morning dressed for a high-end shopping trip: tight-fitting blue jeans and a snug cowl-neck sweater in a beautiful chocolate brown – dark chocolate, not milk chocolate – that showed her figure to great advantage. Not that her figure was ever at a disadvantage, unlike mine, which was becoming a chocolate magnet. Her purse, a soft chestnut-brown leather hobo bag slung across her shoulder, matched her slouchy, pointy-toe boots.

I buzzed her in and gazed at my sorry self in the mirror. I had thrown on faded and worn blue jeans – the ones with a rip in the knee, and not a "fashionable rip" that matched one in the other knee, either. And they were unusually snug. I'd have to watch how fast I sat down in them or I might become suddenly and highly ventilated, and those types of rips were never fashionable, even if you did have hot underwear. I had thrown a comfy tan corduroy jacket over a cap-sleeved baby blue sweater. By comfy I mean ten-years-old with frayed collar; I'd been wearing it since high school. My feet were clad in unremarkable ballet flats. Worn ballet flats, at that. I'd actually worn them in ballet class in my early teens before I got pointe shoes. At least my underwear was new, and black lace, not faded cotton in the "don't ever wear on a date" style.

"Sorry," I said as I opened my apartment door to Stacey's knocking. "I still have to put my purse together."

"Take your time, shugah."

"So where are we going?" I asked as I pulled out my favorite backpack-style purse and began rummaging for my license through wadded-up bills, credit cards, comb, lip balm and uneaten gum lurking in the bottom of the bag. Along the way, I found my fake engagement ring – worn to ward off slimewads – as well as two chunks of surf wax, my favorite screwdriver, pepper spray, a silver whistle and cuticle cream that had on occasion doubled as surf wax.

"Just up the way, Hayes Street," she replied.

I paused in mid-purse dive. Hayes Street encompassed a rather funky and pricy shopping area. "Stace, you realize I'm not thinking of making a serious wardrobe investment in a color which makes me look as if I am a refugee from Chi Rho Pi."

"Chi Rho Pi?"

"CRAP."

"I wasn't thinking you'd buy anything at the high-end places, but Hayes has a few reasonably-priced boutique stores. And if those don't work out, Goodwill is just a couple blocks away on South Van Ness."

"Okay, that's fine," I said, zipping my purse closed – or almost closed with all the stuff I was trying to cram in there (did I really need a screwdriver?) – and throwing it on my back. "But before we start, how 'bout we stop somewhere and get coffee?"

"You're on."

Ten minutes later, we walked into Elixir.

Shaun noticed our entrance; he had a thing for Stacey and was always on the *qui vive* for her arrival. I noted he was once again sporting a full regalia of body piercings: rings, studs, and so forth. Did his girlfriend relent or did Shaun choose jewelry over her? As we joined the line for ordering coffee, Shaun kept turning his head in our direction, trying to catch Stacey's eye.

"Any new developments for Magda? I mean, is an arrest imminent?" Stacey asked.

Ahead of us in line, a fedora-clad Gen Y-er with dreads halfway down her back hauled out her change purse and paid for a skinny chai in pennies.

"I don't know," I replied, watching several of the pennies roll across the counter. "She told me the cops had been 'round asking more questions. I hope she didn't say anything that will make them throw her in jail. You know how blunt she can be."

Stacey stooped down to retrieve several pennies from the floor. "Makes me feel guilty that I'm not able to help you next week. Tall tea and chocolate croissant," Stacey ordered from the girl at the register.

"Make mine a grande double mochachino, extra whipped cream. And a beignet," I said.

"You want sprinkles with that coffee, right?" said Shaun, who'd had an ear to our conversation.

"Why does everybody think I like sprinkles?"

Stacey and Shaun's eyebrows went up in stereo.

"Sometimes I order strong, black coffee, once in awhile, for a change." I was clearly never going to make it as a hard-boiled investigator. Mickey Spillane's Mike Hammer never had sprinkles in his coffee.

Shaun began frothing the milk. He had on a sleeveless black tank that showed off the muscles in his arms to definite advantage. Well-defined triceps. Good delts, too. Not that I'm shallow, but after all the surfing I do, I appreciate a nicely-muscled upper body.

"Is that a new tattoo?" I asked, anxious to get off the sprinkles topic.

"It is; I just got it," Shaun beamed as he held out his upper bicep for a closer view. "It's a Hawaiian design …"

"Ooh, is that *niho mano*?" I interrupted. "It is, isn't it? It's called *niho mano* because the pattern is modeled after shark teeth. My friend Keoni has it only his starts on his pectorals and goes up his chest and onto his …"

Shaun's lower lip quivered.

"It's really nice on you, Shaun," I said.

He continued frothing the milk in silence.

"Keoni, is coming to visit for Christmas. I am sure he'd like to see your tat. You don't see *niho mano* just anywhere, especially not so often on *haoles,* white guys."

Shaun perked up a bit. "Hey, did you notice I got the *artiste* to make the shark's teeth match my eyebrow jewelry?"

I peered at his right eyebrow. The triangular-shaped ring in his eyebrow was the same size as the tattooed teeth on his arm.

Stacey noticed, too. "Oh, that's so cute," she commented, only the last words came out more like "soooo kay-ute" as she laid on the drawl with extra molasses. It had its desired effect. Shaun beamed at as he handed over the coffee. His smile continued as we moved to an empty table nearby.

"You've made his day," I said under my breath as we sat down, not wanting Shaun to hear me.

We chatted about nothing in particular as we sipped our drinks and nibbled at our sweets. I didn't hear Shaun approach.

"I couldn't help but overhear when you were in line," he said. "Sounds like you've got a friend in trouble with the police. Remember when I toldya last summer that I could get you a good lawyer?" Shaun nodded at me but his eyes were on Stacey. "The offer still stands. Got lots of 'em comin' in here all the time. You can tell who the best ones are, cuz they wear the slick suits. Just say the word and I'll be glad to give you an intro."

"Thanks, Shaun," I replied. "I did tell my friend you knew a lot of lawyers, but I think she's finding one for herself."

"Kind of you to offer, though," added Stacey, throwing Shaun a brilliant smile.

"Glad to help. Any time. Say the word. By the way ..."

"Shaun, tall half-skinny extra hot double shot latte with whip!" A sharp call from the counter and Shaun's sentence was left dangling.

"It's *déjà vu* all over again," I quipped. "Everyone knows a good lawyer. Why aren't more people as helpful and promiscuously forthcoming with phone numbers of 'possibles' when one is in a dating slump? Enquiring minds want to know."

"It's clear that San Francisco has too few eligible men and too many lawyers." Stacey observed. "Maybe we need to thin the herd."

"The lawyer herd? Amen to that. Any suggestions how? Issue hunting licenses? Authorize bounties?"

"Tax credits," Stacey replied. "People will do anything to avoid giving the government their money. Offer a $500 tax credit for each lawyer bagged with a maximum of $2,000. Maybe we can dump the bodies in a landfill or use them as compost."

"Sounds good. Recycling begins at home," I said. "Even if lawyers are toxic waste."

"Amen." And with that, Stacey polished off her tea, grabbed her hobo bag and stood up. I seized my half-full cup of coffee and followed her to the car.

THE TRENDY SECTION of Hayes Street is known as Hayes Valley, an area highly self-conscious about being unconventional. Chain stores are prohibited in a several block radius. Years ago, Hayes Street was noted for its crack houses and homeless residents, and any store that didn't involve drug paraphernalia would have been welcomed by the long-suffering non-substance-abusing residents. After the Loma Prieta quake, the extension of the Central Expressway that bifurcated Hayes Valley was torn down. Then, the nouveau riche moved in along with art galleries, boutiques, design studios and high-end hole-in-the-recently-retrofitted-wall restaurants creating a Bohemian ambiance where price was no object – if your company had just IPOed, that is.

In true SF fashion, I found a small parking space only three blocks from the main drag and crammed my Honda CRX into the slot. No actual bumpers were touching but I wouldn't be able to execute a fast getaway.

"Just for fun, let's look at the funky stuff, first," Stacey said as we exited the car. "After all, it's not as if you really care what you wear. I doubt you'll see anyone you know at the protest."

"Anyone I know? While wearing lime green?"

In a scant two minutes, we arrived at the 500 block of Hayes Street, the main shopping drag, where I found a trash receptacle for my now-empty coffee cup. In fact, there were five trash receptacles: recyclable cans and bottles, recyclable plastic bags, recyclable paper, compost and trash. I support recycling, but it was a good thing I had stimulated my neurons with caffeine before being confronted with such a complicated trash-sorting algorithm. Being ecologically correct was hard work. I felt like dumping my trash in a single huffy pile, marked "Whatever."

I should say at the outset that I seem to have been born without a fashion gene, or a shopping one, either. If it weren't for my mother finding "just the cutest thing" on sale in my size and Ariadne dragging me out to "get rid of those mom jeans, already" on occasion, I'd be everyone's leading candidate for the reality TV show *What Not to Wear*.

Which is why, as we trolled from store to store, I found that what passed for fashion was questionable. Over the course of an hour, we dodged in and out of all types of shops selling everything in the fashion realm from "edgy" to "past the edge and right over the cliff." We explored the what's what of fashion: Goth, retro, boho chic, vintage, classic (I wasn't exactly sure what the difference was between "classic" and "vintage" except a couple of decades, or was that a couple of zeros on the price tag?), hip hop and hip replacement. Okay, I made that last one up. There were few if any old lady style shops, though even in San Francisco you were likely to see old ladies in yoga pants and a sports bra. Not to mention the ever popular lower back tattoo, which in the case of old ladies was too often heading south, quickly.

Innumerable clerks descended upon us like well-endowed blondes hanging on a sugar daddy, not only offering to help us but rounding out our fashion vocabulary with words like "kicky," "flirty" and "so-ho" which I think meant "so hot," and not "so like a prostitute." Where was Maria when you needed a slang translator?

After an eternity of fashion floundering, I was heartily sick of hearing "pop," which in fashionista argot apparently means "a heinous color accent which draws special attention to the overall ugliness of your outfit." Even Stacey had had enough when a saleswoman tried to convince us that bare midriffs were 'in' for professional women. Stacey made a rude comment about which profession and declared we were headed for Goodwill.

"And after that, no more lime green or I puke," she said.

"Consider yourself blessed that you don't have to wear it. Could there be a color less flattering on, say, ninety percent of the populace than lime green?"

"Not everything you tried on was that bad. I thought you looked okay in the neon green camouflage pants, or that 1970-ish light green tank top with the peace symbol bejeweled on the chest. What's not to love, besides the outrageous prices?"

"Those skin-tight, ultra-low rise lime green Capris were, relatively speaking, affordable, but they made me feel like a, well ... you know."

"What do you expect when you go in a shop called 'Sex and Me'? Baggy gray sweat pants and a hoody?"

"I wasn't expecting a leather bar or a lime green studded dog collar," I said grumpily. "Anyway, I didn't look at the store names. I just peered in to see if they had anything in lime." I knew I sounded a bit snippy, but I was tired and my feet were beginning to ache from the pounding of the streets. We'd already walked a fair bit and Goodwill was not just around the corner.

"If we don't find anything at Goodwill, you might just have to buy something we've already seen."

"If it comes to that, I'll go with the dog collar. Gorgon can use it when I'm done. As a chew toy."

”

TEN

"All animals are equal, but some animals are more equal than others."

– *Animal Farm*, George Orwell

THE WEEK BEFORE THANKSGIVING is notorious for being slack time at work. The only less productive time on the calendar is the week between Christmas and New Year's Day, when employees who rave about the opportunity to "catch up on things," really mean "get paid for coming in late, watching YouTube videos, working out at the health club, snarfing leftover Christmas cookies and leaving early."

Carson had declared Thanksgiving Monday as "Bring Your Pet to Work Day." A coffee stop on the way to the conference room required stepping over two Mastiffs sprawled in front of the coffee machine. The dogs occupied eighty-seven percent of the kitchenette floor space, but were friendly, judging by the enthusiastic tail thumping, which made the glass sugar bowl on the counter rattle. With coffee in hand, I passed an altercation wherein a dreadlocked employee complained that having to take his boa constrictor, Guido, out of the building was "species-ist," while a petite redhead with a buzzcut argued that the boa created a hostile work environment for her pet rat, Sugarpie. Tragic. I resisted the temptation to say, "Can't we all just get along?"

Knee deep once again in my spreadsheets, I was surprised when Maria asked if I was ready for lunch. I emerged from my numbers-induced coma to discover that everyone else was gone, either to lunch or to meetings.

On the way to the cafe, Maria inquired if I'd discovered anything susfishious over the weekend. I assumed she meant suspicious or fishy and was referring to the investigation.

I'd never read a mystery where God used divine revelation to identify the killer, but I figured it wouldn't hurt to ask, so I went to church on Sunday. Despite my prayers, I hadn't received a burning bush, or even a burning potted plant. Pastor Lucifer – his name attracted a lot of visitors to our church – gave a nice sermon on Jesus raising Lazarus from the dead. But I was pretty sure I wasn't being called to bring Laguna back to ID her killer.

Since God wasn't speaking to me, at least not about Laguna's death, I decided to follow Stacey's advice and talk with Magda's other tenants. Maybe they would tell me something they wouldn't reveal to the police.

Calvin, my third floor neighbor and one of the best-dressed straight men I knew, was just leaving the building when I returned from church. Attired in a black silk suit, black shirt, white carnation in his lapel and a black fedora, he could have been a male model on his way to a photo shoot.

"Got a minute?" I said, corralling him as he stepped out onto the street.

"For you, my love, eternity," he said flashing a wide smile.

"I'm trying to figure out who might have wanted to kill Laguna Butterfield and I thought maybe you could help me."

"I'm sorry, Emma, I work in retail, not the police department. Unless you have a more specific question, like 'did the person who killed Laguna confess to me on his or her way out the door,' I can't help."

"Sorry. What I meant to say was, did you know Laguna at all? I thought since you have all those peace stickers in your window, and Laguna was in the peace movement, that maybe you knew each other."

"My dear Emma, that's like assuming everyone who likes Humboldt Fog cheese knows each other, or participates in cheese rallies at the Ferry Plaza Farmers Market. It may have escaped your notice, but most everyone in San Francisco, except our landlady, supports the peace movement."

"Oh. I was just hoping you might have heard or seen something that would help the police find the perp … er, murderer."

"I saw Laguna and Magda arguing, and of course, I knew it was about the military; I've never heard Magda lose her temper about anything else. Except not cleaning the lint trap on the dryer. Which I always do even if Robert in twenty-six never does. But I find it best to stay out of these things – the arguments, I mean. I like living here and do what I can to stay on Magda's good side. That means I clean the lint trap and don't diss the military."

The disappointment on my face must have been evident.

"I told the same thing to the police except for the laundry discussion, and I don't think they found me very helpful, either," he added.

"Thanks, anyway."

"Later, then." Calvin tipped his hat, turned his back, and strolled down the street with as much elan as Fred Astaire in top hat, white tie and tails. I trudged upstairs to check in with the other neighbors, including Robert in twenty-six who said that he never heard any arguments in the building except in the laundry room. He offered that he was a good citizen about cleaning the lint trap and couldn't understand why Calvin never did.

If either one of them were to show up dead – God forbid I find another corpse anytime soon – I'd suspect Lint Trap Rage.

Paul, Robert's roommate, wasn't in. Paul had lived in the building as long as I had, but I saw him no more than once every couple of months. I preferred to think of him as the recluse, not me. I wasn't even sure what he did. Given his extremely low profile, maybe he was a contract killer, an alien, a Republican, or all of the above. None were predilections you wanted to advertise in this city.

Josh and Sara, a thirty-ish couple on the third floor, had only seen Laguna once or twice. As they worked long-hour financial jobs in the city, I wasn't surprised they hadn't crossed paths with her.

The last tenant I interviewed, Jeanette, was single, in her late forties, always on a diet, and lived across the hall from Laguna. She met me at the door in yoga attire, as she'd been yoga-cising to a DVD.

"I can't say as I knew the woman, but I did run into her a few times on the stairway and at the social Safeway." Jeanette used the local term for the Marina Safeway, so-called because it was alleged to be The Place for the Young, the Single and the Unconnected to connect. I wouldn't know. The only time someone had tried to hit on me was when I had a fake Harley tattoo on my arm; a guy – Italian I think – followed me around the produce department asking whether I'd like to share an artichoke with him. Eew.

"Did you talk with her?"

"Not at all. We nodded and smiled, but we were both busy shopping. You know, I usually shop on Thursdays, after work, so I'm not really in a chatting mood. Though I did notice she had way too much dairy in her cart. Not to mention, a lot of bread. All that gluten is so bad for you. And I didn't see anything like a fresh vegetable. What produce she had wasn't organic, either, and ..."

"So you can't tell me anything about her that might relate to her murder?" I interrupted.

Jeanette shook her head, her loose curls bobbing around her sweatband. "No, but I can tell you she ate a lot of processed foods. She had donuts, some type of kiddie breakfast cereal – that stuff is pure sugar and not even regular sugar but high-fructose corn syrup, imagine! – cookies, soft drinks, non-artisanal cheese and even bologna – über-processed meat is so bad for you – in her cart."

"I see."

"Do you? If that poor woman hadn't been murdered, she would have died an early death from heart disease."

The bottom line, as I told Maria, was that given Laguna's abbreviated tenure in the apartment, it wasn't surprising none of the neighbors could tell me anything about her. I'd given Magda an update to the same effect. Everybody knew Magda and – mostly – loved her. Hardly anybody knew Laguna, other than a flash of her placquards.

WENDELL, SHAFIQ AND ANWAR sat at an outside table, so after grabbing trays and food, Maria and I joined them. The place was a zoo of dogs, cats, rodents in cages, birds and, dare I believe my eyes, a skunk? Or was that a cat with seriously unfortunate birthmarks?

The others engaged in desultory conversation, while I watched the show unfold around me. A border collie, obviously enjoying his work, was successfully herding people – amazing what nips to the heels will do – through the cafeteria line. Just what we needed: a border collie to herd the Carson IT staff.

Fifteen feet from our table, a fat tabby cat lying at its owner's feet eyed a small, colorful bird hopping around its cage on a nearby table. Darn, that was a big cat! Had it been sampling Carson's chocolates? The bird, aware of the nearby danger, chirped excitedly as it bounced from perch, to water dish, to food dish and back again.

"Yup, Zuckers is gonna get you," I said, half to myself.

"What?"

I turned back to my companions. Wendell was staring at me, waiting for an answer.

"I said, it's too bad that such a neat company is going to be swallowed up by Zuckers."

"It's too bad that the owners sold out their employees," Shafiq said, "and the employees are taking it out on us."

"Part of our job description," Wendell said.

The others returned to discussing vacations and I turned away to view the mayhem unfolding near the fountain.

A young but rather rotund woman alternated yelling one moment and madly sneezing the next as she tried to shoo away the off-leash dogs cavorting around her. "Get away, choo! Hel-choo-choo."

Dog allergies, no doubt. The dogs seemed to think her sneezing was a game, and every choo sent them running in crazed circles. A few friends tried to shield her from the dogs and a man grabbed the collar of a Labrador as it raced by. Although he was pulled to the ground, he gamely hung on until the owner, leash in hand, rescued him.

At least a half dozen other people fruitlessly tried to capture the two smaller dogs, a pit bull and Lhasa Apso, still at large. Unlike the Labrador, they easily slipped and weaved around and under chairs and tables. The commotion spread and more people joined the chase while the crazed pair, yapping in excitement, incited other dogs to bark and strain at their leashes to join in. Where were the riot police?

Finally, an older woman knelt down with an outstretched hand cradling roast beef. The Lhasa was the first to pick up the scent. It fell for the trick and the woman soon had the dog in hand. Without a playmate, the pit bull tired and lay down on the stone patio, panting with exhaustion.

I turned around to find my fellow consultants had been oblivious to the show. They were discussing the finer points of cloud computing, the latest in a long line of IT fads that promised a dramatic reduction in costs, faster speed to market, increased flexibility, better functionality and eternal life. Okay, I exaggerate, but so do those proselytizing about it. I left them to it and headed back to work.

Holly was in the conference room when I returned, staring wide-eyed at her Kindle, a half-eaten sandwich dangling from her hand.

"Good book?" I asked.

Holly jumped, nearly dropped her Kindle and did lose her grip on her sandwich. "Uh … uh …" Her face flushed, and as she sputtered for words, the red deepened to the color of a ripe delicious apple. "I uh …"

What in the world? It's almost as if she was, no wait, I got it.

I nodded at her Kindle. "Reading erotica?"

"No! It's a, a, a, *romance*," she said in a loud whisper, peering behind me.

I turned around. No one there. "The others are still eating," I said.

Holly jumped up and scooted over to the door, the Kindle still gripped in her hand. She shut the door and turned to me.

"What's the difference?" I asked, curious to know if she was playing with semantics.

"Romance has love. Erotica is just about the sex."

"So you're reading bodice ripping and heavy breathing?"

"It's more than that," she said defensively. "There's mystery, and history, and ..."

Anwar chose that moment to walk into the room. He already had his ear plugs in and his swaying indicated his iPod was blaring. Although he obviously couldn't hear us, Holly and I said no more, but I gave her a big wink while thinking that cloud computing marketing materials and erotica had a lot in common; each involved heavy breathing and cries of "ooh, baby."

ELEVEN

"Thanksgiving dinners take eighteen hours to prepare. They are consumed in twelve minutes. Half-times take twelve minutes. This is not coincidence."

– Erma Bombeck

THANKSGIVING MORNING FOUND ME in a red silk dress, black heels, a plain black wrap coat and carrying a pumpkin praline pie I'd made with my own two hands, except for the pie crust. Okay, I'd used canned pumpkin: who doesn't? Except for Martha Stewart and she has staff. I hadn't grown my own sugar cane or vanilla bean, either.

I was driving across the bridge to my parents' home in Berkeley so I wasn't literally carrying the pie since I needed both hands on the wheel, but it was safely ensconced in a cardboard box with a couple of bottles of wine at each end to keep the pie from moving around. The wine would keep us all lively at dinner – and after.

I'd watched part of the Macy's Parade while I compulsively read the recipe five times to make sure I didn't do my usual trick of leaving out a critical ingredient. Sugar, for example. (In my defense, don't we all eat too much of it?) I mixed up the praline mixture, dotted the bottom of the pie crust with it, and poured the pumpkin pie filling (canned pumpkin, spices, eggs, evaporated milk and sugar, a recipe that even I couldn't screw up) over it.

The pie came out of the oven an hour-ish later smelling divine and I wondered whether I should tell everyone I bought it at a bakery to increase the chances they'd try it instead of deciding they were too full for dessert. Did I mention I sometimes left ingredients out? I'd helped my culinary skills along by turning off my cell phone. I'd messed up too many recipes when a family member called right between creaming the butter and sugar and adding the flour. (Did I add the baking powder yet? Or was it supposed to be baking soda? What about the salt? *Auwē.*)

I drove up Telegraph Avenue, turned down a couple of side streets and parked across from my parents' house, since Virgil's and Ashley's SUV was already parked in the grass lane that served as the driveway to the detached garage. When I stepped out of my Honda, I promptly sank one of my new spike heels into three inches of mud. I teetered but managed to save the pie from sliding out of the box and into the mud along with my shoe. I muttered under my breath all the way to the porch of the Queen Anne house my parents had lovingly restored. I placed the pie on a convenient chair, removed my shoe and attempted to scrape the heel clean on one of the stairs. I heard scrabbling at the door and the high pitched yipping of Gorgon, followed by Dad's "Gorgon, *silens*!"

"*E Kolakona, ua kulikili*!" I yelled, taking twice as long in Hawaiian to repeat what my father had just said. Gorgon obediently stopped yapping but I still heard him scrabbling to get out.

My father opened the door and a small brown mop with an underbite raced out, jumped on me and promptly caught a claw in my brand new pantyhose.

"*Auwē*, darn, just what I needed, a racing stripe to pull the entire outfit together," I said. "*E noho iho 'oe, e Kolakona.*" I added. Following orders, Gorgon promptly sat, wagged his tail and looked up expectantly.

"It confuses him when you call him – whatever it is you call him and what happened to your shoe?" Dad said.

My father wore a grey cashmere jacket, black slacks, a white linen shirt and a dark blue bow tie emblazoned with little turkeys. I handed him the pie and gave him a kiss on the cheek. "It's *'Kolakona,'* which is a passable Hawaiian transliteration of 'Gorgon' and you noticed he stopped yapping and sat on command. And I stepped in the mud. What is all that by-our-lady mud doing on this street?" I slipped my shoe back on.

"He won't sit for me," Dad said bitterly, ignoring the mud question.

"Because Latin isn't as pretty as Hawaiian, I keep telling you. Teach him Hawaiian and he will be the most obedient dog in the world. *'O wai he keikikāne maika'i*? Who's a good boy?" I added for my father's benefit. Gorgon wriggled his entire body, leapt up and snagged the other leg with his claws, starting a second run.

"I get it, you told him to jump up and ruin your stockings. Nicely done, Gorgon," Dad said. "It serves Emma right for disparaging Latin. '*Rident stolidi verba Latina.*'"

"Only fools laugh at the Latin language," I recited on cue, quoting Ovid, "and thanks a lot for that, Dad."

"Emma, come on in and what on earth happened to you?" my mother exclaimed. She stepped out on the stoop, gave me a hug and then stepped back with a critical eye. "Bruce, dear, put the pie in the kitchen," she said over her shoulder. "Emma, honey, what on earth is that on your shoes? You should take them off before you track mud on the Kerman."

I could see that she wanted to make a comment about the runs in my panty hose, but she stopped herself, perhaps remembering I was no longer thirteen.

I only wore panty hose with very high heels and I almost never wore heels. I wouldn't have ended up with this particular pair of three-inch foot cripplers except Stacey, my shopping enabler, told me they were "so hot." I stepped inside, slipped the shoes off and wriggled my feet in my parents' prized Kerman rug.

As I began struggling out of my coat a pair of strong hands grabbed the back and slid the coat down my arms, lingering just a tad longer than was necessary. "Guess who?"

"Huw? What are you doing here?" I said, turning around, my cheeks blazing. Huw had a black suit on with a black shirt: the first time I'd ever seen him in a suit. His hair was slicked back and he had on a musky cologne. He appeared as if he were about to go clubbing. It was a good look for him but one I'd never seen him affect.

"Emma, is that any way to treat a guest? Huw's plans to go to Boston fell through and we invited him for Thanksgiving," Mother said.

"Chicago actually, to see my, ah, friend. I'm going home to Boston at Christmas. I sure do appreciate being able to spend Thanksgiving with your family, Katherine."

"And we are very happy to have you," said my mother. She raised one eyebrow at me, a signal I'd learned ages ago.

"It is great to see you, Huw," I said, giving him a hug. I was glad to see him, but wondered about this "ah, friend" in Chicago. Must be a girlfriend, I reasoned. I felt a slight pang, which I dismissed as a hit to my ego rather than actual jealousy. We were just friends, so I had nothing to be jealous of.

"I can spot you a pair of shoes," said my sister Ariadne, popping up from the couch in the front room. She bounced over and gave me a hug. Her hair, a Nordic blonde that had never darkened as she got older, unlike the rest of us, was short and shingled. Her impish appearance was accentuated by enormous blue eyes, finely arched eyebrows and sooty eyelashes. She wore a bright blue silk tunic, matching silk pants – last year's Christmas presents from Mother – and silvery heels, with big silver hoops and multiple silver bangles.

"Hey there, vulture snot!" This from Virgil, who also emerged from the front room.

"Love you too, turkey lips."

"Buffalo butt."

"Turtle turd."

"Pus-sac face."

I was about to respond with one of my favorites, "kaka head," when Ashley padded downstairs, rubbing sleep out of her eyes, followed by my niece Rebecca. I swallowed my words. I did have limits in corrupting my niece.

"Got the last word," Virgil whispered. At that moment, Rebecca squealed "Auntie Emma!" and came running, hurling herself into my arms and giving me a wet, but still very welcome kiss.

A few minutes later, Ariadne and I headed upstairs where we found shoes that I could wear that didn't demand pantyhose. Flat black ballet slippers. Boring, but they worked.

I wandered downstairs and into the kitchen, where I found that my mother had already placed seven Waterford champagne flutes on a silver tray. She pointed to a large cardboard box sitting on the counter. I examined my collection of Barbies and weapons while Mother began pouring a splash of cassis in the bottom of each glass, topping it off with champagne.

"Huw's girlfriend dumped him," she said, by way of explanation.

"He told you that?"

"He told your father he was visiting her for Thanksgiving. His plans changed a couple weeks ago, so I invited him for Thanksgiving dinner."

"And what makes you think his girlfriend dumped him?" I asked.

"Educated guess."

Okay, breaks up with girlfriend and invites me to Tahoe to snowboard. Is there a pattern here and am I mad, sad, or glad?

While I was musing on the meaning of it all, Mother dropped a large, luscious blackberry – the fruit, not the smart phone – in each glass, picked up the tray and headed to the living room. I grabbed the box with the Barbies and followed.

Virgil, Huw and Dad were engrossed in a football game, punctuated by the occasional cheer, groan, or slap of a hand to the forehead; Ashley and Ariadne were working on a jigsaw puzzle and were communicating by "ums" and "have you seen any pieces with this color on it?" Rebecca was carrying on a conversation with two of her stuffed animals, neither of which was noticeably verbal.

Virgil turned his lip up a bit at the kirs – he really preferred beer – but ultimately everyone grabbed a cocktail except Ashley.

"I thought you loved champagne?" I said.

"I do, but really, no thanks," Ashley said. "My stomach was a bit upset this morning. Just ice water, please."

While Mother got the water, I set the box on the floor and beckoned to Rebecca. "Auntie Emma has some special toys for you and your Daddy to play with." With any amount of luck, and Auntie Emma's coaching, Barbie would stage a coup, topple G.I. Joe and declare herself dictator for life in this house, say, by Christmas.

In deference to the presence of Rebecca, we managed to make it until desert without discussing murder. Sort of. Dad and Huw engaged in a lively discourse about Troy. When they brought up Hector's dead body being dragged behind a chariot, Mom interrupted stating it was "not a suitable topic for impressionable little girls." Dad protested that it was "classic literature" and therefore suitable for all ages. He lost.

As dessert was being served, Ashley escorted Rebecca to the living room and settled her with her new toys and cookies. "I left her talking to her Barbies about which outfits and weapons they were going to wear," Ashley said upon her return.

"When you get a chance, let her know that an AK-47 is always a good fashion choice and Barbie should carry extra clips, in case G.I. Joe goes rogue or makes a pass at her. Oh, and it's really important to coordinate lethal weapons with her outfits. You know, like bazookas and bikinis don't go together, for instance."

Virgil gave me a dirty look while Ariadne used the opening to put me on the spot. "Speaking of rogue, do you think Magda killed Laguna? And have you offered to provide a character reference? Though maybe since you've been involved with three murders now, that wouldn't be such a good idea. In fact, I'm surprised you haven't been pulled in for more questioning. Or have you?"

I was hoping Mom would protest at this turn of the conversation, but she refrained from commenting, perhaps because Rebecca was now out of the room and she felt like she'd held back the flood as long as she could. Dad wore his quizzical face as if he, too, wanted an update on Laguna's murder.

"By the way," Ariadne continued, "can you pass me a piece of pie, please? You *did* buy this, didn't you, Emma? No offense, but you left the baking powder out of the chocolate cake the last time and it was more like a totally flat chocolate pancake."

"Tastes really good, Emma," Huw said loyally. "And what's this about another murder? Your sister's joking, right?"

"You should have tried the pumpkin bread she made for Christmas last year," said Ariadne, turning toward Huw. "I can see forgetting the cloves, but Emma forgot cloves *and* cinnamon. And no, I'm not joking about the murder. A woman in her apartment building was killed and Emma found the body."

"Maybe Emma is one of the Keres, Greek death spirits," Virgil said.

I sneered at him. "You can forget about any future help with your housing renovations. We death spirits are way too busy dropping woe on people to have time to paint." I wasn't much good with a hammer, but I was the star of the family when it came to masking and painting tricky areas and had already helped Virgil repaint his French door-equipped dining room.

"And to answer your questions, Ariadne, the police have not talked to me again." Thank God for that, although I wouldn't have minded another discussion with the torrid Detective Torres.

"You're not a suspect this time?" Ariadne asked.

"I don't think so. For once, finding the victim doesn't make me the *numero uno* candidate. The police just asked me about how I discovered the body and whether I knew Laguna. Oh, and I talked to them about Laguna's fights with Magda."

"Fights?" my father chimed in.

"You told the police Magda fought with Laguna?" Mother said.

"It wasn't like that. The police knew about the fights, perhaps from Magda herself. They asked me what I knew and I mentioned the blowup where Laguna kicked Chesty, Magda's puppy."

"She kicked a puppy? I'd have beaten her to a pulp," Virgil said, his voice rising.

"Bad E-X-A-M-P-L-E for R-E-B-E-C-C-A!" Ashley said in a sing-song voice, glancing at the doorway to the living room.

"I don't think Laguna meant to kick Chesty," I continued. "She and Magda were going at it and Chesty decided Laguna's protest sign smelled like a tree that needed watering. When he lifted his leg, she tried to shove him away and lost her balance."

"Still," Ariadne said. "It sounds like you threw Magda under the bus."

"What is this, the Spanish Inquisition? I did not throw Magda under the bus. I had to admit I'd seen them arguing." Loyalty to Magda made me refrain from mentioning that I'd heard her threaten to kill Laguna.

"'*Nobody* expects the Spanish Inquisition,'" Virgil said in his best imitation of Michael Palin in a Monty Python skit.

"'Our chief weapon is surprise! Surprise and fear. Fear and surprise. Our two weapons are fear and surprise … and ruthless efficiency! Our three weapons are …'" Ariadne replied, repeating the next lines in the skit.

"Will you two knock it off?" Mother said.

"Nobody appreciates Monty Python anymore," Ariadne groused.

"I suppose Magda is in trouble," Dad said.

"She thinks so. The police saw her for more questioning. Last time I talked to her, she seemed shaken and was thinking of hiring a lawyer," I said.

"Maybe you can help her," Mother said. "Talk to a few people, like you did when Padmanabh was murdered. You might discover a detail that exonerates her or implicates someone else."

What? Mom suggesting I investigate?

"If I were in your shoes, I'd start with the other tenants and the victim's friends," Mother added.

A quick survey of the table revealed other stunned faces, except for Huw. He just looked sheepish, like he'd stepped into a pile of dog poo and was hoping no one would notice.

"Magda needs all the friends she can get right now," Mother continued. "You're probably surprised I'm suggesting this …"

I nodded. 'Surprised' didn't cover it. How about stunned, shocked and speechless? As if Gorgon started speaking Hawaiian. Except Hawaiian was an easy language. If Gorgon started speaking Homeric Greek, that would be surprising.

"But, I expect you'll get involved regardless of what I say. I just ask that you do not directly confront anyone and that if you discover anything relevant, you go immediately to the police. You will, won't you? Go straight to the police?"

I nodded again still not convinced I wasn't hallucinating.

As I cleared the dessert plates, I cogitated about how my mother, the woman who had freaked at my boss's murder, was now encouraging me to investigate a killer. It totally baffled me when my parents didn't act as I expected.

Ariadne and I rinsed dishes and loaded the dishwasher. I almost checked under the sink to see if there were any large seed casings; had my mother been taken over by alien entities springing from gigantic pods?

Ari and I joined the others in the living room where football again held center stage. Mother had set up a tray with liqueur glasses, a bottle of Kona coffee liqueur and chocolate-covered macadamia nuts.

"Keoni sent the liqueur and chocolate," said Mother noticing my arrival. "So sweet of him."

I glanced in Huw's direction, but he was ensconced in the game.

At Mother's urging, my father did the honors, pouring the liqueur into the glasses. Ariadne handed them out while I passed the plate of chocolates.

"None for me, thanks," Ashley said to Ariadne's offer of the liqueur.

"Gone on the wagon?" Ariadne responded. "You become a twelve-stepper?"

"Not exactly," Ashley said with a small smile.

"Then enjoy Keoni's gift," Ariadne said, putting a glass down next to Ashley. "C'mon, it's the holidays."

"Don't be pushing alcohol," Mom chimed in. "I hope you don't do this with your friends at school. After all, you are still underage."

"Puhlease,"Ariadne responded. "As if, like, anyone cares."

"'*Ōkole ma luna* – bottoms up," I said, raising my glass, hoping to end the spat.

Huw, Dad and Ariadne lifted their glasses. Ashley and Virgil made eye contact for a long moment. Mother, watching them, gave a knowing smile as she reached over and pulled the glass away from Ashley.

It was Ashley who spoke. "I wasn't planning on telling you all this yet but here goes; I am on the wagon, so to speak, for the next six months."

"Congratulations." Huw was the first to speak up.

"Great!" I added. Am I getting another niece or a nephy-poo?"

"Holy Mary, mother of ..." This from Ariadne.

"Ariadne!" yelled Mom and Dad at about the same time.

"I didn't mean it that way," she protested. "I mean, uh, it's the season of blessed events? I mean, I feel like shit for giving Ashley a hard time."

"Don't be vulgar," Mother admonished.

"Yes," Virgil added. "'A person of your upbringing should at least use the word 'excrement.'"

"How about 'elephant poop,'" I offered, "as you are in a particularly large pile of excrement?"

"Or say it in ancient Greek; *κόπρος*," Huw said. "Adds a touch of class."

"Enough linguistic scatalogy," said my father in a loud voice. "A toast, to Ashley and Virgil and the blessed event."

And with that, we all raised our glasses in tribute, even if Ashley's was filled with Pellegrino and Rebecca's with a particularly fine vintage Kool-Aid.

TWELVE

"A person who is too nice an observer of the business of the crowd, like one who is too curious in observing the labor of bees, will often be stung for his curiosity."

– Alexander Pope

On any day but Sunday, parking near the Embarcadero is expensive and scarce. On weekdays, with underground parking the only real option, rates run close to ninety dollars for the first three seconds. On Saturdays, the Farmers Market foodie fandom takes every parking space within a twenty-minute walk of the Ferry Building. Taking Muni, the San Francisco Municipal Transit System, eliminates the parking issue, but only if you have time. Lots of time. Days.

Fortuitously, I found a parking space near the Embarcadero after two or three unladylike words and a mere ten minutes circling the block waiting for a Subaru owner to load her organic whatever-the-heck-they-were pallets and go home to Marin.

Maria was waiting for me in front of Paco's, as promised. Outfitted in a pale green leather jacket, matching green head wrap, tight black jeans, and short black boots with pointed toes and stiletto heels, she was a fashion plate compared to the garish crowd swirling a half block away. Maria's olive, flawless skin glowed and her outfit managed to define a new genre, Protest Chic. Now, why couldn't I look like that? In my yellow and lime green plaid hat and scarf set from Goodwill – the price was right even if the hat was too large – I was the living embodiment of a jaunty, leprous leprechaun. And it wasn't even the season for them.

"Sorry I'm late," I said as I came up to Maria carrying my green hat and scarf – I wasn't going to put them on until the absolute last minute. The weather forecast had proved depressingly accurate: cool and intermittent drizzle. At least with the hat, I'd be warmer and my hair might not frizz as much.

Maria was perusing a pamphlet, a large sign resting against her legs. "No problem," she responded, only half looking up from her reading.

"You brought your own sign?"

"Uh-uh. The organizers are in that lime green van, over there." She raised her head long enough to nod toward the corner. "I told them I wanted to help so they gave me this to carry."

She held up the sign so I could read it. "Towson Peabody Destroys" was emblazoned in large black letters dripping with bright red bogus blood. Below was a drawing of the earth with a big chunk missing.

"Okay, then. That's clear enough. No group hug for TP."

"They also gave me this brochure about the Lime Organization. It's fascinating."

"I'll just bet it is."

Ignoring me, Maria continued reading the brochure. "This says that Lime-O was founded by former members of Code Pink."

"Well, that explains the fascination with horrid colors." Just then, a quarter ton of flesh walked by, hand-in-hand, carrying an unoriginal sign proclaiming "Make Love Not War." A muscle shirt covered very little of the guy's *'ōpū nui* (big belly). I could only assume that the rather generous endowment of chest hair kept him warm. Had he dyed it green? I wasn't sure, and I didn't want a second look. His massively overweight companion tested the tensile limits of spandex: neon-green knee length shorts over a pair of black tights, in deference to the weather.

Maria, taking no notice of her surroundings, continued to read from the pamphlet. "'The founders felt that many of the existing peace organizations were losing focus as their organizations became intertwined with other groups supporting environmental causes, women's rights, socialism, animal rights, sustainability, transgender issues ...' Hmm, I think they're missing global warming. No wait, it's here, I just missed a bullet point. 'While personally supporting the goals of these organizations, they felt the need for a pure peace organization that could speak for all.'"

"Global warming is so last decade; it's called 'climate change' now, and 'speak for all' what? Or 'whom,' I guess I should say."

Maria gave me a little smile at this, and continued. "I didn't know this. Lime stands for Love Instead of Military Evil. Hmm, a bit contrived. I wonder why they don't call themselves Limeys?"

"Because it sounds like a product you use to get rid of bathroom scum. Anyway, you can read the literature later," I said growing tired of the history lesson. "You ready?"

Maria nodded, hoisted her sign high and walked briskly towards the heart of the crowd chanting, "I do not like war here or there. I do not like it anywhere. But I like lime green and ham. I do not like war, Sam-I-am."

Had Dr. Seuss been appropriated by the Lime-Os or had Maria just made that up? Sigh. Show time. I took my scarf and wrapped it around my neck, stuck the cap on my head and scooted after Maria. It was all I could do not to chant: "I do not like lime green – no no. Do I look like a preppy ho?"

Forced to dodge the milling protesters, I soon lost Maria in the crowd. Darn. Well, maybe we'd be more effective split up, covering twice the ground.

I recalled a protest I'd participated in months earlier when Magda and I stood in front of City Hall, surrounded by stars and stripes in equally outrageous fashion statements – the embroidered stars on the rear end of a hefty older woman were particulary noteworthy – and picketed for the right of the military to recruit in San Francisco. Now I had joined a group despised by Magda and her friends.

Unlike Stacey and her string of good causes, I was a notable non-joiner. All my experience in community activism was second hand, through supporting my friends. As long as they weren't doing anything that violated my principles, I was happy to help friends proselytize, protest and plant trees. Wearing lime green wasn't anywhere near the strangest thing I'd done in a cause not my own. I'd dumped plastic bags on the mayor's lawn in flash mob action. (I was especially peeved when San Francisco banned plastic bags since they are so useful for lining trash bins, picking up doggie doo, freezing dead animal parts, etc.) I also spent one afternoon counting butterflies. (It was hard to make sure you weren't counting the same ones twice, or fifteen times. If only they'd stay still longer.)

Time to initiate my "did you know Laguna?" spiel. I chose my first target: a graying woman with downcast, pale blue eyes leaning against a lamppost. I was confident she was a veteran of these events; her green sweatshirt emblazoned with the Lime-O logo – a peace symbol inscribed within a lime – was stretched out of shape and faded as if from frequent use.

"Hi, I'm Emma," I said as I approached her, putting out my hand.

"Bev," she replied.

"I'm new to this. You must be a pro," I said, nodding towards her sweatshirt.

"No. I'm not really part of this group."

"But your sweatshirt …"

She laughed softly. "I'm here with my granddaughter. She has to do a community service project for school so she decided on a protest. My daughter, the arch-conservative, refused to take her but asked me if I would, since I spent a lot of time on the lines in the sixties. Isabel was thrilled. That's her," she said, pointing to a young, red-haired girl in a slightly darker green sweatshirt, struggling to hold up a large sign that leaned this way and that in the winds gusting off San Francisco Bay. "Isabel wanted protest outfits, so we found sweatshirts at the Goodwill in the Castro. They have shirts for every protest and every rock concert ever held in San Francisco."

"Oh, I see," I said. I murmured some words of encouragement and moved on. Not to be rude but I was on a mission.

Unlike Bev and her granddaughter, most of the participants appeared to be serious about what they were doing. I didn't find anyone who knew Laguna, but I did find myself in the midst of several heated discussions – Magda would call them fights – between protesters and passers-by on the validity of war and who constituted the enemy. Often venomous, rancorous, and filled with name-calling, these discussions ensured that no minds were changed, but existing opinions were hardened. The one thing almost all of the causes I'd volunteered for seemed to have in common: anyone who didn't agree with the cause was an idiot, unpatriotic and/or totally evil.

After an hour of unproductive searching for information and being subjected to the vitriolic cacophony, I'd had enough. Now, where was Maria?

I spotted her disappearing into a tightly-bunched crowd. I followed, elbowing my way through a sea of puce, dropping a "sorry" here and a "'scuse me" there. What could be so interesting? A nude protester in lime green paint? Nah. That would barely register a raised eyebrow in San Francisco. The answer presented itself when I burst through the last layer of lime and almost ran into a blond woman in a red raincoat chatting with Maria. I couldn't see her face but I knew her voice: Lisa Arillaga, a local TV reporter. As the Channel 8 sob-sister, Lisa could be counted on to cover all urban uprisings and group grievances. She was the master of looking professionally concerned while not adding wrinkles to her forehead.

Lisa held a microphone and stood in front of a camera. Belatedly, I noticed the camera was also pointing in my direction, since I was directly, if inadvertently, behind Lisa. Having trampled on countless feet pushing my way through the throng, I couldn't very well squeeze my way back, and I was much bigger than five foot two, eyes-of-blue Lisa.

Every girl's nightmare is to be trapped on TV in an unflattering outfit. I pulled my beret down over my eyebrows and turned my head to the side. My best side, of course. While I attempted to evade recognition, or at least look good if I were recognized, Maria gaily chatted away for the camera.

"Yes, many groups are here protesting the recruiting of our young people into the armed forces," she said. "We at Lime-O feel that peace in our time is the number one priority for the world. I mean, how can we hope to address the problems of poverty, global warm … er, climate change, health care, and all the other concerns of society when we are pouring the resources of our nation into unnecessary wars?"

"Thank you very much," Lisa replied smiling. "Back to you, Juan," she said staring directly into the camera.

As the cameraman turned away, I pushed forward, but a great din of disparate voices besieged Maria before I could call her name.

"Well, done."

"You go, girl."

"Lime-O! Lime-O!"

By luck, I caught her eye. I pointed to my watch and mouthed the word 'Paco's' before I was shoved aside by the wave of protestors congratulating Maria for her great interview.

I'd have to check out on the six o'clock news to see if I'd been caught by the camera. If by sheer bad luck I made it on TV and my friends and family had seen me, I might be catching it *after* the six o'clock news. There was also YouTube to worry about: old indiscretions never die, they're just ridiculed on the Internet. At least I'd shown my best side.

As Maria might be awhile accepting accolades, I crossed the Embarcadero and wandered through the Ferry Building. I purchased a bit of tea and then checked out the Carson retail store, strictly in pursuit of being a better consultant to them, of course. I know, I know. Why would I buy more chocolate when it's being served up daily at work? But the dark chocolate-covered caramels were to die for, and on sale. I bought eight of them, for chocolate emergencies. And I'd be sure to declare an emergency before they went bad. Maybe even tomorrow.

THIRTEEN

"'Be yourself' is about the worst advice you can give some people."

– Tom Masson

When I returned to Paco's, Maria was inside, had secured a table and already ordered guacamole – the only appetizing thing I'd seen all day in green – and chips. I picked up a thick cut tortilla chip and shoved it into the guac. Mine was a practiced hand at capturing the maximum amount of dip you could get on one chip without spilling it before I crammed the entire thing into my mouth. Delish. The bite of cilantro was exquisite. I almost said "yumster," in honor of Maria.

"You first," she said.

"A bust," I admitted, eyeing another chip. You couldn't really determine the quality of the chips by such a small market sample, so I grabbed another and scooped up more guac. "One non-member who is here with a granddaughter earning community service credits by walking the picket line, three Lime-O members who think Laguna's name is familiar, but don't really know her, and a couple walking their dog who picked the wrong day to dress their Malti-poo in a lime green tutu. I met several people with whom I enjoyed chatting, but none of them knew Laguna. How did you do? Other than getting on TV, that is." I gave in to the guac and loaded up a couple more chips, one for each hand.

Maria shrugged and proceeded to ignore the last part of my question. "I asked one of the people in the van if I could meet the director of Lime-O; you don't ask, you don't get. Anyway, the woman I asked, Cindy Garson, is one of the co-founders and a co-director."

"Did you find out anything about Laguna? Can you introduce me to Cindy?"

"Right now, Cindy's higher than a kite on acid. When I mentioned Laguna, she said that Laguna was a descendant of a sea nymph and would come back to earth as a dolphin."

"In which case she should watch out for those tuna nets," I said. "Cindy must be more flipped out than Flipper."

"I don't know about that but her fashion taste is, well, there's no nice way of putting it. She's wearing Roman sandals, which have never, ever been cool and, if you can believe it, a wool sweater with a fur collar! Real fur!" Maria picked up one of the chips, loaded a scant teaspoon on it, and nibbled it slowly.

"A mega fashion faux pas," I said. "Though you'd think a city as ecologically correct as San Francisco would be happy to embrace 'recycled animal skin.'" Just one more chip, I told myself. Avocados are good for you. Vitamin C, Vitamin K, and all that.

"Speaking of the fashion challenged, I met Laguna's replacement, Janet, and invited her to meet us for a hot drink. Here she comes now."

A short, rounded woman shuffled in. I immediately thought of a mutant mouse. She had blah brown hair clipped short and curled behind her oversized ears, her on-the-small-side brown eyes were covered by wire-rimmed glasses perched on a slightly pointed nose and she wore a faded gray extra large sweatshirt that strained at the seams. Why does every woman thinks she is at least one size smaller than reality? A large mole near her mouth spouted short, spiky black hairs. Eew. All in all, I was glad I wasn't wearing Eau de Cheddar.

Her exterior lime credentials (I wasn't checking the color of anybody's unmentionables) were limited to a cheap, neon green handbag, a fashion brand knock-off of the type sold by discount stores and unsavory street vendors. I immediately put her on my suspects list. Not that being chief accountant of a peace organization was much of a motive, but I had to start with someone.

After the introductions, we ordered drinks from the waitress who glided up almost immediately (lattes for Maria and me and hibiscus-dandelion-orange blossom-chamomile tea for Janet) and more chips. It took me a few moments to move my wrought iron chair into position so it wasn't rocking every time I shifted in the seat. Being a fake Lime-O kept me off balance in more ways than one.

"Thanks for the tea," Janet said to Maria after we were settled with our drinks. "I can't stay long, though. My kids are with the sitter and I have to get back soon."

"Oh, it's so very much my pleasure," Maria responded.

"How old are your kids?" I asked, trying to be friendly and loosen her up.

Four minutes later, I'd been treated to dozens of pictures on her smart phone featuring "sensitive and oh-so-smart" eight-year-old Ryan, "beautiful and bright" six-year old Rhiannan and Raja, a four-year old white Persian who was just "the most playful cat in the world." Did Raja also think "mouse" when he peered at Janet?

Peering at Janet as she gave a running commentary on her children, I found it hard to imagine her ramming a ski pole through Laguna. She didn't appear to be strong enough. On the other hand, I'd heard stories of mothers' ferocity when their families were threatened. Even mousy Janet could become Ratzilla. Whether Laguna had been a threat to her, I had no idea.

"Maria tells me you were both inspired to join our organization by Laguna," Janet said, pocketing her phone with a final loving pat.

"Absolutely," I said. "Laguna was my neighbor. It was so exciting to have her around," I said, thinking about the catfights with Magda. "She was so passionate. It motivated me to try to make a difference, like Laguna did." It would make a big difference to Magda if I could find who really killed Laguna. "While we are both inspired by her work, Maria never got the chance to meet her and I only knew her for a short while. So, we'd love to learn anything you could tell us about her." Such as who wanted to kill her.

"Well," Janet replied, hesitating.

"I know she'd been thinking of leaving Lime-O," I added.

Maria's face registered her surprise. I hadn't told her I'd been in Laguna's apartment yesterday, going through her drawers, closets and computer files.

"Well, yes. I mean, she didn't seem really happy here the past few weeks."

"Perhaps she just needed a change and it was nothing to do with Lime-O." Hey, I was just voicing my opinion.

"That could be it," Janet said. "We're all so sorry she's gone, it's terrible to think someone killed her. It's very gratifying to those of us she worked with that she inspired others to carry on in her place." Janet nodded at us as she made this last pronouncement. Or was she gazing at the nachos at the table next to us – there must have been a pound of cheese on them. I decided to leave the last chip for someone else.

"So right, sister," Maria answered.

"Ditto," I added. We weren't total poseurs. It was true that my primary motivation in temping as a Lime-O was to ensure Magda stayed out of jail. As a side benefit, it would provide a measure of justice for Laguna. She might not have been a friend, but she didn't deserve to be killed with her own protest sign.

As we sipped our drinks, Janet told us stories about protests she'd attended with Laguna. Janet let it slip that she'd broken a few laws (protesting without a permit) but she didn't fess up to felony murder. Dang.

I told her how Laguna and I met ("I fell into a conversation she was having with our landlady") and I mentioned what close friends we were ("I've been to her apartment several times"). Okay, I stretched the truth – all the way to the moon. Heck, all the way to Pluto.

Eventually, Janet started making noises about getting back to her kids. Thinking of Maria's earlier ploy, I asked Janet if the other executives of Lime-O were at the rally today and if Janet would be "ever so kind" to introduce us on her way out. She agreed, walked us to the van and introduced us to Susan Perkins, also a co-founder and co-director and to Cindy, who didn't seem to remember that she'd already met Maria.

Tall and willowy, with stringy brown hair, Cindy sported a plain face on top of a long, thin neck, pale, spindly arms dotted with age spots and gnarled fingers capped by talon-like nails, unpolished. Under her fur-trimmed sweater she wore a drab olive green and dirt brown floor-length dress. Her eyes darted from side to side as she talked to us, and her arms swayed back and forth as she talked. My overall impression was – arboreal. Was there Entish blood coursing through her veins, hroom, hroom? I had no way to know whether her flakiness was drug-induced, as Maria had suggested, or was her natural persona. Heck, I was flaky until I consumed my drug of choice, morning caffeine, in high doses.

Much shorter than Cindy, Susan stood an inch or two over five feet, including her slightly teased hair. She resembled a forty-ish Mrs. Claus, with her cheery voice, large brown eyes, premature white hair and rounded face with red cheeks. Maria took the lead and chatted her up. Soon Susan was telling us about the early days of the organization amidst the numerous interruptions by protest participants stopping by to bid adieu. Cindy barely acknowledged the goodbyes of the crowd and said little as Susan nattered away.

Susan told a story about the nascent group, no more than twenty members at the time, participating in a peace parade in Los Angeles. As they walked by the reviewing stand, manned by a veritable Who's Who of California politics, the announcer hemmed and hawed a bit, and then asked the crowd to give a hand to the Girl Scouts of America. I laughed at the visual image, and asked if there was a Girl Scout badge for promoting peace, but checked my merriment at the flash in Susan's eyes. Was she telling the story for its amusement value, or to illustrate how far she had brought the organization?

When I said that I had known Laguna Butterfield, Susan expressed her sympathies for my loss and put her arm around my shoulders. Cindy scowled.

By the end of our chat, I considered the day modestly successful. Thanks entirely to Maria, I'd met three people who knew Laguna and had potential motives for killing her. Cindy was number one on my suspects list; she could have killed Laguna in a drug-induced state. Janet, I-now-have-a-better-job, came in at number two. I needed at least one male to ensure my suspects list was inclusive, so the boyfriend mentioned by Magda ranked number three and Susan was number four. I couldn't fathom a motive for her. Not exactly as sophisticated analysis as Poirot, but it was the best I could do for now.

I excluded Magda from my list. Only in overly-plotted murder mysteries did the suspect, having enlisted a close friend to investigate and clear her name, turn out to have done it. Magda wasn't that devious. If she thought Laguna deserved to be offed, she'd not only have done it, but would have taken a deep bow for having killed her.

FOURTEEN

"'A'ole mākou a'e minamina i ka pu'u kālā o ke 'aupuni; ua lawa mākou i ka pōhaku i ka 'ai kamaha'o o ka 'āina." (We do not value the government's sums of money; we are satisfied with the stones, astonishing food of the land.)
– "Kaulana Nā Pua," Ellen Keho'ohiwaokalani Wright Prendergast

SINCE THE PROTEST ENDED around noon, I had hopes of surfing that afternoon, but a quick read of the surf report quelled my desire: "A choppy, whitecapped, wind-blown mess with victory-at-sea conditions. Stay home and watch surf movies." Some surfers check elaborate web sites that post buoy readings, wind directions and weather maps and try to divine the surf conditions from reading wax patterns on surf boards. I go for checking SurfScoop.com because they used terms like "poopy surf" instead of "NW wind/groundswell mix on tap as small SW energy blends in." I just want rideable surf that isn't life threatening; I don't care whether the waves are "epic, dude."

The surf being crapola, I stayed home, paid bills and practiced the piano. Paying the bills had the side benefit of being a perfectly respectable way to avoid cleaning my apartment and dealing with spiders resident in the corners. Eew. The dust and detritus in my living room could wait but Mastercard was notoriously unsympathetic to whether I "felt like" corresponding with them.

As for playing the piano, I found it to be almost as effective as surfing in soothing my soul. And music was safer: my piano was unlikely to eat me. On the other hand, it didn't burn a lot of calories or improve muscle tone, except in my fingers and wrists, nor bleach out my hair to surfer-girl blond.

Music requires concentration. Extraneous thoughts must be banished to mental alcoves to allow total focus on the task at hand. I ran through a few scales to warm up, and then began playing Chopin's "Raindrop" Prelude.

Early in the piece the left hand gently taps the bass keys, producing the sound of a soothing summer shower. But today, it did not sooth; it sounded like a hailstorm. Disparate thoughts and memories stomped out of my mental alcoves and kicked open the door into my consciousness. Laguna's white hands clutching the murder weapon, the dried blood blotting her sweater and congealing on the hardwood floor. Chopin's "Funeral March" would have been a more appropriate selection.

My hands struggled with a C-sharp minor section and the bass became ominous as my left hand played a series of chords representing heavy rain and thunder ... echoing the animosity of Carson employees, protesters and passers-by arguing about "just" wars and even Wave Hog cussing me out the last time I encountered him in the lineup. I pounded the keys as the tempest raged.

The music changed direction, returning to tranquility, yet still I struggled with the memories of Magda fighting with Laguna and my uncertainty about Keoni and Huw. I played loudly, jarringly striking one wrong note after another. I stopped, returned to the beginning of the section and tried again to play the piece as it was written. My thoughts were more controlled, my concentration better, my mistakes fewer and my touch softer, yet I ended the piece on an unsatisfying note.

I sat and stared at the keyboard, the ivory wearing thin on the edge of so many keys, as thin as my tolerance. So much for the calming effect of music. Face it, Emma, your life is like the surf conditions and your playing: choppy and oh, so skippable. I closed the lid on the piano and tidied up my music, stacking it just so, spines out, edges even, on the end of my piano bench. One small spot of order in my otherwise disorderly life.

I wandered into the kitchen and put the kettle on, then rummaged through a canister on my counter to find a suitably soothing blend of tea: chamomile and honey. Even my tea canister was a mess. Tea bags of archeological origins mixed with the new, exciting herbal blend I'd just purchased at the Ferry Plaza Farmers Market.

The kettle belted its soprano shriek just when my cell phone launched into "Henehene Kou Aka." Keoni calling. I put my phone on speaker while I poured the water into a mug, swished the teabag through and added a packet of sweetener.

"*Aloha e ku'u pua lilia. Pehea 'oe?*" he said. (Hi, my lily flower, how are you?)

"*Maika'i nō, a 'o 'oe?*" (Good, and you?)

We batted our lives back and forth. I filled him in on what constituted protest chic in San Francisco. I also told him about the schizophrenia of swaying between Carson and Zuckers and that both companies liked to shoot the messengers of bad news. In this case, the GD consultants.

Keoni talked about how Hopena, his Hawaiian music group, was doing. Keoni plays the 'ukelele and guitar, and had formed the trio four years ago with friends. Just last week, Hopena had played at a music festival in Lahaina and had jammed with 'Ike Pono, my favorite group. Keoni and Stan of 'Ike Pono had improvised a rendition of "Dueling Banjos" – in their case, dueling 'ukuleles – and had bridged into "Ka'a Ahi Kahului," a song about the first railroad in Hawai'i and a tribute to King David Kalākaua.

"Oh, and I have great news!" Keoni said. "The Senate Committee on Indian Affairs has passed the Sovereignty for Hawaiians Bill and it will go before the full Senate in the spring!" The Sovereignty for Hawaiians Bill, proposing self-rule for the Hawaiian people, had been bouncing around Washington in one form or another for nearly a decade.

"And what makes you think they'll pass it this time?" I asked.

"Because we are in the right," he said, oblivious that "we" did not include me. "My people were done a great wrong, Emma. You know that."

Keoni proceeded to lecture me on points I already knew. Hawai'i had been an independent country, its royalty recognized and entertained in the courts of Europe. The accomplishments of the government were many and the Hawaiians, far from being backward, were the most literate people in the world at the time of the overthrow of the government. Blah, blah, blah.

What had happened to my Keoni, the one who had made me feel a part of Hawai'i? More importantly, a part of *his* Hawai'i? This Keoni pursued a cause that excluded me because I couldn't trace my ancestry back to the time of the Kamehamehas. Actually, I could trace my ancestry that far back, but I was nowhere near the Kamehamehas unless an anthropologist managed to link *poi*-making to the mashed potato fanaticism of my Irish ancestors. Where was Thor Heyerdahl and his crackpot ethnic migration theories when you needed him?

I said nothing. Perhaps my stony silence finally made it clear that I was not thrilled about his "great news."

"So, how has the surf been lately? Are you getting wet regularly?"

"The surf here is awful – beyond blown out. Water temperature is barely fifty-two and there have been shark sightings where I like to surf. Now, tell me how good the North Shore is ..."

"'*Ae*, I surfed Laniakea this morning and thought of you – there were so many *honu* in the water, I could almost have walked on their shells to the lineup. It was a little windblown but nice, about four feet. You would have loved it, and I would have loved it even more if you'd been here with me." Laniakea was well known for not being as crowded as other North Shore spots and for all the green sea turtles that hung out on the beach. The *honu* even had their own fan club, "Mālama Nā Honu," who used red ropes to provide a perimeter of protection against turtle-infatuated tourists.

After hanging up, I wondered if I'd been too harsh with Keoni. I had always known how proud he was of being Hawaiian. On the other hand, what if the *slippah* were on the other foot, and I became involved with a women's rights group that practiced man-bashing? Would Keoni support me, even to the point of ignoring the group's disrespect to him?

The more I thought about it, the more *huhū* – angry – I became. Keoni should have realized he was being insensitive with a capital 'I' without me having to make a speech about zealotry, especially since I was more Hawaiian than many Hawaiians I knew. I spoke the language, I danced a mean hula, I surfed, I knew all the words to "Hawai'i Pono'ī" and even had a Hawaiian name given to me by Keoni's Auntie Elikapeka: Kealohaikekai. I stormed around the apartment, slamming open drawers shut until I caught the tip of a finger in one. I was still angry, but I stopped slamming drawers.

That night, when I switched off the light after crawling into bed, the last thing I saw before I closed my eyes was a picture on my nightstand of me on Waikīkī, with a beautiful *koa* surf board that Keoni made for me, smiling my delight at the waves and the board, and most especially at the one who had created it.

FIFTEEN

"There are two kinds of people in the world: those who love chocolate, and communists."

– Leslie Moak Murray

LAURA ASSEMBLED THE TEAM for a debrief of her early Monday morning meeting with Grundy. We met in the Zuckers' conference room that GD used for status updates, strategic planning and bitching about the lack of support we were getting from Carson. Make that "expressing concern at the working relationship with the key Carson personnel required to effect a successful integration."

"Grundy wants to know if GD can finish the project earlier," she said. "I think he's feeling pressure to consolidate the systems faster so Zuckers can start realizing cost savings. I explained that the schedule was already tight and we'd be working long hours just to meet established deadlines. More resources would be required to finish earlier, and that would mean a change order and more costs. He's thinking it over, but my bet is he won't pay for the earlier completion."

A few of us muttered less than complementary statements about clients who think they can get more work without incurring additional costs. As if we didn't need to eat, sleep or have a personal life: those were just "free" hours available to clients.

Laura continued. "That means we're still on the old schedule to wrap up phase one by the first week in January. I know it's tight and we're facing the challenge of holiday distractions, so we need to stay on top of things. Any potential slip in meeting a deadline, you let me know immediately, if not sooner."

"Speaking of distractions, those pink slips at Carson won't help," Maria said. "Anybody on the way out the door isn't going to give a two flipbits about the systems transition. The only transition they'll be interested in is the one to the next job."

Flipbits? Maria strikes again.

"Pink slips? I haven't heard that layoffs have started. Did I miss something?" Laura asked, eyes darting around the table.

"My HR contacts at Zuckers told me that it would be another week before they announced them," Holly said.

Laura turned towards Maria. "Well?"

"Carson employees aren't dumb," Maria said. "They know that very few Carson employees have been set up in Zuckers' systems."

A priority activity in any merger is to make sure that the new employees are set up quickly in the new systems so they can access programs and files, and most importantly, get paid. Not being entered in the system was equivalent to being electronically erased. Fired.

"They're probably reading the situation correctly," Laura said. "Zuckers wants to automate the production process and eliminate the 'hand-crafted' part of Carson chocolate creation. I haven't seen the numbers, but I bet fewer than one in ten Carson's employees survive the merger."

I hadn't realized that Carson's candy-making processes were going to be fully automated. "So what's the point of buying a artisinal brand if you're going to automate everything and end up changing the flavor profile?" I asked.

"They didn't consult me," Laura responded, "but I would surmise that owning the Carson brand will give Zuckers more shelf space at stores and more sales. Perhaps they can expand the outlets for Zuckers by pressuring the higher-end retails stores that carry Carson chocolates to stock Zuckers, too. And of course, they'll improve margins and profitability by leveraging their existing production systems for both brands."

"'Leveraging' as in 'firing a bunch of people'?" I said.

Laura shrugged. "It's business. Rules one, two and three are make profits, make profits and make more profits."

After the meeting, Laura returned to her office while Wendell and Anwar left for Carson, leaving the rest of us to our work.

"Why wasn't I invited?" Holly said, just as I was settling in.

I raised my head. Holly stared at Maria.

"Not that I would have attended, but an invitation for such a prominent social event would have been appreciated," she said, turning her head to look at me.

"Beg pardon?"

"You, Maria, braless old bats and protest signs."

Now I understood. "You saw Maria on TV at the protest." And Holly clearly hadn't yet taken the six hours of mandatory diversity and inclusion training, or she'd know they weren't "braless old bats," but "age-empowered women free of the constraints of societal fashion norms."

"What protest?" Shafiq asked, pausing his rapid typing and glancing at the three of us.

"Yup," Holly said. "And you right behind. I didn't know you two were protest types."

"Please don't tell me I was on TV. In that hideous color? Someone shoot me."

"Just for a second, and unless someone looked up at exactly the right time, they'd never have spotted you. And really, you are so forgettable in that hat – completely hideous color on you, if you don't mind my saying so," said Holly.

"What protest?" Shafiq repeated.

"We're not real protesters," Maria said. "We're ringers."

"Am I invisible here? Can someone, anyone, tell me what protest you're talking about?" Shafiq said, even louder.

"I'm helping Emma investigate the murder of the woman in her apartment building," Maria said. "She worked for Lime-O.

Emma thought that if we attended their protest, we might meet people who knew Laguna – that's the victim – and maybe find a motive for murder."

"Finally!" Shafiq said.

"And did you?" Holly asked.

"I don't think we want to say any more about it," I interjected before Maria could give her a complete rundown. "I'm just trying to help a friend who might be a suspect. By finding a better suspect."

Maria shrugged and turned back to her computer.

"Cool. If you need more help, let me know," Holly said, "as long as you're not going to accost the murderer like you did last summer. I heard Brian shot at you and you disarmed him."

"Don't believe everything you hear," I said. "Brian confronted me and I said too much. I ran when it became obvious he was the murderer. Which was coincidentally about the time he threatened my life. Brian chased me, but he never shot at me, and Sanjay, the CIO of Tahiti Tacos, brought him down with a cricket bat."

"For the record," Shafiq said, butting into the conversation, "I know nothing about detective work. And I don't play cricket or engage in protests, either. I am pretty sure Zuckers is a gun-free zone and anyway, disarming threatening managers is not in my position description." At this pronouncement, he ducked his head and went back to work.

I sensed Holly would have liked to talk more, but I followed Shafiq's example, lowered my head and starred at my computer screen. No more questions were forthcoming.

Over the lunch hour, I stepped outside to call Stacey. Stepping outside in this case was akin to entering Hades, since the sun reflecting from the glass windows concentrated their heat upon the concrete inside the ring of buildings where Zuckers had constructed their idea of a courtyard: concrete pavers, concrete benches and a concrete fountain. The only color on the sea of concrete was provided by a few ferns in … wait for it … concrete planters and a discarded candy wrapper for Zuckers' Green Goblin Bar (milk chocolate, pistachios and mint, a revolting concoction). Even with the Sahara-like conditions, "the ring" was still preferable to stepping to the front of the buildings, where in addition to the heat, you'd be serenaded by the "Oakland Quartet": road noise from I-880, the sound of drive-by shootings, homeless people shuffling through trash cans and screeching gulls from the bay.

"Hey, stranger. How was Thanksgiving?" I said when she answered.

"Great time, but too short. Good to see my folks and my brothers, although John couldn't make it."

With four brothers called Matthew, Mark, Luke and John, Stacey had never satisfactorily explained why she hadn't been named Mary or Martha or, God forbid, Dorcas (you just knew she'd be "Dorc" for short).

"And Napa?"

"Mostly fantastarific."

Mariaisms appeared to be contagious. Fortunately, my translation skills were improving with practice. "Glad to hear it. I tried reaching you last night so I wouldn't have to bother you at work ..." I let the sentence hang. I'd placed several calls to Stacey leaving messages to call me, but she hadn't responded.

"We got a late checkout from Napa, and Jake took me for a nice drive back and dinner on the way. I turned off my cell phone."

Late checkout, drive and dinner? Hmm.

"We're still meeting for dinner tonight, right?" I asked.

"Yup. Now tell me about your Thanksgiving. Oh, and how was the protest?"

"Good Turkey Day. Good progress on the investigative front." I gave Stacey a short synopsis of the protest and the people I wanted George to check out.

Stacey was less than impressed with my sleuthing. "So you're telling me that your new suspects include everyone you've met. Have you considered the parking attendants at Embarcadero One, who could be harboring a latent hostility to people who pay in pennies?"

"Very funny. I haven't met Justin yet, and he's on the list."

"Right. Gotta have a token male. Can't just have a female-only suspects list cuz it's not inclusive enough. Any motives or are these women suspects merely because they worked with Laguna? I mean, if it's just because they worked with Laguna, then maybe you could get an organization chart to populate your list," she suggested.

"I'm sure that if you had come with me, Stace, we'd have a confession from someone already. And you'd have the right contact in the SFPD to pass the perp along to, in handcuffs, of course."

"Touché. But you're the one with the police contacts, seeing as this is your third murder. And as for handcuffs, it's San Francisco; you can get handcuffs in metallic pink, leather, fur, with sequins … Hey, maybe you could get one of the cute cops to help you model a few pairs."

"Thanks. Keep it up and I won't share what I learned about Laguna wanting to leave Lime-O."

"Threaten me and you won't get the hot and heavy on Jake."

"You win. Details at seven?"

"So right. See you then."

SIXTEEN

"They keep saying the right person will come along; I think mine got hit by a truck."

– Anonymous

Stacey had proposed The Lead Kitten for dinner based upon glowing reviews by coworkers. The advertised "slick, sleek and modern décor" meant glass and metal chairs, tables and divider walls, and a bar surface that changed colors randomly – from "get lost green" to "seduce me strawberry." I laughed inwardly when I saw the menu. It was over-the-top frou-frou California cuisine: free range something or other, organic roasted strange-herb-you've-never-heard-of sauce, wasabi mashed root vegetable, miso glaze, and grated artisanal cheese (goat, truffled cheddar, or triple cream – definitely no processed cheese product). And that was just one dish!

Stacey insisted on ordering the wine with her new-found oenophilic one-upsmanship, courtesy of the Napa weekend with Jake. When the waitress brought the wine – "a nice sauvignon blanc with overtones of ripe pear, perfection with pesto, not like a too-oaky Chardonnay" – we put in our orders. Stacey asked for a large bowl of chicken, avocado and lime soup and a Monte Cristo. Thinking of how tight my clothes felt, I opted for a grilled pesto chicken salad.

Stacey took a sip of wine and a beatific smile spread across her face. "Just as I remember it. Jake and I had this wine at the Gustafo vineyards. I just love the crisp, tangy taste."

"Enough about the wine, how was the weekend?"

"Napa was heavenly."

"Napa always is. What about Jake? Details, girl."

"Ah, Jake. Well, mostly good."

"'Mostly'? What does 'mostly' mean?"

"It means nearly perfect. Just not totally perfect."

I regarded Stacey with skepticism. She knew that I knew that she wasn't telling me everything. "You know I'll get it out of you eventually," I said.

Stacey caved. "Well, Jake is almost perfect, you know: good looking, wealthy, smart …"

"A high if not record-breaking Key Dating Factors score."

"Right."

"So what's the problem? I get that there are plenty of rich, handsome guys out there that are not exactly prime marriage material, like drug dealers, mobsters and sons of foreign tyrants. Which is Jake?"

The waitress arrived with our orders and we fell silent until she left.

Stacey gave me a small smile. "It's not that bad. There are just little things that bother me. Maybe I'm being hypercritical. Or, maybe I'm expecting he'll ultimately disappoint me like so many boyfriends have, and I'm just trying to guard my feelings."

"Well, what little things are you concerned about? Is he a maniac behind the wheel? That could be a good self-defense strategy in this area. Does he recycle his underwear? You can get around that. Or maybe he likes to wear your underwear. That would be a bit creepy. Even creepier if he looks better in it than you do."

Stacey giggled.

"Bunny tattoo on his *'ōkole*?" I ventured.

"Uses waste water to wash his hair?" Stacey tossed in.

"Clips his toenails in bed? Eew."

"Total turnoff," Stacey agreed.

"Paints his toenails?"

"Clear might be okay. I dated a really hot Iranian guy once who got his nails done. Clear polish. Color is definitely out, though."

"And anything sparkly means he surfs for another sponsor."

Stacey turned serious. "It's nothing like that; the things that are bothering me are more subtle."

"Like?"

Stacey didn't answer immediately and I waited silently, sipping on my wine.

"I know entrepreneurs can't build a business working just nine to five," she said, "but Jake seems obsessed with work. I don't have to be number one all the time but I'd like to be number one at least ten minutes a day."

"Go on."

"When we started going out, he'd get this far away look every so often and I'd ask him what was on his mind. He'd tell me about a business issue he had. Which was okay at first; I thought it was nice that he enjoyed his work so much."

"But?"

"But, when we were in Napa, we visited the San Cristolo winery and sat out on the terrace. It's built into the hillside and flanked by low, stone walls and an Italianate garden. You know the type: Roman statues, fountains, walking paths edged by tall stately pines, lots of rosemary and secluded alcoves where you can gaze into one another's eyes and contemplate future immoral acts. Voted number one on 'Most Romantic Day Trips' by *Bay Area Magazine*."

"Yeah, I know." In fact, I knew very well. Virgil, Ashley, one of Ashley's high school guy friends I found utterly forgettable and I took the wine train one weekend to sip our way through Napa and gone to San Cristolo. I remembered how the road insinuated its way up terraced hillsides, framed by decades old trees high fiving over the road. It was a magical spot, even if it didn't turn whatshisname – Marcus? – into the love of my life.

"Just beyond the garden is a gorgeous view of Napa and we were there as the sun was beginning to set and cast a golden glow over everything."

"Right, Stace, I get the picture. What's the problem?"

"I want to describe all this so you can see that it was perfect. Jake and I were sharing a cheese plate, Pt. Sur Blue and Marin Creamery, served with fresh, crusty bread slathered with olivada and we were sampling San Cristolo's wines."

"Get to the point, Stace. Did Jake belch, spit, pass gas?"

"And," Stacey continued as if she hadn't heard me, "I looked at Jake, and his eyes are focused on a place three counties behind my head, so I asked him what he was thinking about and he starts talking about the fluctuation in fuel prices and how it will affect his shipping costs."

"Ouch." Bad, but it could have been much worse; he could have been thinking about his ex-girlfriend whom he'd taken to the same spot.

"And I made a special effort, wearing a really cute cap-sleeved, yellow and black wrap dress with a matching black silk jacket, yellow patent bag with a gold chain link shoulder strap and black silk slingback shoes …"

I knew that dress. I saw the dress before she did but alas, it suited Stacey and not me.

"And a nice, light perfume, eucalyptus, which Jake is right partial to, and he was thinking of shipping costs. You don't think I'm overreacting, do you?"

"No. For him to admit that he's thinking of work is sending the message that you're not important to him."

"I don't think I'm unimportant to him," Stacey countered. "He's started to talk about moving in together."

"Really? And what have you said?"

"Nothing, yet. I'm not sure where I stand on his priority list."

A small breeze luffed through, rippling the flowers on the table. I though of Keoni, and how I never had to wonder if I was important to him. He loved God more than me, but I came second after God. At least, I used to, but now with Keoni's interest in native Hawaiian rights …

"Emma?"

"Stace, you're a great girl and you deserve a man who adores you. If you're not sure about that with Jake then to heck with him. Besides, maybe he really does clip his toenails in bed."

She nodded. Evidently, Stacey was done talking about Jake because she started interrogating me. I filled her in on Saturday's protest, including Maria's – and my – unexpected TV appearance, in between bites of my dinner. The menu may have been fussy, but the food was excellent.

"Her boyfriend Justin is a part-time stayover," I said, turning to my inspection of Laguna's apartment. "His clothes occupy a few hangers and less than a full drawer. And before you ask, he's into boxers, not briefs. Ugly boxers, in fact." Faded peace symbols, flying pink pigs and marijuana leaves adorned his underwear. And while Laguna's taste was not much better, I didn't mention it, remembering the poor shape of my lingerie when the cops pawed through my underwear drawer last summer.

"I hope you remembered to use gloves when you were snooping through her things. George recommends the disposable latex kind. If, hypothetically, you are in a place you aren't supposed to be in and doing something you hypothetically aren't supposed to be doing."

The waitress chose to arrive at that point to ask if we'd like to see the dessert menu and tell us the dessert specials, all of which were loaded with chocolate.

"Not for me, thanks. I don't want anything chocolate." Eating it every day and being surrounded by the smell had dulled my usual craving, for now. I was sure I'd recover.

"Oh my God! Are you all right? Emma Jones turning down chocolate! Call a doctor! Oh wait, let me tweet it to your faithful followers."

I gave Stacey a dirty look and waited for her to wave off the waitress before continuing.

"Yes, I did wear gloves. Acrylic, not latex, not that it mattered. The place was covered in fingerprint dust. There wasn't anything else obvious to see. I mean, the murder weapon was gone and no threatening letters were lying about. Laguna had an old PC that I managed to get into and …"

"You mean that you managed to break into," Stacey said, interrupting me.

"No, I did not break into her computer. I didn't have to; like a lot of people, she'd written her password down on a list inside the desk drawer. The only thing dumber than keeping it in a drawer is writing it on a sticky on the computer or using numbers or words easily guessed, like their birth date or their dog's na … What?" Stacey's face was flushed, and it wasn't the wine.

"Tell me you don't use a sticky on your computer, Stace."

"I have too many passwords and it's just impossible to remember them all. So sue me."

"Whatever, it's your funeral if anybody wants to break into your digital life. Not that anybody would have to 'break in,' more like 'waltz in through the front door.' Anyway, where was I?"

I explained to Stacey that I'd discovered a file on Laguna's computer containing different versions of her resume, emails she'd sent applying for financial positions, and rejections. Her Internet history and bookmarks confirmed she'd visited job search sites as well as real estate listings in Portland and Seattle the week before she was killed. In other words, she was clearly seeking to leave the area.

"Interesting," Stacey said. "I wonder why was she leaving and did it have anything to do with her death?"

"I don't know. But if you'll join me at the protest this Sunday, maybe we can find out. And if we're really lucky, we might even meet the elusive boyfriend."

SEVENTEEN

"San Francisco is 49 square miles
surrounded by reality."
– Paul Kantner

WHEN I RETURNED HOME that evening, I spent twelve minutes and forty-five seconds searching for a decent parking space until giving up and parking five blocks from my building in a space I happened to know was, technically, red, except for the coat of gray paint that had been added, camouflaging that fact from traffic enforcement. There was enough red showing through that most people wouldn't park there, but enough gray that traffic enforcement wouldn't (I hoped) ticket.

As I trudged through the misty night, the fog began to creep in, though it was more like a rhumba out of *The Fog*: one tendril swallowed the left hand side of the street and another swallowed the right hand side of the street in a diabolical dance. To complete the effect, all that was needed were the hysterical screams of people confronting zombies at the front door. Visibility in the middle of the street was still passable, so when I heard the click-click of footsteps behind me and turned around, I could just make out a hooded figure raising an arm before it began walking more quickly in my direction.

My mind was a bit foggy too, or I would have realized that the clicking was a giveaway for fashionista heels – not a zombie favorite, too hard to stagger mindlessly in them – and the wave of the arm was friendly. Instead, I panicked. I raced around the next corner, reached into my purse and pulled out my Shrieker. I hit the alarm button just as my stalker turned the corner. The ear-splitting and head-pounding screeching from my device was answered by comparable high-decibel screams from my stalker.

Hmm. Not the sort of reaction I would have expected from a mugger. I hit the "Off" button, which merely removed the stereophonic effects as the woman continued screaming for a few more seconds.

This being San Francisco, heads popped out of doors and windows like tortoises, most of which retracted rapidly into their single room shells. One person wanted us to shut the eff up and another yelled, "Martha, head for the bomb shelter." God bless the two people who wanted to know if we were all right.

"False alarm," I shouted. "Sorry! Thanks for checking!"

I observed my would-be assailant as my heartbeat slowed from two hundred beats per minute back to my usual sixty or so. Olive-skinned (hard to tell in the dark) and in her thirties (ditto), she wore spike-heeled short boots, the ubiquitous-in-San-Francisco yoga pants, a loose top and scarf, or hijab, around her head.

"What was that?" she asked after regaining her breath.

"My Shrieker," I showed her the device in my hand.

"Cool. I could use one of these."

"Why were you following me? You were following me, right?"

"Yes, and I'm sorry for upsetting you. I just want your signature on a petition." She pulled a small clipboard out of her backpack and handed it to me. "SaveBig wants to put one of their box stores in this area. I'm getting signatures to register local opposition."

I didn't even glance at the petition before giving it back. "I don't sign petitions. But I don't think you have anything to worry about; I doubt the Board of Supervisors will allow any megastores to move into this neighborhood. We aren't zoned for that." I was almost sure of it, recalling a BooksNMore's attempt to put a large store on Union Street; it was soundly defeated. Nobody was going to bulldoze a half-dozen quaint Victorians to put a concrete monstrosity in the Early Prison architectural style in their place. Especially not if it would contribute to the ruination of more independent bookstores.

"You won't sign a petition supporting it then, will you?"

"Not a chance."

"That's okay, then. You're not against us."

I wasn't one hundred percent for them, either. The downside of the "no chains" mentality was the need to drive out of the city to find a lot of things those stores carried that Mom and Pop didn't. Easy to be high-minded if you can afford the time and gas.

"Can I ask why you are doing this at night?"

She gave a light, airy laugh. "It's my only free time. I work a graveyard shift and sleep from nine in the morning until about five. Besides, during the day people walk right by you. They notice you more at night."

"Indeed. Well, good luck then." I turned and walked away. Whatever her rationale, approaching strangers at night was crazy. Unless she was lying. Maybe she was part of a gang. She'd approach passers-by and then her gang would surround them. Hmm, I don't recall hearing anything about SaveBig moving in. Could she be involved in the break-ins and muggings Magda had mentioned? I glanced around nervously, but didn't see anyone. Nevertheless, I increased my pace.

I was still feeling paranoid over my odd encounter when I followed a strange man into my apartment building. Let me rephrase that. I followed a man, whom I did not know, into the building. The fact that he wore a black cape didn't make him strange. At least not in San Francisco, where a person strolling through the Castro dressed as Kermit the Frog wouldn't register in the upper half of the strange-o-meter. I'd once seen a guy on lower Van Ness wearing a Prussian spike helmet, a leather loin cloth, black thigh-high boots, and nothing else, except a handlebar mustache. There was a dwarf with him who was dressed exactly the same. Including the mustache. The only strange part was that nobody was lookey-looing; it was just another day in San Francisco.

I thought at first that the stranger had been buzzed in by one of the other tenants, but when I reached my door, I could see him at the end of the hall, entering Laguna's apartment. I turned around and went downstairs to knock on Magda's door.

"Hi, Emma. What can I do for you?"

"I just saw a guy enter Laguna's apartment. And unless he's an undercover cop in the drug side of things, I don't think he's a policeman. Can you describe her boyfriend?"

Magda gave a half smile. "Ah, Justin. He's memorable: two or three inches over six feet, sports a dirty blond pony tail, earring, lots of metal, tattoos covering both arms and, based on his sartorial choices, has been mistaken on occasion for Darth Vader. 'Luke, I am your father,'" she offered in stentorian tones, interspersed with the requisite heavy breathing.

"That's the guy. Though I can't verify the tats, I can verify that he wasn't carrying a light saber."

"I've been expecting him to show up," she replied. "I told you he convinced Laguna's parents to let him take care of things on this end for them: packing her things, terminating the lease, processing the change of address and so forth."

"Maybe this would be a good time to introduce myself and ask him if he's the killer."

"Or maybe you could join me on a walk. I was just about to take Chesty for his bedtime stroll. We could talk on the way."

I put my hand around the Shrieker still in my pocket and agreed. I sensed Magda wanted to forestall my interrogation of Justin. Three minutes, fourteen dachshund jumps and one leash entanglement later, we stepped out into the evening.

The apartment building was on the lower part of Russian Hill. Usually, you can see the Bay Bridge from the street corner just up the hill, but the fog had continued to roll in, and nothing more than a block away was visible. Dogs barked in the distance, back and forth, interspersed with choruses of prolonged howls. Chesty answered with a challenge bark.

"Listen to the children of the night," I said in my best Transylvania accent. In San Francisco, vampires would just be another group – the "blood affinity undead" – demanding inclusivity.

Chesty headed for a tree and lifted his leg. Sniffing something intriguing in the air, he dropped his leg while still flowing and took off down the street, dragging Magda behind. Laughing, I walked quickly to keep up.

Chesty darted here and there, occasionally pausing for long smells at prominent poles and a few car tires. I noticed he only picked the cars with anti-military stickers on them. Maybe Magda was telegraphing her preferences through the leash. Twice she had to stop and pick up his deposit. Magda and I kept up an intermittent conversation about mundane matters: books recently read (an account of the battle of Midway for Magda, a *Pride and Prejudice*-inspired novel for me), the latest inanity out of City Hall, and so forth. I also apprised her of the status of my investigation, such as it was, while keeping my eyes open for petition woman, or whoever she was. When Chesty slowed down and made fewer mad dashes, Magda changed the course of the conversation. She mentioned she'd retained a lawyer, Clarence Dale, and recounted his impressive credentials.

"I'm not so sure now that I want you poking around, investigating Laguna's murder," she said.

Chesty strained at the leash, a delicious smell seemingly just outside of range. Magda stepped off the sidewalk to give him more sniffing room.

"Because you now have a lawyer?"

"In a way. I do feel more confident, knowing Clarence is on my side and I don't feel comfortable exposing you to danger. Specifically, Justin."

Chesty stopped at another tree, the third one in a row. He gazed off in the distance. Who would think a little dog had such massive liquid reserves in him?

"The time I confronted Laguna and her friends making protest signs in the courtyard, Justin lost his temper. He screamed at me and strode up to where I was standing, crossed his arms, flexed his vulgar tattoos and puffed himself up. I may be short, but I'm no doormat, so I told him I wasn't afraid of any skinny, ponytailed leftist in a cartoon cape. Laguna yelled at him to back off and he did."

Chesty paused at a tree newly planted by Friends of the Urban Forest. He sniffed one way, then the other, seemingly undecided about which was his good side with which to leave a message.

"He has a short fuse. And who's to say that he's not Laguna's killer?"

Magda turned and headed for home. Chesty strutted along, an extra swagger in his small shoulders. He'd let all the big dogs in the neighborhood know 'Chesty was here.'

"Are you just telling me to be careful, or do you absolutely not want me doing anything?"

A short stretch of silence passed. "The former, I guess," she said.

"Fine. Then I promise I won't confront Justin, or other potentially dangerous suspects, unless I am with others, in a public space, and I've practiced with my pepper spray and baseball bat. Oh and my Shreiker has new batteries that work well, as evidenced in this evening's test run. Does that about cover it?"

Magda nodded.

"Good. Now, can you tell me if you ever heard or saw Justin and Laguna fighting? And did you know Laguna was thinking of leaving the area?"

EIGHTEEN

"These little grey cells. It is 'up to them.'"
– *The Mysterious Affair at Styles*, Agatha Christie

A FEW DAYS LATER, I heard from Stacey's PI friend, George. Despite my protests that a phone report was just fine, he insisted we meet for lunch or dinner.

"I can't wait to meet a real Venus Flytrap," were his exact words.

When I protested that I didn't kill anyone, but only found the bodies, and certainly didn't consume any victims, he amended his statement.

"Okay, that makes you a carrier of death. Let's call you 'Typhoid Emma.' All I know is that I've been a PI for twelve years and I've never worked a murder case, much less discovered a body. You might be at the epicenter of a mysterious force that kills off people you know. Like that woman on TV, the one who lived in Maine. I'm surprised there was anybody left alive in her town by the end of the series. What was it called?"

"Jessica Fletcher, *Murder She Wrote*." My grandmother adored that show. Later in the series, Jessica had moved to or at least spent a lot of time in New York, if I recalled correctly, doubtless because with eight million people in three hundred square miles, NYC wasn't going to run out of potential murder victims as fast as Cabot Cove, Maine.

"That's it. Anyway, it might be dangerous to actually know you, but I'd thought I'd take the risk and maybe you'd let me introduce you to Clyde, my ex-, and I'd hope for the best." He laughed, a thin, rueful laugh.

I smiled in sympathy and because George's laugh was infectious. During my investigation of my boss' murder, Stacy told me that George's former lover Clyde had jettisoned him for a pair of six-pack abs attached to the face of an Adonis. Regardless of one's sexual orientation, nobody wants to be dumped for a newer, shinier and more buffed-out model.

George and I agreed to meet for dinner. "You can meet me at Plataea," he said. "It's the only Greek restaurant in North Beach. Well, the only good one."

"Where the Spartans, Athenians et al. defeated the Persians?"

"Come again?"

"The battle where Xerxes' army … oh, never mind. How about seven-thirty? I'm commuting from the East Bay."

"Done."

George was easy to spot from Stacey's description: in his early forties, big blue eyes, dark curly hair just beginning to recede and a cleft chin. His clothes hung loose on him. Stacey had mentioned that George had lost quite a bit of weight recently, in reaction to Clyde's desertion, although she didn't know whether the weight loss was broken-heart-related or I'm-going-to-shape-up-to-get-back-on-the-market-related. Like so many San Franciscans, George wore Bay Area goth: a black turtleneck, black silk jacket, dark wash designer jeans and black Italian loafers. Stacey's description of me must have been equally precise as he recognized me immediately.

We found a table and George asked if he could order for both of us since he was a regular. I nodded. George waved the waiter over and spent a few minutes catching up with Menis: how was Menis's daughter Kristen getting along at Cal and how was his big baby of a Rottweiler recovering from his ACL tear? Menis in turn asked how the PI business was and whether George liked the new director of the San Francisco Opera.

Once they finished the pleasantries, Menis recited a list of the specials and George ordered two *spanikopitas* for us with a starter of *horiatiki*. I shook my head at his suggestion to split a bottle of wine – it was a week night and I still had to drive home, even if it was less than fifteen blocks – but I did order a glass of unexceptional central coast Chardonnay that Menis brought in a generous wine goblet and placed unobtrusively in front of me. I took a sip on the gulpish side. The commute had been long and nasty and I was glad for a glass of unwinding. George ordered a glass of Barolo.

"So, did you find any smoking guns?" I asked, placing the glass down carefully. The table was really small and I didn't want to knock anything over as I reached for the *tzatziki* and pita bread that Menis had brought "on the house" and placed between us.

"No," George said with a smile, "but I may have unearthed gunpowder."

"Darn. I had hopes that you would discover incriminating information, like Cindy being Laguna's half-sister and next in line for millions from an inheritance."

"No such luck. But I did unearth a few facts that might help you sort out motives. Let's start with the money trail."

Menis delivered a large plate of *horiatiki* while George was explaining the tax filing requirements of a non-profit organization. I found it hard to concentrate on his recital as I dug into the ripe tomatoes, perfect cucumbers and the best Kalamata olives I'd ever tasted.

As a 501c3 organization – or did George say 503c1? – Lime-O had to file each year with the IRS. The filing included basic financial information plus a list of directors, officers, key employees and relevant compensation. For many organizations, these filings are available on the Internet.

George paused in his narrative and watched me attacking the *horiatiki*, fork dangling from the tips of his fingers. "For a little thing, you really know how to shovel it in," he said.

A size eight, I wasn't used to being called "a little thing," so I beamed at the compliment. Clyde had clearly been an idiot.

"Last year," George said, "Lime-O received just over two million dollars in donations and funds from activities. They maintain a full-time paid staff to support fundraising and national programs. Ms. Butterfield was the controller and listed as a key employee on the IRS filing. I must say, even for a non-profit organization, she was poorly paid."

"I think she joined out of devotion to the cause, not for the money."

George pursed his lips. "That may be, but in contrast, the salaries of Ms. Perkins and Ms. Garson, as co-directors, are quite generous given the size of the operation. I'm not an expert, of course; I used some tables compiled by a watchdog organization."

"So Susan and Cindy get paid a lot, but their minions don't. Can't say it doesn't happen in business."

"True. Now might be a good time to talk about those two."

Menis cleared our empty salad plates and brought the *spanikopita*: flaky phyllo, spinach and more yummy feta. Mmm, happy food coma time.

George reached into his jacket pocket, pulled out a few sheets of paper, pushed his plate to the side and placed the papers on the table. He picked at his food while he talked.

"At first blush, Susan Perkins appears to be just your standard radical peace activist: in and out of jail for crossing a police line, unlawful assembly, resisting arrest and assaulting a police officer. Actually, multiple arrests for assaulting police officers. Quite the fighter, that one. Never met a uniform she didn't throw blood on."

"She looks like Mrs. Santa Claus. Maybe someone was trying to deck her halls."

George peered at me over his papers before continuing. He discussed where she'd lived, her education and work history. "Her campaign contributions in the last election were to left-leaning candidates. At least she's consistent in putting her money where her mouth is, although she's not very good at managing it; ten years ago, she filed for personal bankruptcy. She founded Lime-O the following year."

George recounted the unremarkable history of Lime-O, then turned to Susan's personal life. "She and Cindy Garson are registered as domestic partners."

"I didn't pick up on that." But Maria had. When we departed the Lime-O protest, Maria had said that Cindy was possessed by a "green-eyed monster." At the time, I just thought it was a Maria-ism about Cindy's use of weed. But George's domestic partner comment stimulated the old gray matter; Maria had been quoting Shakespeare on jealousy.

"Perkins and Garson live in a two-bedroom apartment on Nob Hill, across from the Pacific Union Club." He glanced up. "That's quite the tony address for a couple of activists. I haven't checked the rents yet, but that has to be three thou a month, easy."

"As for Cindy Garson," George said, turning a page. "Her rap sheet is similar to her partner's, except she hasn't assaulted any cops. Score one for her. No record of financial problems, either."

As George finished rattling off the basics of Cindy's life, Menis came back to clear our plates and ask George if he'd be having his usual double order of *baklava* and a double espresso to go with.

"You know me too well, Menis," said George. "But just a single order of baklava. Have to keep my girlish figure."

"Single of each for me, and make the espresso decaf, please." I said.

In a few minutes, Menis glided up with our *baklava* and espresso. I emptied my usual two blue packet sweeteners into the cup, stirred vigorously, and took a sip after passing the cup under my nose several times. Heavenly. George dropped a cube of raw sugar into his espresso and stirred gently, raising the cup to his mouth with both hands. He set it down, then took a bite of *baklava*. He rolled his eyes in pleasure.

"Never has something so bad for the waistline tasted so good," he said. We sat contentedly for a moment in our private reveries.

"I almost forgot to mention that Cindy, in her copious free time, is the Chief Druid of the Bay Area Grove," George said. "She hosts healing ceremonies that include other California Druid groups, I mean, groves."

"She does come across as a bit peculiar."

"Peculiar is adults traveling with stuffed animals. She's well into weirdo."

I didn't see a thing wrong with adults traveling with stuffed animals. I slept with my stuffed bunny and faithful traveling companion Fred every night. Fred would be very resentful at George's condescension.

"Back to the Lime-O financials; I picked up a whiff of a rumor that Lime-O may soon be receiving a large donation from Jürgen Reimer. Large as in perhaps doubling their current funding level."

I leaned forward. The German-born financier was known for contributing large sums of money to his favorite causes. Writing a big check to Lime-O would be right in line with his previous causes *du jour*. "Money as a motive?"

"Money is always a motive. The question is how does it play here? What connection, if any, could a potentially large donation have to the death of the current controller?"

"Laguna was cooking the books to steer more money to Susan and Cindy. Reimer's people were planning on doing due diligence, and they might discover it."

"How does killing Ms. Butterfield change that?"

"Hmm. Maybe, they wouldn't discover it, because Laguna was too good. But she was planning on telling them."

"Why?"

"I don't know, a sudden attack of conscience? It's a standard plot device in mystery novels."

George laughed. "Maybe more information might help. Let's talk about Ms. Janet Rhoden, former bookkeeper and Laguna's replacement as controller." George consulted his papers. "Before Lime-O, Ms. Rhoden worked for the software company Idgenstar, and got into a spot of trouble. Over $50,000 went missing from the company. Charges were never filed, but several employees in the finance department, including Ms. Rhoden, were 'eased out,' shall we say."

"She stole money?"

"The correct term is 'embezzled.' It's not clear if she was dismissed for embezzling or the negligence that allowed the theft to occur."

"So conceivably, Laguna could have discovered that Janet was embezzling from Lime-O and Janet killed Laguna to keep her quiet."

George appeared skeptical.

"Or," I continued, "Janet had been keeping her nose clean. But she hears of the Reimer donation and figures this is her chance to make a big killing, so to speak. Janet murders Laguna to get her job and be in a better position to embezzle." I sat back triumphantly.

George's skeptical look remained.

"It's a great theory," I said, pleased with myself.

"So do you want to hear more, or have you concluded your investigation?"

"Uh, more, please."

George relayed Janet's life history and current family situation. Janet, a single mom, and her kids had until four months ago shared a three-bedroom apartment in Daly City with Janet's sister, a divorced mother with two kids of her own. "She has since moved out and is renting her own three-bedroom apartment."

"I can understand wanting more space."

"So can I. But how can she afford it? The Lime Organization is advertising for a bookkeeper, presumably the position she held, and offering to pay thirty-five thousand per year, well below the average salary for that position. At that salary and two kids, there's no way she can afford her own apartment."

"You're admitting my theory is right. She's embezzling from Lime-O."

"I admit that it is possible she is embezzling or she has income from an unknown source."

Before I could respond, George launched into Justin. "Now we come to Mr. Thyme. Or maybe we should call him, Mr. 'Deserves-to-do' Thyme. He's a small-time – no pun intended – hacker. Charged but not convicted of attempted blackmail using information he obtained by hacking email. He has been found guilty of defacing websites and unlawful use of employer's information. His convictions resulted in suspended sentences and fines, but no real jail time. The most recent charge is three years old, meaning either he's been on the straight and narrow or he's become more adept at avoiding detection. Thyme now works part time at an electronics store and shares an apartment in Sunnyvale with two other men."

"Doesn't sound like someone I'd like to date. Did you find any charges related to violent behavior?"

"No, why?"

"Just speculating," I said, thinking of Magda's encounter.

Menis cleared the dessert plates and espresso and asked if we'd like anything else. George asked for *ouzo* and the check and I shook my head at Menis' raised eyebrow that was waiter-ese for, "And would Madame like *ouzo* as well?" I'd had enough alcohol for a work night, and my wine glass was still half full.

George concluded his report by telling me that he'd done all the easy work and to dig up more would require a lot more legwork and man-hours. "And I don't think you want to pay for that."

"No. I expect if Magda is actually arrested, her lawyer might do that."

"Don't count on it," George said. "It's only on TV where lawyers try to find the killer. In real life, they just try to get their clients off, frequently though challenging police procedures."

Menis set down a small liqueur glass whose anise-scented contents I could smell from across the table in front of George, together with a red envelope emblazoned "The Damage." *Ouzo* smelled like a glass of black licorice. I love licorice, but wasn't sure I'd like to drink it. Especially when it was fermented.

"Can I get part of that?" I said, nodding at "The Damage" envelope.

"Oh, absolutely not. It was worth the price of dinner to see the infamous 'Emma the Extinguisher.' You've made quite an impression on local police departments. Nobody can remember anyone who was so good at stumbling over dead bodies without ever being responsible for any of them. Though the Pacifica police still think there's something hinky about that surfer's death."

"I trashed his board, not him. He outweighed me by seventy-five pounds at least. How would a weak thing like me do in a big strong bully like him?" I batted my eyes in all innocence.

"Save it for sentencing," he said, smiling. George picked up the *ouzo*, threw his head back and downed the liqueur in one gulp. He grimaced, shook his head, and ran his fingers threw his hair.

"What's your next step?" he asked.

"Based on what you've told me, I'd like to know whether Janet is an embezzler and whether Reimer's purported contribution is real. And I need to meet Justin and spend more time with the Lime-Os to suss out motives and maybe new suspects."

George nodded. "That's a full agenda. Perhaps you can get a few months off from your day job."

"Really? I was hoping to wind this up before Christmas."

George laughed. Hard.

Dang, there had to be a better way. "What about bugging apartments, phones, cars, whatever? Maybe the killer will say something damning." I brightened at this new thought.

"Not a good idea," George said. "Electronic eavesdropping is against the law in California. $2,500 fine and up to a year in jail for your first offense."

"But it's done all the time on TV."

"Right, television again, the killer is tracked down in an hour and the main characters don't go to jail for disregarding the law. Script writers take liberties with enforcing the law. Police and judges in real life don't."

He opened the red envelope, read the damage, and counted out several bills from a sleek black leather wallet.

"But what if the eavesdropping led to finding a murderer? "Or murderess. Is 'murderer' gender-neutral? I'd bet there'd be no jail time."

"Don't count on it. Even if you discover something, you can't use it as evidence if it has been illegally obtained."

My amateur detective bubble deflated.

George looked thoughtful as he read the dejection in my face. "I can't risk my license, but because you're Stacey's friend, we could have a theoretical discussion about equipment that might be used for eavesdropping, if one happened to, ah, use it inappropriately. And of course, we could also hypothetically discuss the ways not-so-law abiding people might disguise such equipment so it's not discovered."

I perked up.

"But," he continued, "if you get caught, we never had this conversation."

"Agreed. Of course I don't want to end up in jail, but I don't want Magda to end up there, either. And I'm willing to cautiously step outside the lines for her."

"I'd do the same for a friend, but don't tell anyone," George said, and gave me a wink.

Later that night, I powered up my computer and went on eBay, George's recommendation, to search for a suitable bug, er, listening device.

Our conversation had exposed more of my naiveté about spying. I'd asked George about using tiny voice-activated bugs. I presumed I could just wait for these bugs to send the recordings to a central spot. Then in my spare time, I'd sift through them until I came across the word "killed" or "murdered." Maybe there was a computer program that would do it for me. Once I found the word – preferably in context, such as "I killed Laguna Butterfield" – I'd have it: a confession! Within a week, I'd have this baby wrapped up and Magda would ever so grateful. I could almost hear her praising my investigative skills and making cheese puffs. Or Moroccan spiced almonds. Nobody said thank you with food the way Magda did.

George trod all over my illusions. He enlightened me as to fiscal and physical realities of listening devices, like the cost rising exponentially as the size of the bug decreases. Inasmuch as small batteries in constant use don't last very long, a voice-activated transmitter was a great idea only if I planned to spend hundreds of dollars. Then there was the issue of range. Unless I wanted to go back and retrieve a recording device, I would have to spend my spare time encamped within a couple hundred meters of the bug transmitter. My years of reading mysteries and watching Female Victims Network movies had led me astray on these points.

I had broached the idea to George of using a high-powered antenna to pick up cell phone conversations; I'd seen one used on a TV show just last week. According to George, that was a non-starter, too, unless I wanted to follow the suspects around hoping they'd call a friend and confess to murder.

After George took my bugging blinders off, I felt really let down by a morass of mystery writers, not to mention a slew of screenwriters.

George's tutorial included the merchandise limitations of the local Radio Shack and spy gear shop, and he volunteered that there was no Home Detective Kit available from the QVC channel. He directed me towards eBay. "If you are hypothetically interested in listening devices that you don't plan to use in an illegal manner." Additionally, George offered advice on how he might hide a listening device if he were in my shoes. And he did admire my designer knockoff sling-back pumps of snake embossed leather with a peep toe and 2 1/2" stacked heels. I looked great in them, if I did say so myself. Even if they weren't gumshoe shoes.

I spent well over an hour on-line locating "monitoring equipment" that met my needs and budget. I settled on a single small unit and receiver that ran on a nine-volt battery and cost less than one hundred dollars. Now, where should I plant it?

Miracles do happen, but asking God to make Janet confess in her sleep while I had a bug in her bedroom was, perhaps, a tetch far-fetched. Justin was in the same bed, er boat. My only hope was that two people had been involved in the murder – say Mrs. Claus and Mother Earth – and would talk about it. Despite the low probability of bugging success – George claimed I'd have as much luck unearthing clues by cracking open Chinese fortune cookies – I felt a surge of optimism as I placed my order for the Transmitter plus Receiver Listening Device, advertised as the "Ideal Baby Monitor." Indeed.

NINETEEN

"A lot of people like snow. I find it to be an unnecessary freezing of water."
– Carl Reiner

I GAZED AT THE GLISTENING SNOW littered with icy "death cookies," ready to trip the unwary. I raised my head and saw Huw, effortlessly balanced on the edge of his snowboard as he waited for me to once again push myself up off the ground. Huw had not a drop of snow on him – had he even fallen once? – while I had snow in every zipper pull, Velcro tab, crease and unspecified opening in my clothing – not to mention body crevices – despite the four layers of clothing I wore. Snow had even inched its way down the back of my ski pants, giving me the sensation of a wet, chilly diaper. Eew.

After losing the battle against traffic all week, I entertained thoughts of backing out on my commitment to go snowboarding with Huw. Don't get me wrong, I wanted to board, but I wasn't thrilled about the Friday night mass migration to Tahoe. But Huw's enthusiasm when he called on Thursday was infectious and I couldn't say no. In retrospect, I should been attentive to his word choice when describing the snowboarding lessons as payback for my surf lessons. "Payback," indeed. "With interest," he should have added on behalf of truth-in-advertising.

I groaned inwardly recalling the endless falls and the up-close-and-personal view of the terrain, as well as the upclose-and–personal view of my *'ōkole* shared with other boarders and skiers. Getting to the lift, I'd slipped and fallen into the guide rope. Then the lift operators had to stop the chair when I tried to get on because I couldn't move up fast enough to catch it. Technically, that wasn't a fall, just a stumble; I only count it as a fall if my *'ōkole* hits the snow – less humiliating that way. Naturally, I'd fallen face first getting off the chair nearly tripping Huw in the process and wiping out the skier who'd been sharing the chair with us. The kid threw me a look of disgust as he pulled himself up, and skied halfway down the slope before I managed to move out of the way so the lift could be restarted. And since then? I think six to eight falls. Maybe I should just count in units of ten.

One would think that with as many tumbles as I'd taken my *'ōkole* would be black and blue. Not being able to see it – and I sure wasn't going to ask Huw to check on it for me – I couldn't speak with authority on its color, but it felt more numb than sore. What really hurt were my arms from pushing myself off the snow. A different set of muscles than I used getting up on my surfboard, apparently. My ego hurt, too and, unlike the bumps and bruises, ibuprofen and an analgesic rub weren't going to help.

I had thought that being a surfer, snowboarding would be a breeze. That's what everybody kept telling me. "You surf, right? You must 'board, too." I heard that often enough I had begun to think surfers-must-board was the Eleventh Commandment. I mean, it's a board, right? How hard could it be? Hah! Surfing and boarding are similar like tennis and football are similar because they both are played outdoors with balls. The odds of concussions and broken bodies are much higher in one versus the other and the reason surfers don't wear helmets and padding, but boarders do.

I looked down slope again. The bottom was nowhere in site, but I could see Huw, patiently waiting, perhaps thinking of all the face plants he'd experienced under my surf-mentor ministrations. But he'd been falling into nice, soft water – with only the occasional reef, sandbar or comfy kelp wad underneath – and not the icy, packed slab of a ski slope known as Sierra Cement.

On the other hand, the scenery was breathtaking. White puffy clouds floated like meringues in the clear blue sky and sheets of sun-glistened snow swept down the slope framed by deep green pines on either side. From the top of the mountain one could see the rich, deep blue of Lake Tahoe, the *pièce de résistance,* beckoning in the distance. Beckoning as in, "here's a place to drown yourself after a really bad day on the slopes."

I dug out my phone, took another photo, shoved it back into my jacket and laid back until my head was on the snow. Flipping my legs and the board up several feet off the ground, giving everyone down slope another good view of my snow-covered rear, I rolled to my left until I was facing into the hill and then pushed myself up onto the edge of the board. Immediately I began to slide across the hill.

The board started to pick up speed as I approached the far edge of the slope. Since my slalom skills were non-existent, I had set a course that avoided the dozen or so snowboarders sprawled across the slope, some newly-fallen and some sitting as if on the beach. Unfortunately, my course also meant I was pointed steeply downhill. If I had been surfing, I would have easily carved turns around obstacles in my way, moving my feet if needed, leaning on my back leg, and using my front to turn the board. Just my luck that it was bass-ackward in snowboarding: my feet were locked in and I was supposed to lean forward. And I could not walk the board to stall it or speed up, as I was used to doing on my longboard. Nearing an imposing stand of trees at the incredible speed of two hundred miles per hour – okay, maybe only eighty – my head kept telling me not – not! – to lean forward, since I would go faster. Overcoming my terror, I leaned forward slightly and whipped the tail of the board around so the front was facing the other direction. Now my back was to the hill and I unconsciously leaned backwards. My forward momentum stopped and I fell back on my *ʻōkole.*

Once again, I peered down slope. Bottom still not in sight. My bottom still parked on the slope. Ego bottomed out. Huw still waiting with bottomless patience. Other skiers and snowboarders still successfully navigating their way down the slope. One definite advantage of surfing over boarding was that, when tired, you could let the whitewater push you in and you didn't even have to stand on the board. With boarding, I'd have to start an avalanche to get a fast trip to the bottom of the hill.

I took a deep breath, put my head back on the snow, lifted my legs and started the whole darn process over again.

We had left after work the night before. We being Huw, Thucydides, and me.

"My neighbor usually takes care of Thucydides for me, but she had a last minute opportunity to go to Vegas. I didn't think you'd mind the company," Huw explained.

Thucydides was a cute twenty pound black-and-white Klee Kai; he looked like a miniature Siberian Husky. When Huw introduced us, I adopted my sing-song voice and started telling him what a smart, handsome dog he was. Thucydides sniffed my fingers, jumped into the back seat and ignored me. Huw just gave a shrug, explaining the breed was typically a bit standoffish.

Since we were getting a late start – I hadn't been able to escape work until after six – Huw had stopped at Tahiti Tacos beforehand and picked up ham and pineapple burritos, two guava malts and coconut fries. Even after I inhaled my dinner, Huw kept the conversation light, avoiding any discussion of my work or his thesis. We discussed good books, good dog breeds, good cities to live in and good places to visit. The traffic was uncharacteristically light instead of the hour-by-hour grind from the Bay Area that is typical for a weekend getaway. I didn't understand how sitting in traffic for eight hours to get to the mountains, not to mention an equally obnoxious slog back, could possibly be considered relaxing, but many Bay Area residents made the trip every weekend.

On the way up, we listened to Huw's jazz playlists, which included large servings of Oscar Peterson and John Coltrane, a heaping measure of Louis Armstrong as seasoning, and a modicum of Billie Holliday for dessert. Most of his jazz selections were of the easy-on-the-ears variety instead of the nervous, over-saxed variety, for which I was grateful.

Arriving late at the ski place, we found ourselves in "high cotton," as my Grandmother Swenson would say. The house had a great view of Lake Tahoe and a fireplace bigger than my dining room. Huw directed me to a spacious bedroom on the upper floor decorated in "mountain modern" with spare, clean-lined furniture and animal accents: a throw pillow sporting an elk silhouette, beaver bookends and watercolors of fish (rainbow trout, cutthroat trout, and salmon). Even the coverlet had a repeating pattern of evergreen trees and bugling elk. I dropped my duffle bag on the floor and hung up my ski parka in the closet, while Huw took Thucydides around the house for his "doggie business."

"Cheers," Huw said as we clinked glasses. He'd brought a nice Merlot and munchies for winding down after the drive.

"*'Ōkole ma luna.* Bottom's up." I didn't know at the time I was prophesying my snowboarding travails.

As I let the alcohol unwind me, Huw bustled about the fireplace, grabbing splits of wood out of a large wicker basket, placing them carefully in the extra large fireplace – you could turn an elk on a spit in there – and lighting it. The wood caught fire, sparked and popped. Huw stood in front of the fire for a moment, warming himself, before returned to the oversize sofa that fronted the hearth. I liked the style of the house but everything was over-scale. Had the builder expected to sell to giants? I preferred cozy, regular-sized rooms and furnishings to "drown in them" tubs, "threesome" showers and "the yeti is coming for cocktails" sofas. On the other hand, the price was right and I wasn't going to complain. Huw pulled two coiled wool blankets from an oversize – what else? – brass urn, and handed one to me.

I do love fires and my apartment in San Francisco lacked a fireplace. I leaned forward into the heat and let it wash over me, especially welcome since the room was so cold and would be until the heat really kicked in. Thucydides must like the cold as he'd moved well away from the fireplace to stretch out on the rug.

After a comfortable silence, Huw spoke. "So, how are you doing in trying to clear Magda's name? I assume since you received your mother's blessing over Thanksgiving that you are up to your neck in a murder investigation. What was her name, Leandra?"

"Laguna. Laguna Butterfield." Entranced by the flickering embers, I fell quiet.

"Or, we can talk about something else if you'd like," he said, taking my silence as a completely uncharacteristic reluctance to talk.

"No, that's okay." The hissing and popping of the fire was strangely soothing, even if the constant, if minor, explosions reminded me too much of the workday. "I've talked to my neighbors about Laguna and snooped about the Lime-O group Laguna worked for." I paused and took another sip of wine. "I've attended one of their protests and met a few of her co-workers. And I've identified but not spoken to her boyfriend."

"That's progress."

"Sort of. George, a PI friend of Stacey's who did background checks for me, didn't find anyone whose CV screams 'potential murderer,' so all I have are suspects who are on the list simply because they knew her."

"So what's next?"

I was drinking the wine entirely too quickly, both because it was a very nice wine – and nicely warming – and because I wanted time to collect my thoughts. I wasn't sure how much I wanted to share with Huw, but the wine loosened my tongue.

"First, I want to swear you to secrecy. No snitching to my parents, even to get in good with my father."

"Your father already likes me, but I won't tell anyone. And, I'll be as faithful to my word as Odysseus, fulfilling my oath, even if it means leaving my homeland to fight Troy."

"The same Odysseus who tried to feign madness to get out of going to war?"

Huw shrugged and smiled.

I took the plunge. "I'm going to plant a bug on a couple of potentials. I'll hide the bug in a houseplant – yes, I get the irony – and present it as a gift. Then I'll tune in from afar and see what they say. Of course, this is all highly illegal and I could get into serious doodoo if I'm caught." I waited for Huw to tell me that I was treading on dangerous ground and shouldn't do it, but he surprised me.

"Sounds like a good plan."

"Really? How much wine have you had?"

"I haven't been keeping up with you. I guess you like merlot."

"Not as much as syrah, but this is pretty nice, whatever it is."

"'Yet a little' as the French say?" He poured me another inch before I could respond. Hey, wine counts as a fruit, right? And red wine has resveratrol, so it's healthy for you. Huw poured the rest of the bottle into his glass and added the now redundant cork to the many corks in a brass bowl on the oversize chest that served as a coffee table.

"You expected me to caution you about planting the bug, right?"

I nodded.

"I know you're not the 'sit back and let it happen' type of girl. After all, I've seen you take on surf bullies twice your size, and win. I've learned not to underestimate you. Your father, in particular, thinks you walk on water. Who am I to disagree?"

I'm sure my jaw dropped at this startling announcement. Huw had been a regular for dinner at my parents' place and it wouldn't surprise me one bit if my mother had been readying my nomination for the Nobel Prize in something-or-other. But my father? He was less effusive with praise – at least, to me. I felt a warm glow, and it wasn't just from the wine.

"Uh, thanks," I said as graciously as I could.

"Wish I could help you, but since my specialty is dead languages, I'm not very good with live people. The only mysteries I really like are historical: Cadfael, Didius Falco and Sherlock Holmes, of course."

Huw and I chatted awhile about mysteries and historical fiction, history, philosophy and so forth, meandering comfortably from one topic to the next. Even after the wine ran dry and the salami and crackers were reduced to skins and crumbs, we could have talked for hours more, but for the yawning that regularly cut into our discourse. It was time to call it a night.

Without saying a word, Huw cleared the empty bottle and our glasses. When he returned from the kitchen, he held out his hand and helped me out of the couch. As I stood up, he pulled me to him and put his arms around me. His soft sweater felt nice against my cheek and his body felt firm – as it appeared in swim trunks – but not as rock hard as Keoni's. Funny. I'd never hugged Keoni in a sweater. I wondered if he'd feel different.

When Huw turned my head to kiss me, I kissed back. When he suggested we could share a room, I demurred. I was happy to see he looked disappointed, but also happy he didn't press it. I wasn't sure I wanted to go there with him. Certainly not now. Maybe not ever. Definitely not unless I felt there were really something there. I might not be pure as the driven snow but I have never been a fan of opportunistic sex. Tempted occasionally, but not a practitioner.

We retired to our respective rooms. I collapsed into bed, my head hit the pillow and … my mind began to race. Sigh. Sometimes wine late at night keeps me awake. Joy.

After what seemed like hours of tossing and turning, I must have dozed off because I awoke to a firm pounding on my door. Huw yelled that it had snowed overnight, conditions were perfect, he'd already had Thucydides out for a long walk and the day was half gone. It was a good thing Huw was a classicist instead of a mathematician, because when I checked the clock, I was pretty sure eight o'clock constituted one third of a day and not one half. Under any mathematical construct, it was entirely too early for anyone who had only drifted off to sleep fourish and hadn't had coffee yet. Not that any amount of coffee would help revive me given the appalling paucity of shut-eye I'd experienced.

Not an auspicious start to the day.

"I'M SORRY YOU DIDN'T have a good time," Huw said loudly as we slumped in oak captain's chairs in the small Tyrolean-style restaurant at the base of the mountain. The outdoor deck was packed with skiers basking in the warmth of the sun and consuming large glasses of warmer-uppers, so we had to take a seat indoors next to the bar. Noise radiated around us: clomping boots, high fives, the TV blaring a sporting event and a chorus of "dudes" from teens who appeared to be part of a school group.

"I've always wanted to try snowboarding. Now I can say I have," I yelled back, attempting to put a bit of cheer in my voice. I think I'd used the same tone when asked how I liked eating raw oysters, which are just nasty: I kept expecting one of them to come back to life and start burrowing into my brain.

Sabrina from Germany – and yes, she did wear a dirndl skirt and too-tight white, embroidered blouse – brought us our beers and food. Pasta for me. Burger for Huw. While she arranged the food on the table, I peered out the wood-mullioned windows up slope, observing skiers and boarders swooping down towards the base and the lift lines. A snowboarder headed for the edge of the slope waved his arms frantically before diving head first into the snow. I winced in sympathetic pain.

"You were starting to master it at the end there," Huw said encouragingly after Sabrina left.

"'Master' as in master falling?"

"No, really, you were doing much better on the Shirley Lake run," Huw fiddled with his drink and avoided looking at me directly. He was a patient instructor but a bad liar. I could tell by the way he tried to keep from smiling – oh, and there went the eyebrow twitch – that he wasn't totally sold on what he was saying.

"Well, I wasn't falling as much," I admitted, "but I was just so dang tired that I couldn't go on."

"Tell me about it," he said. "I felt the same way after the first surfing lesson. I almost didn't try it again."

But he had, showing more tenacity than I was feeling. I was convinced Shirley Lake was named for a deceased beginning snowboarder who was buried at the foot of the chairlift named for her. And why had Huw taken me down a blue run instead of a green one? "Surfing is a lot more forgiving unless you fall right on top of the reef. Or hit a rock," I said. "Or run over someone who beats the tar out of you on the beach."

"There are no sharks on the ski slope," Huw countered. For some reason, perhaps he's seen the movie *Jaws* once too often, Huw had an inordinate fear of sharks. I'd told him that he was more likely to be in an auto accident on the way to work. He grimly replied he'd never seen an SUV eat another car. It hadn't helped that one of the guys in the lineup told Huw about the eighty-eight stitches it took to sew up a shark bite he took surfing at Stinson Beach. When he started in on the number of pints of blood he'd needed, I moved us down the beach, to a gentler break with fewer shark bite victims. I assumed it was fewer, but it wasn't a survey I cared to make: "So, who here in today's lineup has been part of the aquatic food chain?"

It was getting harder to communicate over the noise, so I didn't feel guilty when I took out my phone to check voicemail, messages and other electronic intrusions. Five voicemails, six texts, three applications that needed upgrading, and twenty-eight new messages. One of the messages was from Stacey, reaffirming her commitment to join me at the Lime-O protest the next day. Good. Meghann had sent a reminder that "The Event" was only six months away and had attached the latest *Nuptuals Newsletter* covering her wedding preparations. I must have groaned audibly.

"What?" ask Huw.

"It's Meghann, a high school girl friend with a message about her upcoming wedding."

"You don't like weddings?"

"Not when the couple thinks they're royalty. Meghann's getting married in Grace Cathedral with a full choir, eight hundred invitees and twelve bridesmaids. She posts updates of her plans on Facebook *and* sends bi-weekly newsletters to all members of the wedding party. You get the idea."

Huw shook his head. "All some women want is the wedding," he said. "The guy is just an accessory."

The bitterness came through loud and clear. I didn't pry, but wondered if his attitude stemmed from his recent breakup.

Huw checked his watch. "I think it's time to rescue Thucydides and head back."

"Fine," I said and took a long look at the mountain of white snow. Tomorrow's challenge would be lime green.

TWENTY

"What's so funny 'bout peace love & understanding?"
– Elvis Costello

STACEY AND I MET UP that Sunday morning at Berkeley Labs. It felt strange joining a protest against a company that had interviewed me for a job. On the other hand, they hadn't hired me, so I didn't feel all that guilty. A premier research and development organization, Berkeley Labs – unaffiliated with the University of California, Berkeley – worked almost solely on projects for the U.S. Government that pertained to defense and national security matters. I knew from the prep work for my job interview that Berkeley software programmers had access the most powerful computers in the world. What grade-A geek wouldn't want to work there?

I'd approached Berkeley when I decided to move back to the mainland after graduating from the University of Hawai'i. It was rare that Berkeley hired anyone without work experience, so I was thrilled when I got the initial interview. By the time they got back to me with a rejection – moving as glacially as molasses in January (okay, molasses in January in Minnesota) – I already had a job offer with GD at a much higher salary. So there.

"I brought coffee for you, hon, a salted caramel mocha. Whipped cream. Artisanal caramel drizzles. What?" Stacey said in response to my raised eyebrows.

"Do you have any idea how many calories that has? Oh, and are there any sprinkles?"

"This from a woman who snarfs a 16-ounce mocha, with whipped cream, caramel and two kinds of sprinkles and wipes the cup out with her finger so she doesn't miss a drop?"

"I read an article online last night about coffee drinks. I could eat a Big Mac with jumbo fries for what the average mocha anything costs me in an expanded waistline. Now I know where my extra winter insulation comes from – egg nog lattes. Plus, I've been eating a lot of chocolate lately, so I'm trying to cut calories in other areas. So, does it have sprinkles? Sprinkles don't add many calories so I don't have to give them up."

"It doesn't have sprinkles because salted caramel mochas do not have sprinkles. It's in the Coffee Bible – 'thou shalt not add sprinkles to a salted caramel mocha.' As for the calories, don't worry; I had them make a skinny one."

"Uh, okay. Thanks, Stace," I said, guiltily. "And this is for you." I handed her my plaid yellow and lime green beret.

"Isn't this the cutest littl' ol' hat?" Stacey slapped it on her head. "So, how does this thing work?"

"First, you adjust the hat so it's at an angle. You don't want it too far forward on your forehead and you don't want it on the back of your head, either. Let me show you."

"Very funny. You know I meant. I don't care about beret etiquette. I'm never going to look like anything except a fashion-deprived bagpiper in this. And how long have you been an expert on beret placement?"

"Ever since I spent four years in the Wilderness Girls. I made it all the way to Bullfrog. You couldn't make it past Tadpole if you didn't wear the beret correctly." I decided not to mention it was four years and out for me after I flunked the Nature Appreciation Hike. I smuggled a can of Raid insect spray into my backpack and used it on everything that buzzed, including our Troop Leader's cell phone in an unfortunate accident. It wasn't my fault Mrs. Snodgrass's ring tone was set to "mosquito."

"So, what are we doing?" Stacey said, bringing me out of the woods.

"Sorry. We'll go over to that green van, protest central, and I'll introduce you. We'll grab a couple of placards and then mill around and see if we can sniff out anything in between chanting and acting outraged."

"The only things I've sniffed out so far are an excess of spandex and truly heinous outfits that are worse than what you see on St. Patty's Day. Come to think of it, I have seen a couple of green bowler hats. At least St. Patty's Day green has positive associations."

"Like?"

"Like lying on soft grass – the sod kind, not the pot kind – and watching the clouds go by."

"I thought you were going to say 'green beer,'" I said, remembering our foray into an Irish bar – and endless renditions of "Cockles and Mussels, Alive Alive-O" – after the first corpse I'd found. I was trying to pump Maria for information at the time. No surreptitious investigation was worth that much bad Irish music.

Stacey must have been thinking of the same thing. "As you may recall, I'm more of a green Chardonnay type."

Coffees in hand, we headed towards the action.

Berkeley Labs resides in a brick building fronted by white Corinthian columns spanning all three storeys. Though not part of the university, it has a campus-like feel about it: a large expanse of thick grass surrounds the building and an arboreal canopy of towering oak trees shelters the brick paths. Appearances could be deceiving. I knew from my interview with them that the interior of the building is gleaming steel and glass. Only the shell of the old building was preserved to satisfy the Berkeley Historical Preservation Society or, as my father referred to them after one too many neighborhood battles, the "Berkeley Hysterical Preservation Society."

The Lime-O mobile protest van was parked prominently on the street in front – the parking lot was controlled access – in all its headache-inducing glory, like an apparition you might have after a surfeit of gin and tonics. The police had closed off one lane of the road and the van functioned as a hive, with lime-clad worker bees milling about, waiting on the queen bee, Cindy. Today she was channeling her inner Druid priestess in a sheer voluminous dress embroidered with figures of trees, a necklace of – were those carrots? – and a crown of pine cones and greens encircling her head. Mother Earth in her finest.

I put on my sincerest fake smile as I pushed determinedly through the crowd, like a salmon through headwaters. "Hey, Cindy! I'd like to introduce you to my best friend Stacey. She's a fellow committed Lime-O warrior."

We were met by sullenness and a mumbled hello. Cindy turned around, her diaphanous dress shimmering like Tinkerbell's fading light. She reached back in the van, grabbed two signs and shoved them at us.

"Thanks," I said with another brilliantly insincere smile, and turned to go.

"That is an interesting necklace you have on, Cindy," Stacey said. "I do believe it's made out of vegetables."

"Uh-huh," Cindy responded. "Asparagus ends, dried peas, yellow squash and carrots. All of them were grown in the Community Garden here in Berkeley. Organic, of course."

"Quite practical." Stacey flashed an approving smile. "Y'all can donate it to the local soup kitchen after the protest: two good causes from one necklace, peachy! Thank you kindly for the signs. I'm lookin' forward to raisin' Cain." She turned and wriggled her fingers in a cheery wave as Cindy smiled and nodded.

We moved towards bodies chanting mantras and marching.

"Laying on that Southern syrup awfully thick, aren't ya, 'sugah'?" I said dryly.

"My mama taught me you catch more flies with honey than vinegar."

"I'll remember that if we have a plague of flies." I still preferred Raid, quick and lethal.

Protesters with placards were striding up and down the grass in front of the lab, a series of orange traffic cones connected by yellow tape separating then from a half dozen security guards, clearly bored by the proceedings but staying well clear of the protesters. I looked up at my protest sign and groaned.

"What?" said Stacey, turning to look at me, her beret slipping over one eyebrow. She shoved it back in place with a glare.

I pointed to my sign. Stacey was beset with an attack of the giggles. Her beret slipped over the other eyebrow. She reached up, grabbed her beret with and yanked it over her ear. One of Stacey's few unfashionable moments.

"It's not that funny," I protested.

"But it is because it is soooo true."

On a bright blue poster board, someone had carefully written in large block letters: "I Like Men Out of Uniform."

Stacey's laugh was infectious, and I started giggling, too. "Okay, I agree it's true, but I generally don't like to advertise. And what does yours say?"

Stacey turned her sign so we could read it. "Berkeley Labs Sucks" was scrawled almost illegibly in black marker. An upside down American flag was hastily drawn in the lower left corner.

"Hmm, short and to the point," I said.

"Wanna trade?"

"No, thanks. I think I got the better end of the deal."

We joined the lackadaisical parade of twenty or so protesters. More joined over time, but the participants were fewer in number than at the Embarcadero, younger (perhaps drawing students from the university) and, dare I say, better dressed. A few girls actually looked cute. They were brunettes, of course. We blonds just can't handle the color.

Stacey and I dropped in and out of groups as we walked around, meeting people who knew Laguna, but none who had known her well.

Stacey took a few pictures with her phone, including one of a protestor wearing a Kermit the frog hat, green bow tie and gloves. I overheard him complaining to his friend about the power bill from charging his electric car. I could almost hear the TV Kermit singing the chorus of "It's Not Easy Being Green."

"I have to post some of these," Stacey said. "My Texas friends will think I've gone native." I refused to let her take one of me, but let her hold my sign while I took her photo.

I spotted Janet heading for the protest line, her head adorned with a large straw hat – black, in a delightful departure from the prevalent color – and we veered to intercept her.

"Hey, Janet," I said as we got close. "It's Emma. I'm so glad to see you again. I'd like to introduce you to my friend Stacey. This is her first Lime-O event."

Nothing is supposed to move faster than the speed of light. I wasn't big into science, taking just what I needed to satisfy minimum requirements at University of Hawai'i, but I do remember that. However, the rapidity with which Stacey managed to insinuate herself into Janet's good graces threatened to upend all Einsteinian constraints.

She started with the Texas charm: "Ahm sooo glad to meet you" and "Isn't this just thrilling?" Stacey name dropped various causes she'd been involved with including Friends of Urban Arbors (tree planting in San Francisco which I'd done and enjoyed, too), Feed Our Friends (helping animal shelters) and Save Ocean Beach (Stacey quit when she realized SOB's ultimate goal was to make Ocean Beach off-limits to anything that wasn't indigenous flora and fauna, including all hikers, runners, surfers and dogs).

Stacey asked Janet how she liked Lime-O and whether it was a good place to work. Janet was non-committal until Stacey asked whether a friend of hers should apply for the bookkeeper position being advertised.

"Well, it doesn't pay all that well," Janet admitted. "NGOs generally don't. But the other employees are the nicest people I've ever worked with and there's a lot of flexibility in work hours. When you have kids, or other interests, it's nice to have that latitude."

When Stacey enquired about Janet's children, I drifted away. I wasn't contributing anything to the conversation and I'd heard enough about her kids and Raja, the white Persian.

I located Susan standing in the shade under a large trees with a young woman and an apparition that could only be Justin. The young woman was wearing lime green leather pants – hadn't I seen that identical pair when shopping with Stacey? – and was draped all over Justin who had ditched the black cape for a green one with a big L on the back. His black turtleneck and too-tight jeans left nothing left to the imagination. Black sneakers completed the super-hero wannabe ensemble.

I parked my sign against a fire hydrant and strode up to them.

"Emma. Great to see you here. I'd like you to meet Caitlin. And I presume you know Justin. Emma was a friend of Laguna," she said to Caitlin, by way of explanation.

"Ah, Justin and I haven't formally met. Hi, I'm Emma ... Laguna's neighbor."

"Oh, I just thought you'd naturally know each other since you both knew Laguna and you're both in technology," Susan said.

Justin eyed me curiously and Caitlin mumbled what I think was a hello, but I didn't hear the last syllable.

"I didn't know Laguna long," I said. "And I guess she never had the chance to formally introduce us. But she did mention you work in IT. What area?" I hoped talking about technology would keep Justin from inquiring further into my supposed friendship with Laguna.

Justin didn't respond immediately and Susan jumped into the gap. "Laguna brought Justin by to help with our PCs, and since then, he's done all sorts of things for us like update our software, maintain our web site, and he even finds targets for us, like Berkeley Labs. Oh, and he twitters our events."

"Tweets," Justin corrected her.

The conversation came to a dead stop as Susan seemed out of ideas and Justin wasn't volunteering anything.

I turned to Caitlin. "Did you know Laguna?"

"Not well," she mumbled.

Pause in conversation again. Susan excused herself, stating it was about time for her speech.

"Gotta work, too," Justin said. He unwound himself from Caitlin's arms and headed for the green van.

Caitlin followed his retreating back with her eyes.

I observed her carefully. Like Maria, her dark hair and olive complexion weren't overwhelmed by neon-lime green. She was definitely younger and prettier than Laguna.

"I guess you two are an item, now." I said, bringing Caitlin's eyes snapping back to meet mine.

"I suppose you think I stole him away from Laguna," she said, thrusting her chin in the air. "Well, I didn't. He's loved me for a long time. He just didn't know how to break it off with Laguna."

"I see," I said in my most sympathetic manner, taking Stacey's "you catch more flies with honey than vinegar" advice to heart. "You look good together."

Caitlin's face registered disgust. She turned and stalked away.

Too much honey, or not enough? Well, I'm not giving up yet.

I sauntered over to the driver's door of the Lime-O van. Justin was in the front passenger seat with a notebook computer open, madly typing away. I stuck my head in the open window.

"Hello, again."

Justin nearly jumped out of his skin and looked none too happy to see me.

"What?"

"I just wanted to see how the tweet was going."

"Fine."

This was going as well as my chat with Caitlin.

"I expect you have a lot of followers."

"Don't keep track."

Can this guy even form a whole sentence?

"So, Laguna got you into this protest stuff, huh?"

"Yeah."

"Me, too." God is my witness. That was the truth. Not the whole truth, but it would do for now.

"She never mentioned you."

There it is! A sentence!

"Well, it was her example that inspired me, actually."

"Good for you. I gotta work." He put his head down and started typing again. I was half surprised that he didn't reach over and put up the window.

"Uh, just one more thing. What's the hashtag?"

"Why do you need it? You're here."

"Just to pass on to my friends. I'm sure they'd like to follow you."

"#Limeo," he said as he turned the ignition key and hit the close switch on the automatic window. It closed so quickly I had to yank my head back into my sweater like a very startled turtle.

I wandered back to the crowd and joined the retinue surrounding a podium that was being set up for Susan. A tall, distinguished African-American woman, whom I recalled seeing at the Towson-Peabody protest, seemed popular; many of the protestors stopped and chatted with her for a few moments. I wished I were half as pulled together as she in her stunning lime green jeans and cable cardigan over a crisp white linen blouse. The multiple silver bangles on each wrist and cascading silver earrings added a touch of class.

We exchanged introductions and she said her name was Estelle. I commented that the crowd here was smaller and less overtly enthusiastic than I'd seen the prior week. Estelle responded that Berkeley Labs had become a routine protest site, but before she could explain further, Susan began speaking.

Susan spoke for no more than fifteen minutes, and the responsive applause was a bit more than mere politeness would dictate.

"Isn't she wonderful?" Estelle said.

"Dynamic."

"I've known Susan since early Lime-O days and she never fails to inspire."

Okay, I'm going to try this honey thing one more time and if it doesn't work, I'm going back to my go-straight-for-the-swat approach.

"You must be so proud of how the organization is growing," I said. "Tell me, is it true Jürgen Reimer is going to make a large donation soon?"

Estelle expressed surprise that I'd heard the news but confirmed that Reimer's people were performing due diligence on Lime-O's management and that Lime-O was hoping for a "significant sum" of money, although no specific amount had been mentioned.

"I guess Laguna Butterfield's murder looks bad, then," I said, without thinking. "I mean, if her death had anything to do with Lime-O's finances."

Estelle looked startled. "Pure conjecture on your part, I must say." Her tone was not friendly.

Oops, too much vinegar.

"Estelle's right. Laguna's death has nothing to do with us," spat out a voice. It was Susan who had come up from behind. "Excuse us. Estelle and I have things to discuss." She put her arm around Estelle's shoulders, guided her away and I was left standing alone amidst the crowd.

So much for honey and vinegar.

TWENTY-ONE

"This is unexpected as squirt from aggressive grapefruit."
– *Charlie Chan's Chance,* Earl Derr Biggers

STACEY AND I SURFED that afternoon in blissfully uncrowded conditions at one of our favorite secret spots: an unnamed, unreported surf spot still safe from clods posting Internet videos with all-too-recognizable landmarks. May they all be strangled with their own surf leashes and each buried with a bar of surf wax in his mouth. Rancid surf wax.

Happily enough, the traffic was light. With Christmas just around the corner, most of the Bay Area residents were apparently in the malls, elbowing one another for the latest must-have gift to commemorate the birthday of the Prince of Peace. I was glad to have done most of my shopping in bookstores and in Hawai'i last summer.

The stark, steel sky reflected the gray, glassy water. Though nothing like Hawai'i in appearance, the ocean still had a rugged beauty all its own. As waves were few and far between, we spent most of our time in companionable silence.

Until Harrison joined us. He had the entire coastline between San Francisco and Santa Cruz so wired that there were no secret spots safe from him: he knew them all. Stacey seemed to enjoy his near constant talking and they prattled on while I made a few abortive attempts to catch waves. Too many waves looked promising coming in, but just as they were breaking, the wind blew the board up the face of the wave and you could not make the drop. Just like dating: looks good, but doesn't deliver.

The cold eventually penetrated deep within and I paddled back to the lineup one last time to let Stacey know I was going in. Stacey's lips were purple and Harrison was shaking, so we all decided to quit for the day.

Harrison was first in. He had changed, racked his board and was striding over while Stacey and I were still struggling out of our wet suits into the beauty that is fleece wear.

"Stace here tells me you solve murders," he said when he arrived, without preamble. "Why don't you figure out what happened to Shamu? Who killed him, I mean. Just cuz the guy was an effin' moron doesn't mean he deserved to be murdered. Stace here says you're pretty good. And you did find his body. Course, I guess you couldn't miss it since he was under your car. You don't seem like a woman who'd drive over a guy. Even if he did drop in on you out in the water all the time. Effin' moron."

I eyed Stacey, who radiated embarrassment. Having seen Harrison at work, I wasn't surprised at how quickly he'd managed to get her to reveal her deepest darkest secrets. I wondered if the CIA could use his talents: "wangle state secrets out of anybody, without waterboarding, in ten minutes or less." Come to think of it, maybe I should ask Harrison to help me in my current investigation. He'd get a confession a mere ten sentences after "Hi, nice to meet you."

"I'm not a real investigator ..."

"You're successful. That's what counts. And from what your friend has told me, you're a sharp lady. Now, if there's a problem with money, I expect we could case the lineup and get people to contribute. Not a lot, of course, but maybe expense money. Shamu was a pain in the ass but he was *our* pain in the ass."

"No, no," I protested. "Money isn't the problem."

"Then you'll do it. Great. That'll be good news to the guys. Been great hangin' with ya, but I gotta go. Here's my card. Remember, give me a buzz next time you're coming."

A quick wave and he was off, striding towards the parking lot like a man with a purpose.

That evening I signed into Twitter (I'd established an account long ago, just to see what all the fuss was about) and checked the Lime-O hash tag. There were a dozen tweets, most of them from @numerounogeek, who I presume was Justin, and a couple from supporters. They at least seemed to be into the protest.

"#Limeo will bring down Berkeley Labs Killers of Humanity!" screamed one. "#Limeo says no war no war no war no no no," another wrote.

Justin's tweets, in contrast, radiated dullness: "Join #Limeo today from ten to noon, protest at Berkeley Labs" and "Enthusiasm growing #Limeo protest as Susan Perkins speaks" and so forth. Not much to them. Not an hours' worth of sitting on one's *ʻōkole* with a computer, anyway.

Ten years earlier, a shady character on a computer in a van parked near a defense contractor would likely be trying to sniff out the contractor's wireless network. Not today when even home-based networks are secured. So, what was he up to? Using a GPS-based hookup application to find cute girls nearby? Watching a sports game on streaming video? Whatever it was, I couldn't see the relevance to Laguna's murder. And what, if anything, had I learned today that was?

During our drive down the coast, Stacey and I had shared our investigative progress, or lack thereof. Stacey's probing of Janet hadn't turned up anything; we were still in the dark as to her financial situation and whether she was augmenting it through embezzling, or growing and selling a new strain of pot in lime green.

Stacey claimed a "fruitful" chat with Cindy, which I thought at first meant they'd talked about Cindy's wardrobe. But no, Stacey had steered the conversation to Justin, and received an earful. Cindy called him superficially charming, but an opportunistic limpet: once he attached himself to you, it would take a crowbar to dislodge him.

A motive for murder, I'd said. Justin's sugar mommy was leaving the area, leaving him.

Stacey wasn't convinced. "First of all, you don't have any proof Laguna was leaving Justin behind. Secondly, even if she was, killing Laguna does what for him exactly? She can't support his lifestyle when she's dead. And third, if losing sugar mommy or sugar daddy were a motive for murder, we'd have a bloodbath in every city, every day. Breaking up might be hard to do, but it's a lot easier than getting blood out of your living room carpet and hiding a body."

When I didn't respond immediately, Stacey knew I didn't have a good answer. "Game, set and match to me."

All I could show for my sleuthing was reluctance on Susan's part to have me probe the Reimer-Laguna connection – totally understandable, as Stacey pointed out – and Caitlin's infatuation with Justin. Jealously as motive for murder? Caitlin as murderess? Perhaps it could use further examination, except for the eensy fact that Ms. Super Ace Detective didn't get Caitlin's last name. Even Nancy Drew's slightly dim bulb chum Bess didn't make that mistake. It must have been severe chocolate deprivation: my neurons weren't firing.

Clearly, my sojourn into detective work was showcasing my limited ability to suss out potential perps. Why couldn't I be more like Miss Marple – in ability, not in age – whose insights into people's characters provided a sound basis for her conclusions? Or Amelia Peabody, whose ratiocination – a word not even my comparative literature professor mother had taught me – allowed her to reason her way through a morass of clues in between unearthing tombs of pharaohs whose names I could never remember but they all sounded like Amenchorus, or was that Amenhodad?

If not for Maria, Stacey and George, I'd be "up a crick without a paddle," as Grandma Swenson would say. On the other hand, maybe I needed more paddles, more friends to help. And I knew just who to call: Meghann, my friend from high school active in the peace movement. How she, a committed Californian leftist and I, an apolitical Midwesterner, had become friends puzzled many.

For my part, I had always found Meghann's political opinions free of self-delusion and I admired her for her willingness to act on her beliefs and for not trying to convert me to her causes. And for her part? Meghann said I made her laugh.

After playing catch-up pong – trading greetings and status (great, good, just okay) – I told Meghann that I was calling her because I was involved with Lime-O. She was shocked, of course, until I gave her the highlights and lowlights of Laguna's murder and explained my desire to help Magda.

"Sounds a bit dangerous, but right in line with your tendency to jump first, think later. And don't deny it; you know it's true. Anyway, what do you want from me? Anti-war chants in three-part harmony?"

I explained I needed any information that might reflect badly on the founders or the organization's activity that wasn't common knowledge. Meghann promised she'd make a few discreet, yet nosy, inquiries and get back to me.

I hoped for Magda's sake that the police were making more progress than I was.

SUBSEQUENT TO GETTING BACK together last summer Keoni has called me Sunday evening unless the surf was killer and he was out there and on it. This evening, his call didn't come. I waited for the phone to ring, considered calling him, checked the O'ahu surf report (ugly) and ultimately went to bed disappointed.

I slept soundly until morning when my subconscious spewed forth a chaotic dream: Keoni in a cape, Justin in a bigger cape, a bull charging both of them, Caitlin throwing herself at Keoni, Susan riding the bull, waves pounding a green van against the rocks ... pounding ... pounding. The pounding penetrated my sleep. I arose, wild images half-remembered, to a near constant banging on my door. I grabbed my pepper spray key chain, stumbled to the door – almost tripping over the end of a protruding surfboard – and peered through the peephole before opening the door to Magda.

"I'm sorry to wake you, my dear, but the police are here to take me to the station and charge me with Laguna's murder. Could you possibly … if it's not too much … that is, I desperately need you to take care of Chesty and Edsel." Tears welled up in her eyes. I threw my arms around her and hoped that I was still dreaming.

TWENTY-TWO

"Niniau 'eha ka pua o Koai'e. 'Eha i ka anu. Ka nahele 'o Waika." (Wearied and bruised is the flower Koai'e. Stung by the frost. The herbiage of Waika.)

– "Waika," John Spencer

"Chesty's had his walk this morning, but probably needs to go out one more time. I've already called Elise, my hairdresser, and she's agreed to stop by around one o'clock each day and take Chesty for a short walk. Could you take him for his evening walk? He likes to visit the row of bottlebrush trees on Green Street ..." Magda's voice broke.

I nodded my head, tears filling my eyes. Get a grip, Emma. Mike Hammer didn't cry. Crying detectives can't solve cases. I patted Magda's arm in sympathy.

Magda took several deep breaths, composing herself. "Elise will also turn the TV on so Chesty and Edson have some distraction in the afternoon. But absolutely no soap operas or reality TV. *Animal Planet* is verboten, too – those programs about abused animals upset them too much. And if you wouldn't mind sitting with them in the evening, just so they have company besides each other, you know. It's probably too much to ask you to spend the night ..." She looked to me for an answer.

"Of course I'll stay overnight with them. But how long are the police going to keep you in jail? Won't they let you out on bail?"

"I hope so, but I don't know how it works. Clarence, my lawyer, will meet me at the station, so I'll know more when we've spoken. I just hope they'll allow me to visit my son in San Diego for Christmas," Magda said, her voice breaking again.

"Magda, I'm so sorry." I'd never seen Magda when she wasn't totally sure of herself, or sure she could bypass, end run, or run over whatever obstacles stood in her way.

I could feel the tension in her entire body as she gave me one last hug. "I have to go; they're waiting for me."

Indeed, I could see a man in a dark suit standing in the hallway, keeping an eye on Magda. As we broke from the hug I grabbed her arms. "I'm still on the case."

"I'm sure you are doing your best, Emma. Don't worry too much. Things will work out." Her words expressed more confidence than her mien betrayed. I wasn't sure if Magda was trying to convince me or convince herself. "Please, take good care of Chesty and Edson until I get back."

"I will, I promise," I said as she turned and left.

I made a quick call to Laura, explaining why I'd be late. When I told her a friend had been arrested and I had to take care of her animals, she was speechless.

Laura was a relatively tolerant of my occasionally odd work hours, but I knew missing the client deadline because of poop patrol wouldn't fly. I promised to get into work as soon as I possibly could and, in hopes of reassuring Laura, reiterated that this latest diversion would not keep me from making my deadlines.

I fixed a cup of coffee and went downstairs to check on Edson and Chesty. They looked none the worse for wear. In fact, I think both were napping comfortably until I came in. I rousted Chesty for a short walk – as short as it could be considering he marked every blade of grass within a two-block radius – checked to make sure they both had water and *kau-kau* for the duration and then headed into work.

I arrived at Carson an hour late, but just in time for Laura's staff meeting. Laura, fresh off her meeting with a grumpy Grundy, announced that layoffs at Carson were officially starting. She added, before we could interject, that we couldn't use the lack of help from Carson employees as an excuse for not finishing the transition on time.

"At least they haven't turned to active sabotage," Wendell said.

"You haven't heard?" Maria asked.

We all looked questioningly at Maria, except for Laura.

"A number of Zuckers' executives were here late on Friday for a meeting about Carson's brand and sales channels," Maria said. "An employee hacked into the PC that was being used for the presentation and edited the slides with some X-rated images and accompanying sound overlays."

With Maria's news in mind, we worked as quickly as we could to extract data from Carson's systems. It was nearly seven o'clock when I got home, and not until I was searching for a parking space did I remember that I had two little creatures depending on me, one of whom probably was standing by the door, holding himself. Or would be if he had opposable thumbs. I found a space two blocks away, grabbed my computer bag and ran. Sure enough, when I opened Magda's apartment door, Chesty was immediately underfoot, his whole body wiggling. I didn't for one minute think that the excitement was all about seeing me. I hooked him up to the leash and whisked him to the building's small, flower-lined courtyard. Chesty lifted his leg on the first four things he passed: the edge of the stairs, a flower pot, a Meyer lemon tree and the edge of a wrought iron bench. Small dog, large bladder. He used the tiny patch of grass to deposit some organic fertilizer. Fortunately, I found a loose plastic bag in the corner of the courtyard to remove his contribution to the environment.

Once inside, Chesty was ready to eat and play, in that order. By the time I'd taken care of Chesty's needs (eat, play, go for a walk, play again) and Edson's needs (peel me a shrimp right this second and then leave me alone to scarf it) and fed myself, it was nine o'clock. Chesty was curled up on the sofa, snoozing away while Edson had long since disappeared into Magda's bedroom and was,

I presume, engaging in the same activity. There wasn't much to watch on TV and I was just mulling over not hearing from Keoni the night before when my phone rang.

"Emma! *Welina! Pehea 'oe? Maika'i nō?*" (Greetings! How are you? Good?)

"Keoni! You didn't call yesterday. Are you okay?"

Keoni's joy at hearing my voice was evident. Jeez, Emma, one day late in calling you and you freak out. High school heart; shake it off, dudette.

"I'm good. Sorry to have worried you. We played a wedding reception yesterday and a birthday party. I have been very busy lately with my music. Stan Oshiro is letting me sub for him with 'Ike Pono while he's on the mainland for a few days. I'll be playing with Michael and Bobby at their regular Friday night gig in Waipahu and the farmers market in Waimanalo on Saturday."

I was thrilled. Keoni knew that 'Ike Pono was one of my favorite groups. We settled in for a comfortable chat and discussed 'Ike Pono as well as Keoni's own group, Hopena.

I told him about Magda's arrest and the lack of real progress in my investigation. Keoni listened without offering advice and assured me that I could only do my best. He'd learned the hard way – I admit I can be a bit tetchy at times – that if I didn't ask directly for his input, I didn't want it.

Not once did Keoni mention his Uncle Kimo and Native Hawaiian rights, which meant our conversation was blissfully free of controversy.

After we said *a hui hou*, I pulled up Hopena's web site. I hadn't checked it out for ages. The news section mentioned the group would soon release a CD, which "will include songs that express the aspirations and sorrows of the Hawaiian people." The playlist included songs written by Keoni. Why hadn't he mentioned this earlier? This couldn't be the big news he planned to share with me at Christmas, could it? Keoni had written both the title song, *He 'Uhane Hawai'i*, described as a "soulful melody about the longing of the Hawaiian heart," and *Mahele,* about "the unlawful seizure of

Hawaiian land." Much to my dismay, protests songs comprised the entire CD. Other than *Kaulana Nā Pua,* none could be considered a Hawaiian standard.

I felt like I'd been kicked in the chest. There was not one song celebrating the Hawai'i that I knew and loved: the beauties of Kaua'i (*Nani Hanalei, Koke'e*), or the cowboy culture (*Waiomina, 'Ulupalakua*), even the regrets of Hawaiian warriors facing their deaths (*Waika*). And nothing of the beautiful plants and creatures of Hawai'i (*Ka Uluwehi O Ke Kai, Wai O Ke Aniani*), or of love (*Ku'u Lei 'Awapuhi, Pua Hone*).

The times when Keoni would joke about my *'aumakua* (ancestor gods) as if I were Hawaiian seemed long past and far, far away. *Mahea ka piko o kona pu'uwai?* Where is the window of his heart? *A'ole au e 'ike.* I didn't know.

I WAS THE RECIPIENT of a five a.m. dachshund wakeup call the next morning. Even after tending to Chesty's and Edson's needs, I still made it into work unusually early, for me. Magda texted me during the day that she'd been released and would be headed home to "spring my kids from house arrest," so I stayed late again, not arriving home until after eight. Exhausted as I was, I stopped by to see her.

The scent of freshly-baked cookies greeted me as Magda opened the door and invited me in for tea and flycatcher cookies, a blond brownie with chocolate chips.

"Most humiliating thing I've ever been through," she said after we sat down with the refreshments. "And that includes childbirth in a teaching hospital. But I guess you wouldn't understand that reference."

"I think I get the idea. What was it like? Jail, I mean. Not childbirth."

"They take everything away and give you an orange jumpsuit to wear."

"How 1970s," I responded. "Fashion-wise, that is."

"Yes, well, that about captures it."

"Did you have anything to read or eat?" I think my own worst fear about being arrested, besides the possibility of a cop testifying under oath about the state of my underwear drawer, was to be left without anything to do. Bad enough I wouldn't have my phone or an Internet connection. Take away books and TV and I'd be climbing the walls, barbed wire and all. I'd beg my visitors to bring me an ile-fay in an ake-cay. One with extra frosting and sprinkles.

"I didn't have that much free time. There was a TV in the waiting room tuned to ESPN. But there was the whole process of being booked, and then talking with Clarence."

Magda revealed that the bail arranged at her arraignment had been set rather low, according to Clarence. He also thought the charge of voluntary manslaughter instead of second-degree murder seemed "unambitious." Voluntary manslaughter implied Laguna provided provocation that would have caused an average person to act rashly. The pretrial hearing, the next step in the process, was two months hence. Clarence thought the soft charge and lack of trial urgency indicated the prosecution just wanted to show they'd made an arrest, not as if they really believed they had a solid case. I hoped he was correct.

"Thank you for taking care of Edson and Chesty."

"Not a problem. I bet they were glad to see you."

"Overjoyed. Or in Chesty's case, overflowed."

"And I thought it was just my parent's dog, Gorgon, who had that problem."

"I like to think of it as a fountain of love." Magda smiled as she scratched Chesty's ears. His tail thumped weakly and he flopped over for a slavish belly rub.

On the way upstairs, I stopped at the front hall table to collect my mail. Magda had obviously not had time to sort it. Amazing what accumulates just in a day. I plowed through the pile of flyers, local rags, bills and catalogs and tossed the timeshare offer and Victoria's Secret catalog, as I was nowhere near their target audience: anorectic eighteen-year-olds. Two packages were buried at the bottom. One stamped "Addressee Unknown: Return to Sender" had come from Laguna, who'd used an iPhone box judging by the badly ripped brown wrapper. She'd never know about her errant gift.

The other package was – yes! My bug had arrived!

TWENTY-THREE

"Call on me and I will answer you, and tell you great and wondrous things you have not known."
– Jeremiah 33:3

THE NEXT NIGHT FOUND ME parked in an only slightly illegal spot listening to my "not for illegal eavedropping" but "perfect for baby monitoring" device. Yessiree, it was just the ticket to listen in on those nine-month old babblers: prevent insurrections in the nursery, stop Junior callously throwing his teddy bear against the wall and solve the case of the missing pacifier.

On George's advice, I'd encased the bug in a plastic bag and taped it to the bottom of a plant in a cheap plastic pot. A spathiphyllum to be precise, also known as a peace lily. I could enjoy the irony as I listened in, I mean, "monitored" the slightly big babies. I'd put the lily in a slightly larger plastic container using super glue to secure the pots; I didn't want Susan or Cindy separating the containers to reuse them, and thereby discovering the bug. Magda had allowed me to test the bug by eavesdropping on Chesty and Edson – putting the plant on a table so Chesty wouldn't water it – while I sat upstairs. Edson was the silent type. Chesty yipped whenever Magda moved from one room to another, but he didn't give up any state secrets like where he'd buried his latest bone.

I'd looked up their address on the Internet and delivered the plant to Cindy and Susan earlier that evening. Susan, dressed comfortably in black yoga pants and a black T-shirt, was surprised at my appearance on her apartment doorstep but greeted me warmly.

Cindy, arriving second at the door in mommy jeans and a Muppets sweatshirt, nodded but didn't say hello, less than thrilled at my arrival. I told them how much I was enjoying Lime-O, how many nice people I'd met, and that nothing says friendship like a plant. Cindy still didn't look happy; did she think I was a stalker, or was she druidically opposed to the imprisonment of plants?

Susan invited me in and soon I was seated on a long black leather couch sipping an herbal tea that tasted like roasted toadstools – green ones, which doubtless had more antioxidents, if they weren't outright poisonous. I admired their décor – or said I did. Their 'Mid Sixties Malcontent' style included tie-dyed bean bag chairs with matching curtains.

I asked a few questions about Lime-O's activities and Susan launched into a well-rehearsed pitch about the number of military bases whose gates they had closed, military recruiters whose operations were derailed because Lime-O blocked their doors and even binges where they'd pasted Lime-O stickers over Department of Defense decals, without which a car couldn't get onto a military base. She was clearly proud of their successes. "We now have chapters in fifteen states, thousands of members and are growing rapidly," she crowed.

"It's so thrilling," I said, trying to look wide-eyed and eager. Well, I was eager to dump the wretched toadstool tea. "I just can't think of the last time I was this excited. That's why I just don't understand about Laguna."

"What about Laguna?" Cindy snapped. I turned to face her as she put her teacup down and leaned so far forward in her chair, I expected her to tip over.

"Well, you know, she didn't seem into Lime-O. The weeks before she died, I mean."

"Dear Laguna," Susan said, a forced smile upon her lips that didn't reach her eyes, "was going through a rough patch, that's all. Justin can be a trial."

"Really? She was leaving Lime-O because of Justin?"

"We all dream at times about running away from our problems," Susan responded. "I'd convinced her to stay at Lime-O – despite Justin – and then the poor thing was killed by a maniac."

"So you think it was a random killing."

"What else could it be? If I were you, I'd be concerned about how a lunatic got into your building, and whether he or she will do it again."

"My landlady had all the security rechecked after Laguna was killed."

"Well then, you should be safe. Oh, look at the time. You did say you couldn't stay long." Susan rose to her feet.

I put my tea down, hoping I had an antacid – or ipecac in the unlikely event it really was toadstool tea – in my purse, and followed her towards the door. I thanked them both for their hospitality – which sounds so much more polite than "thanks for trying to poison me" – and left.

I was grateful my Honda was parked only a block away; the light rain that was falling upon my arrival had become a deluge and I quickly became a sodden mess. I started the car, turned on the heater and then switched on the listening device. Goody, an argument, which, as everyone who reads murder mysteries knows, might lead to a spontaneous confession. Quickly, I hoped, so I could go home and wash the taste of toadstools out of my mouth with a nice cup of cocoa, laced with Kahlua to warm me up.

"I don't want a thing to do with her or her plant."

"She was just trying to be nice," Susan replied calmly.

"She says she was Laguna's friend. Why the hell didn't Laguna ever mention her? Phony as a two-dollar bill."

"There actually are two-dollar bills, sweetie. Jefferson is on them. Emma could be a new friend that Laguna didn't have a chance to mention."

"Yeah, well, why does she keep bringing up Laguna? She talks more about Laguna than about Lime-O. And her friend Stacey kept mentioning Laguna, too. I don't trust either one of them."

"Isn't that a bit paranoid?"

"'Paranoid'?" Cindy's voice moved into a higher register. "You know as well as I do that Laguna was going to leave. She said she'd tell Jürgen Reimer about your out-of-control spending if you didn't give her a good recommendation. Wasn't it just oh-so-convenient that someone shut her up permanently?"

"The only reason she was worried about a recommendation was because of your screaming about treason and threatening to fire her before she could quit. You can't blame her for that: it's a small non-profit world and people talk."

I heard a loud bang and then silence. My heart raced. I persuaded myself that the bang was the slamming of a door and not a gunshot. If it were a gunshot, there would be a scream and the sound of a body hitting the floor, which I'd definitely hear because their apartment had hardwood floors instead of plush, body-absorbing carpeting.

Did Cindy just accuse Susan of killing Laguna? Or did Cindy imply that she had killed Laguna to save Susan and the funding? Why can't murderers give nice, clear confessions, preferably in front of a crowd where one person has a smart phone recording the argument?

Fear of carbon monoxide poisoning forced me to turn off the engine and heater. I sat in silence.

"Side effects include fatigue, trouble sleeping, hair loss, facial paralysis, incontinence, increased risk of heart attack ..."

The TV had been turned on. Good. Confirmation that no one had been shot. Or at least, the one who had done the shooting felt like watching mindless television. I wish I had caught the name of the drug whose side effects were being enunciated to make sure I never took it. Tough luck. I could hardly call up Susan and Cindy and ask if they had TiVoed the commercial.

Five annoying commercials later, the main feature came on: a reality TV show entitled *Who Wants to be a Trophy Wife?* Contestants vied to become the arm candy of a rich old guy more interested in cup size than IQ. It didn't seem to be the type of program Susan or Cindy would like, but then, what do I know? In this episode, contestants each spent a rather generous allowance to improve their appearance. No surprise that every contestant went for semi-permanent cosmetic improvement, from Botoxing frown lines to cheek enhancements. "Cheek" as in wanting to look good in a thong. Eew.

I was just as happy that I didn't have to actually see the show; listening was bad enough, particularly when one contestent showed off her new dress and proclaimed in a New Jersey accent that "gold lamé is so [bleep]-ass classy!" I was beginning to root for Madison over Kimberly – doubtless spelled "Kymberleigh" – when whoever had stormed out returned. Susan and Cindy traded apologies; bygones were bygones. The TV was shut off and they retired to bed. That was my cue, and I did, too.

The next morning I rose early to greet a cold, foggy day. Early being five. I could hear the foghorns moaning in San Francisco Bay at regular intervals, like a prehistoric dinosaur calling for his girlfriend. I picked up a grande coffee from a place that didn't do sprinkles, a dark chocolate croissant and a newspaper before heading out for my next eavesdropping session. I brought a hoodie to stay warm and a mindless celebrity magazine so I could keep up on who was shacking up with whom, who was practicing serial polygamy, who was planning a mega-bucks wedding and who was doing all of the aforementioned activities.

I had been encamped in the car for over an hour before I heard the first sounds of life: a door closing, a big sigh, a fast sprinkle of water – no wonder she was sighing, it sounded like a painfully slow attempt at making coffee – and then the unmistakable flush of a low flow toilet. Followed by a second and then a third flush since "low flow" usually equates to "no go."

The squeal of a water faucet being turned on – she couldn't have really washed her hands thoroughly – and then the whooshing sound of a shower penetrated my headphones. "Imagine there's no countries. It isn't hard to do. Nothing to kill or die for. And no religion too. Imagine all the people living life in peace. Ooo-ooo-ooo."

Like so many things in life, the Hawaiian language version was so much better.

"So why was the plant in the bathroom?" Stacey asked when I talked to her later that morning. I was trying to suppress the mental images that went with the sound effects, especially the post-breakfast bathroom break. One of them had way too much fiber in her diet. Eew.

"It's a tropical plant. Maybe they thought it would do better in a humid environment. I just hope it's temporary. As it was, all I got was the bullfrog singing, more bickering and swearing from both of them."

"Swearing? Are they on the outs?"

"Uh, I should have been clearer." I remembered the sound of metal being dragged over the floor, then a long tapering scream, followed by swearing interspersed with "I cannot *believe* it! It's not fair! I hate myself."

"Cindy weighed herself and wasn't pleased with the results. She swore. There were words I'd never heard before," I said.

"Totally understandable."

"Susan was in the midst of butchering 'Imagine' when she started cussing. I don't know why. Maybe she cut her legs shaving."

"I really don't need to hear any more," Stacey said.

"Me, neither, but I have to go back this evening. George warned me that the batteries on these things don't last long, so I need to take advantage of what little time I have."

"Tragic."

"Butchering 'Imagine' or the battery life of bu…er…'nursery checking devices'?"

"Both."

"Want to take my place?"

"No thanks. But I have info for you about Janet Rhoden."

"Do tell."

"Remember meeting my sorority sister, Amber?"

"I think so. Wasn't she at your Derby Day party last year? Short, curly red hair?"

"That's the one. She works in finance for a medium-sized company in Santa Clara. I know from her LinkedIn profile that she is a Vice President of BAFPA, the Bay Area Financial Professionals Association, and has connections to a lot of companies. I called her and asked if she knew anyone from Idgenstar, Janet's old company, who might be willing to talk about the embezzlement. Turns out, she knows the Idgenstar controller, so Amber gave her a call."

"And?"

"The current controller was hired after Janet and the others were asked to leave. But based on what she has heard since working there and read in the documents, she told Amber, off the record of course, that she thinks Janet was guilty of being stupid, nothing more. Of course, that's just her opinion."

"Thanks, Stace. Appreciate the info, although it would have been more helpful to discover that Janet was a serial embezzler with a penchant for violence."

"Sorry, hon, but I don't want her to be guilty. If she were convicted, who would take care of her children and Raja?"

"NOT VERY MANY PEOPLE at work, today," I said as I joined Shafiq, Holly, Anwar and Wendell in the Carson conference room. "Are the employees resigning en masse?"

"Who knows?" Holly responded. "Channukah starts tonight, so some employees may already be on vacation. Or at the mall. Carson gives their employees a full day off for holiday shopping."

"Or looking for new jobs," Wendell said. "Two of the systems guys I've been working aren't waiting around to get axed. One got a job offer and has already resigned. The other is going through his third round of interviews."

"I'd do the same thing in their situation," I said. "It's just so stupidly shortsighted of Zuckers. You would think they'd be concerned about key person dependencies."

"I dunno. Since Zuckers is absorbing the data and eliminating the systems, everyone in IT is pretty much expendable," Shafiq countered.

"I'm not talking about just the IT people. What about the sales people who have great relationships with retailers, or lawyers who know where the bodies are buried?"

"Bodies? Did you discover another dead body?" Maria had just entered the room.

"We've been over this ground," Shafiq said, ignoring Maria. "Like Laura said, this is just a brand name for Zuckers to add to their stable. And before we crawl all over Zuckers for their treatment of Carson employees, let's remember it's Steve Carson and pals who sold out the company and are now sitting fat and happy with their millions. Carson employees should be blaming Steve Carson for their situation."

I couldn't disagree, so we settled into work.

My plans to return to the stakeout that evening were delayed when Laura called an end-of-day staff meeting to review progress. I shared a large spreadsheet that identified the outstanding issues we had, who on the GD team was responsible for getting the information and who in Carson could provide the data. We spent nearly two hours going through each painful line, discussing the status of every item. The once full candy bowl was reduced to holding a half-dozen Carson Coconut Delight bars: chocolate-covered coconut cookies. Blech.

Shafiq complained about the mega problems he was having in eliciting information about the procurement system. The Carson IT guys had realized that Zuckers had no interest in using Carson's home-grown system. They clammed up and wouldn't give Shafiq the time of day. Shafiq's solution was to start digging through the software himself. And he wanted my help.

Oh good, digging through someone else's code was as exciting as checking Gorgon for ticks. I suggested a reasonable alternative would be to waterboard the IT guys. Or force them to eat Zuckers mass market, industrially-produced milk chocolate. The horror. "We'll get the information we need in no time."

Laura told Shafiq that I had plenty on my plate so he'd have to deal with things on his own. In celebration, I reached for a chocolate infusion and against my better judgement took a bite of a Coconut Delight. Mammoth mistake. The sensation on my tongue made me think of cat hair – tropical cat hair.

By the time we finished (after eight) I'd consumed my daily caloric allowance in chocolate so I skipped dinner and went straight to the stakeout. I couldn't afford to put on weight before Keoni came. I didn't want any teasing, even in fun, about love handles.

After fifteen minutes of driving around the neighborhood, I found a parking space I could just fit into. If nobody happened to notice I was about five feet closer to a fire hydrant than the statutes allowed and nobody in the building I parked in front of had a larger-than-compact car they needed to back out, I was home free. I was parked about five blocks away from Susan's and Cindy's apartment.

I set up the unit, clapped on my earphones and tuned in. Not unexpectedly at that distance, the reception was poor. But I didn't want to leave the car. I was parked in a sketchy area on the edge of Tenderloin, which meant if I left, I couldn't be sure the tires would be here when I returned. Or the rest of the car.

From what I could hear, the plant was back in the living room. Maybe they just gave it a bathroom break overnight. I was in time to catch the start-up of a searching-for-a-house show. I listened in as a young couple toured homes close to downtown Boston. The wife complained about the lack of an open floor plan, granite countertops and updated bathrooms. Oh, and a spa tub was an absolutely must-have. She wanted all that on a budget of $300,000. Good luck, sister. Cindy's and Susan's exchanges were confined to who was going to get up during the commercials and get the evening snack. At least they weren't screeching at each other.

I was just about to hear whether the couple was opting for house one, two or three when there was a tap on my car window. I jumped a foot. Okay, maybe just an inch or two. But in my excitement, I hit the horn, and the unexpected blast caused me to jump another inch. Sigh.

The source of the tapping was a policewoman peering in the passenger door window.

"Are you all right in there?" she asked when I rolled down the window.

"Yes, I'm fine."

"I noticed you've been sitting here for awhile and I just wanted to make sure everything was okay."

Did I imagine it, or was her initial concern for me changing to suspicion of what I was up to. Just what I needed, police attention. "Really, I'm fine. I, uh, had a fight with my friend and I, uh, just needed to go someplace and think." There, that sounded reasonable. "And listen to music," I added to explain the headphones.

"A coffee house would be safer."

"It's quieter here," I said. "And coffee keeps me awake."

"Then I suggest you either discover decaf or keep your doors locked." She glanced at the too-close fire hydrant, but didn't say anything. She turned away and shook her head as if she thought I was slightly deranged.

Oh please! This is a city where weirdness reigns. Just last week on Mission Street I saw a man walking his pug dog. Both were wearing leather jackets and pink tutus. And this cop thought a woman sitting in a car at night with headphones on was weird? She must be new to San Francisco.

I slapped my headphones back on. They were now watching a *Law and Order* rerun about insurance fraud and murder – I'd seen it multiple times. Would the on-screen drama with police and lawyers trigger a discussion of Laguna's murder and how Susan and or Cindy had foiled the police? No such luck. They did speculate about the murderer on TV, but they were so wrong about who did it. It was always the evil corporate type, c'mon.

When again I heard tapping on the passenger side window, I barely twitched. This time a panhandler stared in. I intensely disliked the aggressiveness of the beggars – the "residentially challenged" – in San Francisco, and normally gave them nothing but a cold shoulder. This time I made the mistake of looking into his eyes, "the window to the soul" according to an old proverb. I reached into my purse and pulled out a ten-dollar bill. I rolled the window down just far enough to slip the money into his grime-encrusted fingers. He gave me a brief smile, revealing the loss of several teeth, nodded at me, and moved on. The vagaries of life give some people more than adequate food, housing, love and the blessings of prosperity, while others lie in the street knowing not whether tomorrow will be better, if it comes at all. I was one of the lucky ones.

Back to listening. McCoy was questioning an expert witness about swoop and squat – an insurance fraud technique, not a bathroom break method – and then the unit died. Total silence.

Now what?

TWENTY-FOUR

"I have a 'carpe diem' mug and, truthfully, at six in the morning the words do not make me want to seize the day. They make me want to slap a dead poet."

– Joanne Sherman

I REGARDED MY LITTLE RED CHARIOT in dismay. The side windows were smashed and the front tires were slashed. I had been singled out; the other cars parked on the street in front of my apartment building appeared undisturbed. Still in disbelief, I walked to the side of my car and looked in. Other than the glass on the front seats and floor mats, there didn't appear to be any other damage. The upholstery was in one piece – even if worn – and the radio/CD player was still intact. My poor little car. My eyes teared in pure frustration. Wait, my Hawaiian music CDs! I had a brief moment of panic and feared the loss of my older, difficult to replace recordings, such as the Kalima Brothers ("1000 Pounds of Melody"). I pulled open the passenger door and spotted my CDs discarded on the floor by a vandal who, it appeared, didn't like my taste in music. Only a rap CD that I'd always hated – a gift from Ariadne – was missing. Who knew the lawless in San Francisco preferred headbanger music?

Yet again I had to call Laura and tell her I'd be late for work.

"Please don't tell me you've now found the dead body of your landlady, or you've been arrested, or any story involving the police, FBI, CIA or the Mafia."

The Mafia? Did Laura think I was involved with organized crime?

"Just a flat tire," I said. Hey, it was true.

"Fine. I'll see you when you get here."

After dealing with the indifferent police, the barely responsive insurance company and the "won't be ready until after the New Year because we're hung over from all the holiday cheer" repair shop, I felt entitled to treat myself to a gingerbread spice latte at Elixir of Life. I also felt entitled to an almond croissant and a half dozen *macarons* (French for "just apply this straight to your hips"), but, thinking of Keoni's arrival, I eschewed the goodies that I'd really rather be chewing.

Shaun was on duty at Elixir and lit up when he saw me. We'd barely said hello when I received the second major shock of the morning.

"Say hey to Stacey for me and tell her I'm psyched about our date."

"Huh?"

"I said," he began.

"Date?" My best friend has a new man in her life and you spring it on me before caffeine and sprinkles?

"Yeah. Did she call it something else?"

"Uh, no. Fact is I haven't talked to Stacey in awhile. Been busy at work." Almost my last free evening had been the stakeout, nearly a week ago. Since then, I'd been staying late evey day and even worked through the weekend. Except for a couple phone calls, one from Mother and one from Huw, my family, friends and investigation had occupied the dim recesses of my memory.

Shaun handed me my drink. I must have appeared dubious as I peered at the chocolate sprinkles.

"There's white chocolate in the latte," he explained. "The sprinkles bring out the sweetness of the gingerbread."

"Okaaaay." I took a sip and he was right. I didn't really taste the chocolate, just an enhanced gingerbread effect. "So, you and Stacey?"

"Uh-huh. We're gonna check out this jazz club after the holidays. Stacey ..."

"Shaun." The woman behind the counter nodded at Shaun and then the empty cups stacked on the counter and the waiting customers.

"Haveagoodday," he mumbled and turned back to his work.

First my car, now Stacey dating Shaun. At this rate, a 6.5 magnitude earthquake couldn't jolt me. Provided I remembered to stand in a doorway jam. It was time to have a chat with my best friend.

"What's this about – oof – you and Shaun?" I asked Stacey. I had called her while driving to Carson in a rented Hyundai with blown shocks where I felt every bump. My insurance covered a midsized car, but nothing was available, so I was offered a full-sized option: a Chevy Impala. While it might carry the surfboard a bit easier, I knew I'd have a harder time finding parking on the street near my apartment. Scratch that. I'd have to park in Sausalito. I opted for the Hyundai instead.

"And 'hello' to you, too," answered Stacey.

"Okay, hello. Now, what's this I hear from Shaun about you two dating?"

"'Date' is a bit strong. We're going to listen to jazz. I was in there this past weekend and he asked, so I said yes."

"When were you planning on telling me and anyway, what about Jake?"

"Mr. 'it's all about me'? We had a fight last week. He wanted to use some of my corporate contacts to boost his business. He said he didn't want to take advantage of me, and he'd be happy to pay me based on how the contacts worked out. Bad enough having everyone at work think I'll introduce them to the sports figure or celebrity chef of their dreams, now guys I am dating want the same privilege? I'm so mad I could just strangle him."

"I'll be happy to run him over with my car and make it look like an accident. Better yet, I'll use this rental. It'll be another body I can discover."

"I was angry enough with Jake that when Shaun asked me if I'd like to go with him to listen to jazz I thought, why not? He won't be thinking about lattes, cappuccinos, espressos or frappés when he's with me. And he isn't a football fan so I won't have to listen to him gush about Darrell. I said I'd love to go. For heaven's sake, it's not like he asked me to go to a tattoo parlor with him."

I had to hang up then, not because of anything she'd said, but because I had turned off the highway onto the badly-in-need-of-repair streets in Marin and I required two hands to keep the annoying car on the road. Did I mention the car tended to drift to the left, into oncoming traffic? And rattled at every bump? Had snakes in the back seat and mating gerbils under the hood? Okay, I made that last one up.

"Who did it?" Maria asked after I explained why arriving late was becoming a habit.

"I can think of several possibilities."

"So, like, what?"

I started to tick them off. "First, there's been crime in the area. More than usual," I added, seeing Maria's raised eyebrows. "Several muggings and two apartment building break-ins in our block this month, according to my landlady. It does seem odd, though, that this would be connected, especially since mine was the only car hit. Unless the vandals are focused on Honda CRXs in particular." Or hated the military. I didn't tell Maria that my beloved Honda sported a bright red bumper sticker that read "Semper Fi: Support our Troops" given to me by Magda after I joined her for a pro-military demonstration last summer. I'm not one for advertising causes on my car, but I couldn't not put the sticker on with Magda hanging over my shoulder and telling me where to put it.

"Secondly, it could be someone from Carson; maybe that guy who lives near me."

"I remember him from lunch; he was weird."

"Right. Although I would expect something more pointed, like pouring artisanal chocolate all over my upholstery and garnishing it with candied violets."

"Organically grown," Maria said, picking up on the levity.

"Natch."

"Maybe we can do some investigating here and find proof that he did it."

"Third," I continued, ignoring the snooping opportunity, "it could be someone connected to Lime-O."

"Like who?"

"No idea. I don't know that anyone is on to what I'm doing, or knows the car I drive."

"But someone does know where you live; you told Cindy that Laguna was a neighbor."

I nodded in agreement.

"Does this mean you'll be hiring a body guard soon?"

"I'd don't think so. Maybe I should feel more scared, but right now I'm just angry. I love that little car and I'm Tee-owed about the smashed the windows."

"Don't you mean Pee-Owed?"

"Tee-owed, ticked off. My parents were strict about swearing and crude language."

"Yeah, I've noticed your 'gosh darns.' Have you made any more progress on your investigation? Can I help?"

"Uh, actually, you could. You don't have to. I mean, only if you have time."

"Give me the jeeptions."

"Huh?"

"The GPS directions. What you want me to do and where you want me to go."

"There is another protest this Sunday, and since I can't go, it would be great if you could check out a few things for me." I told Maria about my encounter with Justin and Caitlin and my failure to get any useful information out of either one of them. "I want to know about Justin's relationship with Laguna before she died. Were they still an item? Were they arguing about her leaving? And is he even the type that could kill? But," I said, thinking of Justin's attempt to intimidate Magda, "he could be dangerous, so feel free to say no."

"Puh-lease. I've done dangerous. Dated a guy once who was a mixed martial arts fighter."

"Do I want to ask why?"

"Brother of sorority sister. Did it as a favor. One date was enough. He had tattoos over his entire chest and half his back. I like well-thought out tattoos, not indiscriminate masses. I wasn't even sure he could spell half the words on his left arm."

"Doesn't sound dangerous."

"He was lecherous and aggressive; one step below rapist. I had to kick him in his tattoo-free zone. No second date, but I didn't have to call the police, either. I think I can handle this guy Justin."

"Great, thanks."

"And while I'm at it, I'll check out Justin's new girlfriend. Maybe she's a green hornet."

"A comic book character?"

Maria shook her head, looking mildly disdainful. "Jealous. And her sting can kill."

TWENTY-FIVE

"Empty?! You took all the cookies!"
"They were crying to get out of the jar …
Cookies get claustrophobia too, you know!"
– Charles M. Schulz

On Friday I left straight from work to meet Huw. He had called earlier in the week to invite me to dinner before he headed off on Christmas break. I agreed to meet at a restaurant in Berkeley and I was intrigued when he mentioned which one. Frascati was on most Top Ten in the Bay Area lists, and was known for its locavorism. Berkeley had held a food festival and a near riot had ensued when it was discovered that one of the Frascati chefs used pork from Sacramento instead of the Bay Area. (Barbecue the heretic!)

Huw was waiting in front of the restaurant for me when I pulled up in the ghastly Hyundai and as soon as we were seated, I told him the sad story of my CRX. Before he could ask, I told him I didn't know if it was related to my investigation, or was totally random.

"I think that …" Huw was interrupted by the arrival of our waitress.

"A gracious good evening. My name is Kayla and I'll be the culinary advisor for your repast. May I get you drinks or appetizers to entertain your palate?"

No wonder the prices were thirty percent higher than anyplace else I'd eaten: elocution lessons for the staff. I guess it was an improvement on, "Hiya, whatcha gonna eat? Awesome!"

Huw picked out a bottle of Washington State white that had a mere four sentences of description in the wine menu and an order of chutney-marinated shrimp on curried rice with kava-marinated coconut for us to share. I wasn't entirely sure that wasn't one ingredient too many, but I was willing to try anything once. Except oysters or *'opihi*, a slimy shellfish Hawaiians considered a delicacy. Eew.

"Now, where were we?" Huw said as the waitress – er, culinary advisor – flounced off. Not that I had a sense for these things but she seemed to linger over Huw, unfolding the menu for him (leaving me to fend for myself, risking a severe paper cut), adding a few extraneous "sirs," and extolling the texture of their mâche – was that a come-on? – with no obvious evidence interest by Huw who, I happened to know, was an arugula man. So there.

"You were about to tell me you were concerned for my safety and I should give up trying to help Magda," I said, after Ms. Salad Porn left to bring us the wine.

"Not a bit of it."

"Really? Don't you care about my safety?"

"Of course I do, but we've had this conversation. You're going to do whatever you want, despite what others say, right?"

"Pretty much."

"Okay then. What I started to say was that the Hyundai you're driving does nothing for your image. Since I'm leaving tomorrow morning, do you want to borrow my car while I'm gone?"

"Really?" The thought of driving Huw's sporty red Acura was tempting. But what if the attacker struck again? Even more importantly, what did it say about our relationship if I were to accept his offer? Hmm. Didn't want to go there, yet. *Yet?*

"That's sweet of you, Huw, but I don't want anything to happen to it, and until I can find out whether this was a random or directed attack, I'd rather drive a less valuable car. The Hyundai is perfect for that."

"Are you on Facebook?"

I nodded, surprised at the non-sequiter.

"I'd like you to friend me. I'll be worrying about you over Christmas, and it will be nice to be able to check up on you without bugging you, if you get what I mean."

After my eavesdropping experience, I'd never hear the word "bug" in quite the same way again. In word association games for the next year, I'd be answering "toilet," or worse, "bathroom scale."

"Sure," I said, and gave him the info he needed to friend me.

The remainder of the evening was almost perfect. The seafood was delish, the wine gave me just a hint of a buzz and Huw and I discussed everything under the sun. After a second glass of wine, I managed to ignore Darla, or Kaycee, or whatshername, who was attempting to seduce Huw.

When Huw said he had a Christmas gift for me, I was not caught unawares. I wasn't entirely oblivious to his changing feelings toward me and I figured this get-together might involve an exchange of presents. I came prepared with a nice book on the fundamentals of surfing, including history and culture of the sport, humorous surfing stories and exercises to develop better balance and to build up the muscles needed for paddling. I hoped it struck the right tone as a personal gift without sending a romantic message.

Huw sang from a different hymnal.

He handed me a small box elegantly wrapped in silver paper.

Uh-oh. Jewelry. Normally, I'm a ripper, tearing off the wrapping to get to the present inside. As it didn't seem appropriate to attack what might be a romantic gift, I carefully unwrapped the tiny package, and slowly opened the felt covered box it revealed.

Nestled on a satin bed was a tiny silver chain with a silver pendant bearing the form of a famous statue of Aphrodite.

"It's gorgeous," I said. "Thank you, Huw."

Huw cleared his throat. Was he blushing?

"I'm glad you like it, but I almost didn't get it for you. I don't want you to read too much into the fact that it's Aphrodite."

"Because she is the goddess of beauty, or because she is the goddess of love? Or," I added, "because she is associated with ritual prostitution?"

"See, this is the problem giving a gift like this to a classicist's daughter. Let's just say I thought it was pretty and would look nice on you. I did notice that, when not in surfing gear, you wear small pendants. Case in point," he said, nodding to the blue glass dolphin currently hanging from a black silk cord around my neck.

"It's perfect," I said.

Huw seemed pleased with his gift and took the opportunity to lean over and kiss me. I didn't encourage him, but I didn't resist, either. And when he said he'd like to take me out for New Year's Eve, I was pleased.

I GROGGILY RAISED MY HEAD from the pillow and eyed my ringing cell phone. I'd ignored it the first time it went off, letting voice mail take it. The second time I opened one eye and gave it a murderous stare. The third time I reached over, fumbled around the nightstand and turned the clock radio around so I could read the time: 7:08. Who could be calling me at such an ungodly hour on a Saturday morning? I picked up my phone and checked. Ariadne! I was immediately awake. Something bad must have happened.

"Ariadne. What's the matter? Are you okay? Are Mom and Dad all right? How is Gorgon?"

"I'm good. Mom and Dad are good. Gorgon is devouring a Latin grammar book, literally. We're all fine."

"Then why are you calling me so by-our-lady early?" I said, my anxiety turning to anger. "And why are you up before noon? Didn't you have a big party last night."

"I did, but I couldn't sleep in this morning. I, or rather, *we* may be in a bit of trouble."

"Trouble?" My mind churned as it tried to identify a plausible reason we could both be in hot water. I couldn't think of anything questionable I'd done in the past couple weeks that involved Ariadne, but then, all my neurons weren't firing and wouldn't be until I got a large dose of caffeine cavorting through my corpuscles.

"You know that tin of Christmas cookies with the special Santas for my party?"

"Uh-huh."

"I couldn't find it last night. There were only two tins left and neither was the right one," she said. "I think Mom mixed them up. She said she'd delivered a tin to Virgil and sent the rest of them to the church."

I groaned and fell back on my pillow.

Mother had called last Sunday evening to remind me that Ariadne would be home from school on Thursday and I was expected for dinner and cookie-making. Mother's Christmas baking traditionally began right after Thanksgiving. Most of her output – the part that wasn't cordoned for the Professor Jones's Blowout Christmas Party – went to the Second Avenue Methodist Church Baked Goods Sale. For years, Ariadne and I had been drafted into sugar cookie duty. Mother would make up the dough, quadrupling the recipe, and the rest was up to us. My telling her that slavery had been illegal since 1865 earned me nothing more than the annual reminder of Ephesians 2:10: "For we are God's workmanship, created in Christ Jesus to do good works, which God prepared in advance for us to do." Reminding her that she prepared the dough, not God, never worked.

Grandma Swenson could complete a marathon in the time it took us to roll, cut, bake and decorate the dozens of Santas, reindeer, camels, trees, bells, stars of David (in the interests of ecumenicalism) and well, you get the idea. We drew the line at Festivus, Kwanzaa or Winter Solstice cookies on the grounds that if we were too ecumenical, we wouldn't finish making our "winter holiday cookies" until well past Easter.

By the time I arrived for cookie duty (working late, yet again) Araidne had done the rolling, cutting and baking, and the cookies were laid out for frosting.

"I assume Mom hasn't seen these," I said as I picked up a Santa Claus that had been modified to show an "anatomically correct" Claus-man.

Ariadne giggled. "Nope. She told me she'd done enough baking and I could manage on my own, so I decided to have a little fun. I'll put them in the tin I'm taking to a party tomorrow night."

"Just to be careful not to mix these up with the church cookies."

"No problem," said Ariadne. "Mother has labeled the cookie cans: five for the church, one for Virgil and Ashley, one for Christmas Day and one for my party."

"Must be some party."

"Yup. A combination Christmas and Halloween party. We'll watch *The Nightmare Before Christmas* and eat bizarre food. Last year, someone brought headless gingerbread men and rum balls decorated like eyeballs. I'm going to dress as a zombie elf."

"Whatever. Let's get to it."

For the next two hours, we mixed up icing, colored it, frosted cookies, and added sprinkles and other decorations. Ariadne filled me in on her fall semester, including issues with her roommate and "Siamese twin boyfriend: joined at the lips. Way too much PDA, to say nothing of their nauseating terms of endearment for each other; she's Schnoogenhaufen and he's Booberry. Gag me."

White and pink went on the candy canes as I gave her a rundown of my murder investigation. "I'm stuck on what to do next. All I can think of is to keep attending the protests and hope someone spills something."

"How about seducing the caped crusader?"

"Justin?"

"Sure, what have you got to lose, besides your self-respect? And didn't that go out the window when you went to the junior prom with Cecil?"

I recalled the mistake of equating a seventeen-year-old's English accent, slightly crooked smile and shyness with being a nice guy. "I went with him out of kindness," I said. "Who knew he would morph into an overachieving octopus." I'd buried the memories of his sweaty hands all over me during the slow dances and every time we sat down. When we drove home, he purportedly ran out of gas. That's when I first learned the utility of self-defense gizmos. The silver studs on my evening bag made quite an impression when swung at a sweaty, leering face at high velocity. Hey, I did him a favor; the studs popped a few of his pimples.

"Dad did his best imitation of an Indy 500 driver when you called," Ariadne said.

"I'd just as soon forget about it if you don't mind. Or I might have to tell Mom and Dad the *real* story about how the grandfather clock was knocked over."

I continued with the white and the pink frostings, now slathering them on the bells.

"Well, what about it? What about seducing Justin?" Ariadne said as she took the chocolate and frosted reindeer.

"He gave me a big brush off when we first met, so I doubt seduction would work, if I were so inclined, which I'm not."

I fell silent, thinking about my stalled investigation. Meanwhile, Ariadne was off on another tack: what was Keoni up to, when had I last heard from him, and does his coming for Christmas mean he is going to pop the question.

"He said he had something to share, but I doubt it's a marriage proposal. We've only just started seeing each other again. Besides, there's still the geographic issue."

"How about Huw? No geographic issue there," Ariadne said with a sly look.

"He's a friend, nothing more."

"Uh-huh," Ariadne said in her most skeptical voice.

Bells done, I moved to the Santas. Ariadne had already done the chocolate backpack and boots. The pink suit and white beard were my jobs. I'd done a half dozen when I picked up one of the 'manly' Santas. I hesitated and then passed it to Ariadne.

"Your Santas, you frost them."

"Fine," she said, and gathered up her special Santas.

Mother chose that moment to call me away from the kitchen for assistance in hanging the Christmas tree lights. She needed someone taller than her five foot three stature and she didn't want to wake my father who had gone to bed early. When I returned to the kitchen the frosting was done and Ariadne was filling the cans.

"What are we going to do?" she said, dragging me back into a too-early Saturday morning discussion.

I couldn't help it, I started to giggle. "Can you see one of the church volunteers coming across your Santas? What a moral dilemma. Can one reject a cookie given in the name of the Lord? Or maybe no one notices and it ends up in a tin purchased by an eighty-five year old woman who is so shocked that she has a heart attack. There's a new option for murderers: death by cookie porn." The giggles intensified.

Ariadne laughed, too. "Can you imagine the pastor speaking to Mom, trying to guide her down the right path?"

"Next sermon: 'Are Sweets Instruments of the Devil?'"

The giggles intensified as we traded "what ifs." Eventually, the laughter subsided and Ariadne voiced serious concerns about the possible fall out. "C'mon sis, I need some ideas. Mom's gonna kill me if she finds out."

I didn't much care about Ariadne getting into trouble. Truth be told, I'd like to see her take a bit of flack as back payment for all the things she'd gotten away with over the years. However, I didn't want Mom to be totally embarrassed at church. "You might try going to church today and helping with the cookie sorting. You may get lucky and be able to pull the offensive Santas before anyone else sees them."

Ariadne groaned. "Spend a whole day of my vacation with the church ladies? I'd rather kill myself."

"Go ahead, but do it some place public. I don't want to be the one to discover the body. 'Sides, if you really did mix up the tins, Mom may do the deed for you so you won't have to worry about how to commit ritual *seppuku* with a cookie cutter." And with that, I hung up on my sister and turned back to my pillow.

But I couldn't get back to sleep. My mind was churning like a ten-foot shore break: not something anybody could get past without getting worked, big-time. Huw clearly had me in his sights. Keoni had "big news" to share – which might or might not be about his CD – and would be here tomorrow. I wasn't sure what I wanted out of either of them. Well, one thing I might want, but only from one of them. I could handle dating two men but I wasn't going to sleep with two of them. Course, at present, I wasn't sleeping with either of them. And both were pretty attractive. Really attractive.

The only hot, hairy animal in my bed these days was my bunny Fred. He'd been with me since age twelve and had survived being put through the washer with my sheets once by mistake – though his whiskers were forever frizzed – and Ariadne's hanging him from my canopy bed one year as a Halloween prank. Fred had overcome the trauma but I never let Ariadne near him again.

My phone rang. Why were people calling me so darn early in the morning? It was Virgil.

"Hi buffalo butt," I said.

"I need to talk to you," he replied in a no-nonsense voice.

"What's up?"

"I know you and Ariadne made the sugar cookies for Mom, and I need to find out if I need to yell at both of you, or just Ariadne."

Understanding and the giggles hit me at the same time. "Ariadne. I was the good child."

"Hanging is too good for her."

Fred would agree with him. "Your best revenge might be to say nothing, and let her sweat it out," I said when I caught my breath. "She called me in a panic, worried her 'Santa studs' were in the tins that went to the church. She's trying to decide now whether to give up her morning to go over there and help sort the cookies, in hopes she can retrieve the bad Santas. Make that 'really bad Santas.'" Again I was hit with the giggles.

I could hear Virgil snorting back a laugh. "I had to explain to Rebecca that there had been an accident while baking Santa Claus. I removed all the Santas, and told her she could have new ones when we went to Grammy's house, and Auntie Ariadne will make them just for her."

"What about calling Ari to tell her you have the Santas?"

"I will, about seven this evening. In the meantime, she can sweat."

TWENTY-SIX

"Only those who will risk going too far can
possibly find out how far they can go."
– T.S. Eliot

I SPENT MOST OF THE DAY preparing for Keoni's arrival. Dust bunnies were rounded up, books stacked in neat piles, sheets changed, refrigerator stocked and I even draped my breakfast table with a pretty red cloth upon which I placed two brass candlesticks with red candles and a Christmas nutcracker. That was the fun part. It took two hours of scrubbing, three broken nails and three different types of cleaners to turn my bathroom into a place my mother would use to wash her hands. It still looked dingy, but I was confident it was clean; only a super bug could survive all the chemicals I used.

My reward was to be able to attend my high school friends get-together that night with a clear conscience. In fact, I felt positively virtuous. I wouldn't need to clean again for another four months, maybe six.

Jennifer was hosting the event at her one-bedroom apartment in an older, low-rise building located on one of the streets in Palo Alto that were named after poets and writers: Cowper, in her case. The quiet streetscape of old, no-more-than-two-storey stucco buildings with established plantings seemed to have escaped the late nineties McMansion plague in which people tore down small, funky houses to enact Windsor Castle replicas (complete with guards in funny costumes) on much less land.

I'd barely gotten in the door of Jennifer's second storey apartment when "Emma Jones! Howyerdoingirl? Lookin' good!" and other greetings rang out. The apartment was already crowded – Jennifer, Meghann, Megan, Charlotte, Amanda, Tram and me – and more friends were expected.

The main topics of conversation were boyfriends and weddings. Only a few years ago we'd been discussing graduate school acceptances and office size, but the intent was the same: comparing lives. How fast am I moving up the ladder and am I doing better than the next woman? Although I pretended to be above it all, I was equally guilty of playing the comparison game.

Invariably, I had to answer the Keoni questions: yes, we're in touch and he's actually visiting for Christmas; no, we're not exclusive; yes, I'm dating other men from time to time.

Part way through the evening, Meghann pulled me aside, literally, and we closeted ourselves in Jennifer's bedroom for privacy. A bedroom, I should note, that was not nearly as clean and picked up as mine. Okay, mine as of noon, when I finished my last act of compulsive cleanliness in tossing twenty-eight back issues of *Surfer*, from when I still took the print edition.

"I wanted to get back to you about your Lime-O question," Meghann said. "I've talked to a few contacts. You were right about Reimer giving them a chunk of money. Lime-O plans to launch a major expansion in January by announcing chapters in more cities. Susan's got publicity gigs set up along the east coast with prominent journalists and bloggers."

"Rumor or fact?"

"Fact. A friend of a friend is in PR and has helped to organize the tour. She says Susan is going first class as in pricey hotels, limos, etc. And there's more. Susan is co-hosting these events with environmental groups in DC, New York and Boston. So much for Lime-O's being a pure peace organization."

I pondered Meghann's revelations. "So Susan has her hands on a lot of money and is joining forces with other groups. Interesting, but I don't have a clue as to how it relates to Laguna's murder."

"Nor do I. If I worked for Lime-O, I'd be thrilled. All this money means funded chapters, a higher profile organization, the opportunity to reach more people with the peace message and from a personal standpoint, a more significant role in a large and growing organization. What's not to like?"

I sensed something in Meghann's voice. "How do your friends at Peace Now feel?"

"Angry. Honestly, part of it is just jealousy because we're all competing for the same money. The other part is resentment that after criticizing Peace Now and other groups for working with environmental and anti-hunger groups, Susan's now doing the same thing."

"Not to mention going first class? Who says you can't be green and glam? Or should that be peaceful and posh?"

"There's that, too," Meghann admitted.

I was deep in thought when we emerged from the bedroom, but not so deep as to miss the squealing as a crowd – three more friends had arrived – pressed around Jennifer. We soon discovered that she had announced her engagement and was brandishing "the rock." Jennifer proclaimed that those of us still single would be invited to be bridesmaids in her Gothic-themed wedding. She'd already selected our dresses: "amethyst purple with a princess-cut bodice covered in black lace, long sleeved with a lace flounce." What was a flounce, besides what I felt like doing at the thought of being a bridesmaid again? Did my closet lack for ugly, unwearable dresses that made me resemble a satin buffalo? When she added that the entire wedding party would do "Thriller" for the first dance and practices would be held on Saturday mornings starting in February, I could hardly contain my joy. I was not, I repeat, *not* going to spend Saturday mornings practicing dance steps. No way, not gonna happen.

SUNDAY MORNING AT LAST. With Keoni's arrival imminent, all thoughts of dance rehearsals, murder investigations and work travails disappeared. I was giddy with joy and practically dancing, though not to "Thriller," as I moved around the apartment doing meaningless tasks. I checked the flight schedule online four times to confirm his arrival time. Meanwhile, I phoned a half-dozen florists to find one that could do a ti leaf and plumeria *lei*.

I greeted Keoni with a fresh *lei* and a kiss. Okay, a lot of kisses. Keoni had brought me a *lei* as well, *tiare*, made by his Auntie Elikapeka, with *aloha*. To save money, Keoni had traveled overnight and come through Phoenix. Short on sleep, he still looked good in a black leather jacket, black slacks and a white linen shirt. Almost corporate. I was so used to seeing him in board shorts and *slippahs,* or an *aloha* shirt and slacks, that I'd forgotten how good he looked in mainlander clothing. Very nice, indeed.

We drove back into the city, playing 'Ike Pono's *Deep Waters* CD. I took Keoni straight to Elixir of Life both for the shot of caffeine that would keep Keoni going and to make good on my promise to Shaun to bring Keoni by so they could talk *niho mano* (shark teeth) tattoos. Shaun and Keoni were comparing tats in no time: inks, needles, which anatomical part hurt worse to get tattooed (eew) and so forth. Not that Keoni whipped off his shirt or anything but he did give the patrons a quick flash of his very nicely developed and tastfully tatted pectorals.

I'm okay with tattoos (or "tramp stamps" as Mother calls them) as long as they're small and tastefully done. Not that I'd ever get one. Magda had filled my head with descriptions of sagging tattoos on the wrinkly skin of old, retired sailors. Ugh. Now, if I had skin the color of a perfect salted caramel mocha – I speak as a veteran consumer at least 150 of them – like Keoni, I might consider getting one.

Keoni mentioned to Shaun that he had a cousin who grew coffee on the Big Island – not Kona, but the up-and-coming Ka'u district – who was interested in selling to selected coffee shops on the mainland. Shaun gave Keoni the name of his boss, who was the coffee buyer for Elixir, and put a near-record number of sprinkles on my Wakeup, Already (three shots espresso, skim milk, a shot of toffee syrup and toffee sprinkles on top) as a token of appreciation.

The surf report was lousy, "blown to heck," so when we finished our caffeine fix, Keoni and I opted for a hike of Mt. Tamalpais. Not as warm, and without the tropical foliage of hikes in Hawai'i, but on the other hand, the only pigs we had to dodge on the trail were drunken college students with Bud Lights in their fanny packs. We hiked from Muir Woods up a long trail through the trees until we had an incredible view of the ocean. Large rocks toasted in the sun made perfect perches from which to view the shimmering white caps in the dark aquamarine sea. Keoni's hand crept up the inside of my sleeve and he rubbed my arm softly before pulling me towards him.

We separated, rather breathlessly, only when an Australian couple clomped up the trail, pausing to take a number of pictures and for the woman to repeatedly express her phobia about ticks attaching themselves to various extremities and sucking her blood. I didn't quite understand her concern considering she came from a country that boasted it was home of the deadliest spiders in the world. The bottom of her pant legs were cinched so tightly I was concerned she'd succumb to lack of circulation in the extremities long before a tick could start sucking.

When the Australian couple moved on, after an exchange of "g'day" and "*aloha*," Keoni opened his backpack and pulled out fresh bread, cheese and a bottle of champagne. "I stocked up at the store next to Elixir when you were getting the car."

He didn't have glasses along, so we chugged from the bottle of champagne. After my second swig, I said, "So, what's the big news we are supposed to be drinking to? Now that you've dragged me all the way up the trail, seems like a good time to spill. Did I mention that your ride back might be contingent on letting me in on the big secret?"

Keoni grabbed the champagne bottle and tipped it in my direction. "*Mahalo nui loa* for a lovely day, even without surfing." He took a big swig and wiped his mouth on his sleeve. "The big news is that I hope to have many more wonderful days with you," he said, handing the bottle back to me. "I plan to spend much more time in San Francisco."

I just held the bottle, stunned. "Uh, if you're moving in with me, you do need to ask."

"Well, it's not quite like that. I know Fred would not agree to be permanently displaced to the couch."

"I don't understand."

Keoni gazed over the valley and watched a red tail hawk laze in circles, eyes peeled for today's rodent blue plate special. "I know that my interest in Hawaiian tribal rights has been upsetting to you."

"Look, I …"

"*E ʻoluʻolu ʻoe* – please, hear me out. *E* Emma, just because I feel the injustices done to my people does not mean I think that *haoles,* and especially you, are the enemy. But Hawaiians prize *hoʻoponopono*, making things right, very highly. I want to make things right, after so much wrong has been done."

The hawk hovered, then dove sharply. I didn't hear a cry of expiration, but I suspected there was one less mouse on the Mt. Tam "local and sustainable" menu.

Keoni took a deep breath. "I've decided to become a lawyer, like Uncle Kimo. And like Uncle Kimo, I will use my skills to serve the Hawaiian people. ʻ*Kulia i ka nuʻu*'. Strive for the summit. That was Queen Kapiʻolani's motto. She did so much for Hawaiʻi. Can I do less than she did?"

"Have you taken the LSATs yet? I have a friend in Mililani who tutors …"

"Too late." His broad smile set me back on my heels, or would have if I weren't already sitting cross-legged on a warm rock.

"*He aha? He aha? I keia manawa*!" I said, lapsing into impatient Hawaiian.

"Champagne?" he said, handing me the bottle.

"Keoni, I mean this in the nicest possible way. If you don't tell me right this second what you have to tell me, I'm going to smash the bottle over your head and then it will be four corpses in six months. Spill. Your secret, not the champagne," I said, taking another large swig.

"Okay, here goes. I have applied for, and been accepted to the Hastings School of Law here in San Francisco, starting with the January semester. *Maikaʻi nō*?"

When we got back to my apartment, we were both tired and sweaty from the hike. I told Keoni how thrilled I was that he'd be in San Francisco. In truth, I was shocked and didn't know quite what I thought. It was clear that Keoni chose to come to San Francisco in part because of me. But was *I* ready to reignite our relationship? And then what? Three years of law school and he'd go back to Hawaiʻi. Either we'd be married and I'd go, too, or we'd break up again.

I offered to let Keoni use the shower first while I put dinner together.

"My *makuahine* always told me 'ladies first,'" he said.

"Your mother is right, but in this case, I'd like to get dinner underway. I can stick the chicken in the oven and throw a salad together while you clean up." My voice trailed off as he pulled his shirt over his head.

He dropped it on the floor, gave me a wink and said, "Or, we could *mālama i ka ʻāina* – care for the land – by cleaning up together. Just to save water, you know."

Who knew water conservation could be such a wonderful, dreamy idea.

So Fred spent the night on the couch instead of Keoni, but he didn't seem to mind.

The next morning, Keoni got up with me and fixed fried rice Hawaiʻi style – where did he get the can of Spam? – eggs and coffee. "*Kuʻu ipo*, you need to take care of yourself and not rely on chocolate for energy." Keoni was a bit of a health nut, radiating mild disapproval from time to time at my eating habits.

I left Keoni with the dishes and headed out the door. He gave me a quick kiss and said we'd talk more that evening about his move to San Francisco. But he said it with a wink, as if talking was not first on his agenda.

TWENTY-SEVEN

"Back up my hard drive? How do I put it
in reverse?"
– Anonymous

"Good morning," I said, entering the Carson conference room where the GD team had gathered.

"Morning, yes; good, no," Wendell said, lifting his head from his discussion with Anwar.

"Why? What happened?"

"Logic bomb," Wendell replied.

I groaned and slid into a chair next to Shafiq, just as Laura strode in, appearing a bit frazzled.

"Right," she said. "Logic bomb. Discovered by Shafiq, fortunately," she added as she took a seat at the head of the table.

"Shafiq, you rock!" Maria said.

"How did you discover it?" I asked.

"I had a bad feeling about the Carson procurement system, so I've been auditing the system for several weeks. Late last night I noticed that there had been some changes to one of the scripts."

Since Zuckers was nuking Carson's systems – not planning on using them going forward – Carson employees had been told to perform no programming work whatsoever. Changing a script (a program or sequence of instructions) was in violation of those instructions, and grounds for suspicion. Companies more experienced than Zuckers in acquisitions (and less trusting) immediately change the security settings so no one at the acquired company could make mischief or mayhem in the systems.

Shafiq was still talking. "I went line by line through the script. Someone had inserted instructions to delete large stores of Carson's data based on a trigger date of December twenty-fifth, three days before we are due to transfer the data to Zuckers' systems."

"Merry Christmas and a Happy Deleted Data Year," Maria said.

"Indeed," Laura said. "I met with Grundy and team earlier this morning, and they will free up resources to help identify the saboteur. I know you all have your plates full with making our deadlines, but you also need to be vigilant for any signs that Carson employees are trying to sabotage the merger including refusing to provide information or access to information, or feeding us false information. If you encounter any resistence that could jeopardize us meeting our objectives, I want to know about it yesterday. Clear?"

We all nodded.

"Then get to it."

There was very little non-work conversation for the next several hours. I admit to not being entirely focused on work; I was occupied by the thought of Keoni living in San Francisco for the next few years. Clearly, Keoni saw me in his future. But his future was in Hawai'i. Was Hawai'i my future? What about Huw? Well, what about Huw? It's not like we were dating, really. Just the occasional kiss and checking out his pecs.

It was during one of my daydreaming sessions when Maria tapped me on the arm. "Got a few minutes? I thought you might like to hear about my encounter with Justin and Caitlin yesterday."

OMG. I'd totally forgotten about Maria attending the Lime-O protest in my stead. I glanced around the conference room, empty for the moment except for Anwar and his ubiquitous head phones. His head was moving like a dashboard bobble dog, fast enough that I suspected he was listening to one of the unintelligible rap artists he favored with names like H8U or What.A.Crock.

He wasn't going to overhear anything we said. "Sure, what did you find out?"

"Justin and Caitlin are sort of engaged."

"Sort of?"

"Caitlin says they are. Justin doesn't say much. But Caitlin's a barnagirl, so she'll probably get her way."

Barn and girl? She's an animal. A cow? She didn't look like a cow. A pig? No, not that either.

"Uh ..."

It was obvious to Maria that I didn't have a clue. "Listen," she said. "When I first got there, I walked over to chat with Justin. He was easy to find, although he wasn't the only one wearing a cape; there was a chihuahua wearing one and a guy dressed as a Lime Green Lantern. Anyway, Justin turned on the charm, and I gotta say, he's good at it. So we're having this great conversation and this girl comes up and grabs his arm. Justin drops the charm like last year's fashion. Caitlin introduces herself as Justin's fiancée, clearly warning me off. Justin clams up and Caitlin's all over him like a barnacle until he heads for the van."

"Barnagirl. Got it," I said. "So mostly, the protest was a waste of time."

"I didn't say that. I chatted up a guy I met at the protest. Tino. We had lunch at a cute restaurant down the street. A place called Ernesto's. They had a really awesome BLT: heirloom tomatoes, fried pancetta and mache, on ciabatta, with homemade mayo with just a touch of roasted garlic, and the sweet potato with sea salt French fries were ..."

"I'm happy for you. What I meant was, you didn't find out anything else about Justin."

"Well, no, but I found out Cindy has problems with paranoia and aggression."

"What?"

"Cindy's a long time user of marijuana and has developed paranoia issues. When she tries to back off the marijuana, she gets really aggressive. Physically aggressive, sometimes."

Where did she pick up this stuff?

Maria noticed skepticism writ large upon my face. She proceeded to explain that while she and Tino discussed what brought them to Lime-O, Tino had said that his politics had been influenced by his Aunt Cindy. Yes, that Cindy. Maria probed and Tino described Cindy as funny, smart and incredibly caring. But, he also revealed her problems brought on by smoking pot.

I wasn't sure where this new information left me. It certainly didn't close out any suspects. Cindy had never been high, so to speak, on my list, but an aggressive paranoid faced with someone quitting her beloved organization was a different kettle of weed. Caitlin's jealousy was a plausible motive. And Justin? He had my sympathy if he was spending time in the van to escape Caitlin.

Maria had no more to offer except that she and Tino were going out to dinner early in the New Year at a place that specialized in heirloom tomatoes since they both liked them.

Work and the murder continued to intrude on my "think about Keoni time," which was *he mea li'ili'i* (a little thing) next to what Zuckers' management had to contend with that afternoon; the Carson's home page on the Internet was corrupted. Pictures of high quality chocolates fading in and out and dreamy music playing had been replaced with a cartoon of a three-headed drooling dragon defecating into a vat of Carson chocolate. The flashing "it's why our new chocolate is so creamy and dreamy!" caption was a nice touch. I could have done without the background music, which sounded like a remix of "Carmina Burana" and the theme from *Jaws*.

Carson's e-commerce manager, ostensibly the source of the defacement, resigned to avoid being fired. The unconfirmed rumor was that in addition to trashing the home page, he'd broken into and locked the plant managers out of the industrial systems that controlled Carson's chocolate manufacturing. As the denouement to his "not go gentle into that good night" act, the perpetrator had contacted all the local media outlets before Carson's and Zuckers' executives were even aware they had a problem. Icing on the ganache, you might say.

TWENTY-EIGHT

"Someday he'll come along, The man I love
And he'll be big and strong, The man I love
And when he comes my way
I'll do my best to make him stay."
– "The Man I Love," Ira Gershwin

By the time I'd made my way home, dodging the mayhem of frenetic last-minute Christmas shoppers on the roads, I'd come to a mature decision. Contrary to my nature, I was going to enjoy the next few days as they came and not over-analyze my relationship with Keoni, or anything else.

At least, that was my intent. I didn't count on seeing Susan walking along my street as I was searching for a parking space. What was she doing here? Had she been trying to visit me, or just passing by? I was still thinking about her when going through the mail on the front hall table where letters, flyers, a dozen packages and a slew of catalogs were scattered. Two DVDs I'd ordered had arrived. Good. They'd promised delivery by Christmas, but I hadn't totally trusted them. Hmm, Laguna's mail hadn't been stopped yet; several bills and a half-dozen catalogs (including *Victoria's Secret*) were addressed to her as well as another returned package, marked "addressee unknown." I puzzled over the address on the package. Who did Laguna know, or think she knew, in Berkeley Labs and what had she mailed there? Surely she wasn't sending mail bombs. I turned the package over and began picking at the tape on the back.

"Emma!" Keoni called from above. My heart beat a bit faster. Not just because it was Keoni, but because I'd almost done something really stupid, like open a package to check for a bomb. Worse, open someone else's package to check for a bomb. I should clearly only be opening my own incendiary devices. What was I thinking?

"Emma!" Keoni was on the landing, peering down at me. "I saw you coming in the door. I've poured you a glass of coconut milk and put out a *pupu* platter. What is taking you so long? *'Āwīwī!*"

"I'm coming." I put down the package and hurried upstairs to receive Keoni's welcome home hug followed by his putting a cold glass of white wine – 'coconut milk' – in my hand.

I thrust the wine back. "We need to talk. There may be a mail bomb in the front hall."

Keoni raised his eyebrows: a look I'd seem many times when he didn't quite believe me.

"Really." I gave him a quick explanation of why I thought it might be a bomb. Before calling the bomb squad and risking *ho'ohilahila* (embarrassment), Keoni wanted to take a look at the package.

We were making our way down the stairs when Justin entered the building. Dressed in his avenging dark angel outfit – black shirt, jeans and cape – he strode purposefully across the front hall toward the mail table. Snatching up the returned package, he whirled around to see us watching him.

"What's your problem?" he sneered.

"That package," I responded.

Justin shoved the package behind his back. "None of your business."

I felt Keoni stiffen beside me. "Is it a bomb?" I asked.

Justin started. "Don't be stupid."

"What else would Laguna or you have sent to Berkeley Labs?"

"It's really none of your business."

"Not my business, but maybe police business. Perhaps I should call the bomb squad."

Justin starred at me, his hostility radiating like a rolling thunderhead; I waited for the discharge of electricity.

Keoni took a deep breath, moved closer to me and spoke. "If you open the package now, you could prove it's not a bomb."

Justin glanced from Keoni to me and back again. His lip uncurled, only slightly. "Sure, pretty boy. No problem."

Justin talked rapidly as he tore off the brown wrapper.

"A friend of Laguna's brother works there. As a favor, Laguna got the guy a deal on an iPhone. She's got a college friend at Apple and they get employee discounts. I guess she just didn't address it correctly."

I watched his movements intently, barely registering what he said.

"See," he said, holding up an iPhone box.

"Open it," I said.

Justin paused for a moment, then ripped off the end of the box.

I leaned back into Keoni.

Fumbling with the box, he reached in, grabbed something, carefully pulled it out and held it up for us to see. Even with his big fist wrapped around it, I could tell it was an iPhone.

"I've done what you wanted. Now, get the hell out of my way," he said.

Keoni and I retreated upstairs to my apartment, but not before Keoni pulled himself up to his full six foot three height. I could feel his *mana* flow around me, protecting us both.

"We will speak of this later," Keoni said after returning the white wine to my hand and leading me into the living room. "So *pua nani* (beautiful flower), how was your day?"

"Not good. I don't want to talk about it, now. How about yours? What did you do?"

"I found a few potential places to live. I would like you to visit them with me."

Keoni pulled out a map and showed me the locations of some of the apartments. We were discussing them when there was a knock at the door. Magda.

"I wanted to say goodbye before leaving for the holidays and give you a Christmas present," said Magda as she handed me a red tin with snowflakes on the lid.

I had a sudden vision of Ariadne's cookies and stifled the impulse to laugh.

"This is so sweet. Thank you, Magda."

"And," she said, leaning forward so I could hear her whisper, "I want to meet your Hawaiian honey."

"Why don't you come in," I said in my best polite voice, winking at her. "I'd like you to meet my friend, Keoni."

Keoni emerged from the living room and I made introductions. After the usual pleasantries, I asked Magda if she'd like to join us in a glass of wine.

"I'll sit with you for a few moments," she said, moving into the living room and selecting a chair. "But nothing to drink, thanks. I don't drink at all when I have to drive and I'm leaving for San Diego within the hour. But you should open your present. It's my Moroccan spiced almonds: perfect with any type of alcohol."

Magda peppered Keoni with questions about his life in Hawai'i, which he politely answered. When he let slip he was moving to San Francisco, Magda's eyebrows lifted dramatically, but all she said was, "That's so nice. I know Emma will enjoy having you nearer." Surprised that she didn't press Keoni for details, I soon realized Magda had something else on her mind.

"I'm a bit worried about Emma," she said, her eyes fixed on Keoni. As I stared at her in puzzlement, she continued. "The movers were here today and packed up all of Laguna's things. I checked the apartment and it's clean. Of her stuff, that is. Of course it will need painting and a few repairs before the next tenant moves in."

"Sooooo?" I said. But Magda didn't turn her head; her eyes stayed on Keoni.

"The point is that Laguna's lease terminates as of today. That means her boyfriend has no right to be here. And I can't see any reason he would be, except he was very funny about setting a date to close up Laguna's apartment."

I thought for sure that Keoni would mention the incident in the front hallway, but he didn't. He just nodded at Magda to continue.

"He was in no hurry to terminate the lease. It was her parents who called me, demanding that everything be out of there this month. They didn't want to pay for another month's rental."

"Who can blame them?" I said.

Magda glanced at me. "Justin wanted to do the move on the last day of the month. I explained that I had to be here to accept the keys and today was the last day I could do that."

"I still don't see …"

"What has he been doing hanging around here for the last three plus weeks?" Magda said, as if she hadn't heard me. "She didn't have that much stuff to pack up. Was he homeless and using her place? I checked out her apartment one day to ensure he hadn't started growing marijuana or running a meth lab. I don't know what he's doing, but I don't trust him. And I don't trust Emma to keep out of his way."

"Just a minute," I said, or tried to say. Keoni cut in over my protest.

"I will protect her while I am here," he said, locking eyes with Magda and totally ignoring me.

"Good," said Magda, nodding her head in agreement. "I know enough about you from what Emma has said to know that I can count on you. Now I have to be off."

Keoni and I followed her to the door and I gave her a hug goodbye and wished her a Merry Christmas.

As the door closed behind her, Keoni put his hands on my shoulders and turned me towards him. "We'll discuss apartments later," he said grimly. "It's time for you to tell me everything about this investigation of yours."

TWENTY-NINE

"Ah, but in case I stand one little chance
Here comes the jackpot question in advance:
What are you doing New Year's
New Year's Eve?"
– "What Are You Doing New Year's Eve," Frank Loesser

I EYED THE SMALL BAG in the corner of my bedroom as I slipped on my dress. Keoni's things. "I'll be back in two weeks," he said when he left yesterday, "so I'll just leave them here."

The bag represented the looming change in my life. I needed Stacey back ASAP so we could talk. I had tried chatting with her on the telephone after Christmas, but she was always on her way out with her mom or just sitting down to a meal. We needed face-to-face girl time over a stiff drink. Double espresso or a Mai Tai. Or both.

I put on my earrings and rummaged in my closet for evening shoes. They were buried under shopping bags of stuff I'd received for Christmas: sweaters, bubble bath, slippers, biking gloves with plastic roaches stuffed in them (Virgil's contribution), and a fleece top from San Diego State (Ariadne). I made it a rule not to use any presents until I'd written thank-you notes for them. It was one way of forcing myself to do the right thing – or should I say "write" thing – lest the spirit of Grandmother Swenson (not that she's dead, yet) haunt me for my bad manners. Meanwhile, the presents sat in my closet.

I slipped on my heels and studied the image in the mirror, shifting poses to observe various angles. A cute blond in a long, black scooped-neck dress stared back at me. Turning sideways, I could see the dress just hugged my rear end and the low cut back with draping fabric showed off a smooth-skinned back. No doubt about it, I looked good. The shoes – black, with a rhinestone strap – and my rhinestone drop earrings were the only touches of bling. My evening bag was black with black sequins over lace. Festive, but not garish, and big enough to hold lipstick, a couple of credit cards and a keychain with small mace spray – enough to fend off an extremely large rodent after my cheese and cracker.

I looked really well put together, but my bedroom was a mess. In addition to Keoni's bag in the corner, I had a stack of books from Christmas on the floor next to my bed. My rule about writing thank-yous didn't apply to books. It was too much like not eating chocolate when it was sitting right in front of you. (I'd already devoured three of my new bars, er, books.)

Keoni's present was on display in my living room. The *lei o mano* was an ancient Hawaiian weapon in the form of a short paddle ringed with shark's teeth. Keoni had made it himself: carving the *koa* wood and stringing more than a dozen shark's teeth. The handle came to a point, so the *lei o mano* also could be used as a dagger, allowing the wielder to stab his opponent and then rake him with the shark's teeth on other end. It was beautifully bellicose. I wondered if in the future his lawyer self would insist on putting product instructions and liability waivers with the weapons he manufactured.

I grabbed my sequined clutch bag, made sure I had my keys in hand and headed out. When Huw invited me out for New Year's Eve he'd promised a place where I could dress up, a late supper and a view of the fireworks. I didn't want him wasting time searching for a parking space so I told him I'd wait outside my building. The phone rang just as I started down the stairs.

"Huw?"

"Yup. I'm a block away."

"Your timing is perfect. I'm just leaving … what the heck is he doing here?" I said as I espied Justin pawing through the mail on the table. "Just a minute," I said to Huw.

Hearing me, Justin gave a start and grabbed a parcel off the table.

"What are you up to?" I said angrily. "And why do you still have a key to the apartment building?"

"None of your business," he said defiantly.

"Magda asked me to keep an eye on things," I responded with equal hostility. "And you have absolutely no business being here. Get out right now or I'll call the police."

Justin let loose with a number of profanities, directed at me, ending with: "and don't threaten me with the cops." He took several steps toward the bottom of the stairs.

I stopped. Descending the stairs, that is. I should have stopped my mouth from running rampant.

"Why not? Afraid they might ask why you're reading Laguna's mail and packages? That's another returned iPhone, isn't it?" I said, recognizing the size and shape of the parcel in his hand. "What's going on? You're acting awfully susviciously." Great, now I was channeling Maria.

Speaking without thinking has all too often put me in hot water. In my favorite mysteries, the heroines get away with it: said heroine confronts the murderer, tells him/her that all is discovered and, after a desperate scene where the heroine's life is in danger for a page and a half, escapes with a bit of derring-do. But this wasn't a nice cozy mystery. I hadn't yet read the ending to make sure the heroine survived. Challenging Justin while outfitted in a long dress with nothing more than a sequined evening bag for defense was a definite "derring-don't."

Justin started toward the stairs spewing more profanities and I back pedaled. No small feat in high heels.

His face glowered. "You and that old cow have no right to keep me from Laguna's place."

I had the sense enough to be scared now, but not enough sense to scream. Instead, I turned and ran upstairs. Dang, why was this dress so tight? Hadn't I learned from Pad's murder not to challenge a perp when wearing tight clothes? I'd just unlocked the door when Justin slammed me up against the door jam. He grabbed me, turned me around, put his hand on my throat, pushed me into the apartment and threw me against the wall. I banged against the hall table, slowing my momentum enough to prevent my skull from fracturing as it hit the wall, but guaranteeing additional bruises on my backside. He kicked the door closed while I gasped for breath and threw his body against mine, pinning me.

Panicked now, I struggled to free myself, wriggling frantically and trying to get my arms up to scratch at his face, his eyes.

"Stop it, bitch, or I'll end it now," he growled, tightening his grip on my neck.

Managing for a moment to hold back the waves of panic, I stopped struggling.

"What are you planning on telling the cops?" he asked. "What do you think you know?"

The intercom buzzed. Huw. Damn. He didn't have a key.

"Ggg," I croaked. Justin eased the pressure on my throat and I tried again. "Nothing," I managed to get out as the buzzer sounded again.

Justin didn't seem to hear it. He narrowed his eyes. I tried to look innocent, at least as innocent as possible when one's neck is in a vise.

"Women always lie," he stated firmly.

"Honest, nothing," I protested.

"Always lie," he repeated. His eyes looked right through me, as if he were seeing something else. "Say something, but don't mean it. Like Laguna. Yeah, lovely little Laguna. Said she wanted to help me when she thought the hacking was just a prank. But then she changed her mind."

I said nothing. His stranglehold was loosening ever so slightly as he talked. The buzzer, yet again. I hoped it wouldn't break Justin's concentration. If he just continued to talk and ease his grip, maybe I could break free.

"She betrayed me," he said, his eyes still glazed. "I coulda made a bundle selling the info I got. Found a Chinese buyer for it. But she got all patriotic on me," he sneered. "Erased what I'd collected and told me just cuz she hated war didn't mean she hated her country. And now she's dead. Bitch!"

He added a few more words about Laguna that I'd never heard before and I knew it was only moments before he realized he'd have to kill me, too. It was now or never. I swung my hands up swiftly to poke him in the eyes with my thumbs. Being right handed, I was relatively successful with that hand. My left arm was slower and got the bridge of his nose as he snapped his head back. Wrenching free from his grip, I slammed again into the hall table and fell to the floor. I scrabbled up and ran further into my apartment, hoping I could beat him into my bedroom and lock the door. My purse and cell phone – the only phone I had – had been lost in the scuffle by the front door. The walls were nearly soundproof, but I could open the bedroom window and call for help. Hopefully, someone would hear and not mistake me for an enthusiastic New Year's Eve reveler. It was my only shot.

I didn't even come close to making it. Two steps along the hallway and I fell off my three-inch, rhinestone t-strap heels and twisted my ankle. Justin grabbed me from behind and threw me into the living room. I slammed into my coffee table, which was no more than a large brass tray on a wooden stand. No doubt about it, I had too much furniture in this place, but then, when I'd furnished my apartment, I hadn't exactly thought about evasive maneuvers in avoidance of a murderer. I ended up in a heap as the coffee table and all its accoutrements went crashing to the floor. Even the sound of a five-foot gong wasn't enough to rouse my neighbors. So, I did what every helpless female does when she's about to be ravaged, or worse. I screamed.

I've never thought of myself as a screamer. We didn't yell in my family. A frown, shake of the head, or a stern warning from a parent was enough to bring us in line. If not, there was always the shoulder pinch or the very occasional swat on the rear end. Consequently, I'd never wound up a really good old-fashioned, ear-piercing, glass-breaking, call-the-cops scream before. Until that moment, I wasn't sure I knew how. I can now faithfully report that a woman's ability to produce a heart-pounding scream is innate. The tonal quality and volume surprised even me.

It was useless. Justin paused only momentarily, and lunged at me. I struggled to my knees and began picking up the debris on the floor and throwing it at him: my Hawaiian dictionary – another reason to buy in hardcover instead of going digital – a brass candlestick with a stub of a red candle, the rest of the red candle, two mystery books from the library (also hardcovers, fortunately) that made a satisfying thump as they connected, a pillow with a Hawaiian quilt cover (useless) and an eight-inch sandalwood carving of a surfboard. Then I grabbed the *lei o mano.* I felt a surprising burst of power ripple through my hand, to my arm, and to my shoulder. Using the couch as leverage, I rose to my feet. Suddenly, I felt brave. My scream changed. No longer a shriek, it was a *ka'a* – a war cry – as I held the *lei o mano* over my head. Justin took a half step back, sensing the change. I stepped towards him and in a swift movement with power I didn't know I had, brought the *lei o mano* down. He turned away, but I caught him on the shoulder and the shark's teeth ripped through his shirt, opening up a large jagged wound. He fell to the ground, screaming. Skirting his body, I ran for the door, flung it open and tore into the corridor.

Huw, who after unsuccessfully buzzing all the apartments had managed to break through the front door – his 'Hulk Hogan moment,' he called it – and was halfway up the stairs when I emerged.

"*Make!*" I yelled, "Death," for someone who had already taken life and had tried to take mine.

THIRTY

"They can conquer who believe they can."

– Virgil

"Explain in English, please," Magda said.

"Yeah, no multi-syllabic words or techno-abbreviations," Stacey added.

Stacey, Magda, Maria and I were gathered in Magda's apartment enjoying drinks, dinner and a debrief. When I had called Magda at her son's home in San Diego to explain that Justin had been arrested for killing Laguna and had been the only land-based victim of a shark attack that the San Francisco General Hospital had ever seen, she had expressed great relief. "I'm off the hook, or should I say no longer in the hoosegow on my way to the noose, and you're okay. What better way to start the New Year? When I get back I'll fix dinner for you and whoever else helped and you can tell me the whole story then." While anxious to get back to playing Worlds of Warcraft with her teenage grandson, she nonetheless spent several minutes thanking me, with great effusiveness, for establishing her innocence. When she hung up, I was left wondering what else I didn't know about Magda beside her fetish for WoW.

Now, two weeks later, it was just us girls (George begged off with a prior engagement) discussing the *post mortem*, much of which was dedicated to how I avoided *my mortem*. Maria and I were also celebrating finishing the Zuckers assignment with no more surprises, except for a visit from Grundy to personally and enthusiastically thank each and every member of the GD team for their valuable contributions. That was a shocker, actually.

We were well into drinks (G and Ts with Junipero, my favorite) and appetizers (crab dip for Edsel and us, kibble for Chesty) when I began to explain "the case" in between snarfing crab dip with a sesame cracker or two. Or five.

"I don't know the sequence of events, whether Justin liked Laguna and only realized the hacking opportunity later, or whether he got close to Laguna so he could make her an unwitting hack enabler. In any event, Justin used the fact that Lime-O parked their van next to these military or quasi-military facilities for hours at a time; perfect cover when you are trying sniff out and hack wireless networks. Uh, 'sniff' means 'check the airwaves,' and not for a rap music station."

"But don't all wireless networks have security," Stacey said. "Like when I power up at Elixir of Life I see those little lock symbols next to the names of available networks."

"Right. To log in, your computer has to be recognized by the network and you may need a key to prove you are who you say you are," Maria said.

"Key?" Magda asked.

"A password, or a code of some sort. So to connect to a network – unless it is wide open, like leaving your front door open for just anybody to walk through – you have to guess or otherwise discover the password. That's not so easy," Maria added.

"So cut to the chase, sister," Stacey said. "How was Justin able to hack into networks? And why? To support the Lime-O cause?"

I took another sip of my drink and tried to organize my thoughts. "The 'why' first. And this is just my theory based on things Justin said. Initially, he told Laguna his hacking was a prank. Maybe he claimed he wanted to disrupt the network, perhaps through a denial of service by overloading the network so the users had trouble getting their work done."

"No denial of service here," said Magda as she tossed some kibble to an anxious-looking Chesty. He quickly gobbled up the two pieces she had tossed and gave her another pleading look followed by an insistent 'woof.' I swear he sucked in his cheeks to appear thinner.

"Whatever he told her, money was the real motive. Justin thought he could sell information he obtained over the networks. And before you get concerned about the vulnerability of the Department of Defense network, I should explain that most companies working for the DoD have their own network for company business, like email, human resources and finance. My guess is that Justin hacked into the company networks and found what he thought was valuable information. Maybe classified documents that shouldn't have been there, or maybe just sensitive information that could be useful to the right kind of buyer."

Maria nodded her head. "I've heard of network breaches at DoD contractors by foreign entities and sophisticated teams. As the saying goes, 'there are only two kinds of companies: those who have been hacked, and those who are going to be hacked.'"

"I don't know if Justin did find anything significant or even whether he was part of a group. The police don't seem inclined to tell me their findings."

"You still haven't explained how Justin got access," Stacey said. "Did he get a job with the company? Bribe someone for an ID and password?"

"Neither. He used a rather clever ploy, which I should have figured out earlier. Twice when I went to pick up my mail I spotted packages being returned to Laguna. The second time, I paid more attention because it was from Berkeley Labs. Keoni and I found Justin with the box, and he showed us it was just a misaddressed iPhone that Laguna had purchased for someone. It sounded fishy, but I was too busy with Keoni and Christmas to figure it out."

"Oh, I see," Maria said. "Very clever."

"Emma, darlin', how about spellin' it for the rest of us?" Stacey said.

"Right, sorry. Justin was using iPhones to sniff out wireless networks. Cindy mentioned that Justin liked to do research and recommend targets for Lime-O protests. What he was really doing was identifying targets he wanted to hack, like Berkeley Labs. He'd buy an iPhone and rig it to detect wireless activity; all it takes is a few adjustments. He'd then send it to a fictitious employee at the targeted company. In most organizations, a package without a recognized name on it will sit in the mail room for awhile as they do a check to see if the name is misspelled, or the person is someone coming on board soon, or whatever. Meanwhile, the phone would listen and collect information about the network. Justin may have had the phone rigged to call out regularly, like once a day, and transfer the information it had collected so it didn't have to store all the data. Anyway, by the time the mailroom determines the package is undeliverable and sends it back, the iPhone has collected and sent a ton of data."

"What about the battery life?" Maria said. "I can't imagine he'd get more than a day's worth of data."

"True. Apple hasn't gone after the espionage market yet. Justin must have rigged up some external batteries." I explained about how Keoni and I had confronted Justin and he'd fumbled with the box while pulling out the iPhone. "He may have disconnected the batteries or covered them with his hand when he showed us the phone."

I paused for breath and to take a sip of my drink. Magda appeared thoughtful and even Stacey don't-bother-me-with-tech-stuff seemed interested.

"But getting the data is only the first step," I continued. "Justin had to analyze it to discover what he needed to get into the network. I expect he used a number of programs that are available over the Internet, plus he may have developed his own algorithm. He'd have to get the data analyzed by the time Lime-O had their protest so he would have what he needed to break in. Then he'd sit in his truck with his computer, pretending to tweet, and ..."

"Tweet?" Magda said.

"Provide live commentary on the protest that others can read on the Internet."

"Okay."

"So he produces a couple tweets but what he is really doing is hacking into the network."

"I still don't see the motive for killing Laguna. I mean, presumably he'd be pis … er, perturbed that Laguna was quitting Lime-O, but he could have continued," Stacey said.

"When Justin was choking me," I said, rubbing my neck self-consciously, "he revealed that Laguna had discovered that he planned to sell information he'd obtained to the Chinese. In Laguna's mind, being anti-war was not the same thing as betraying her country. She erased Justin's data and threatened to expose him, so Justin killed her."

We sat silently for a moment. Finally Maria spoke up. "Did Justin smash your car windows, too?"

I shook my head. "I don't know." I had just got the car back two days ago, looking good as, well, as good as it could being a seventeen-year old car with 150,000 miles. "It could have been random violence, or as we talked about earlier, even that guy from Carson, angry about losing his job."

Magda reached over and put her hand on my arm. "I'm just so glad you're all right, dear. I never wanted you to risk your life to keep me out of jail."

"Hmph," Stacey said. "The cops blew that one, trying to pin it on Magda."

"I'm not so sure they were trying to, as you say, pin it on me," Magda said thoughtfully, tossing another piece of kibble to Chesty and providing a touch of crab dip to Edsel who gently licked it off her finger. "My lawyer said that the case against me was weak and that the prosecution seemed indifferent about going forward with it. He wondered if I were just a convenient person to bring in to show they were doing something. After all, their evidence against me consisted of fights with Laguna, my overt patriotism and my infamous temper," she added with a smile. "Not to mention, my ferocious, rabid dog that I sicced on her," she said, scratching Chesty's ears. He thumped his tail and licked her hand.

"Well, the police should be happy that you found their killer for them. Right?" Maria said, turning to me.

"Not exactly," I said. "They gave me a hard time about confronting Justin. Said I should have called them with my suspicions and 'let law enforcement professionals do their jobs.'"

"Not your style, is it?" Stacey said.

I wanted to protest, but knew she was right.

"I'm grateful for what you did, Emma," Magda said.

"Speaking of gratitude, I had a visit from Susan and Cindy yesterday," I said as I lifted my glass and took a sip. Junipero was as smooth as melting ice cream only better for you. Juniper berries count as a fruit, right?

"And?" Stacey prodded.

"And they wanted to thank me for catching Laguna's killer. It was sweet, really. They may have figured out that I was joining their protests as a pretext for snooping, because they wanted to assure me that I and my friends," I winked at Maria and Stacey, "were always welcome at Lime-O events."

"That is nice," Stacey agreed.

"Oh yes, they gave me a house plant, too."

Stacey started giggling and I couldn't help it, I began cracking up too. "D'ya think," she gasped, pausing between giggles, "they knew?"

Maria looked puzzled at the exchange. When I finally managed to stop laughing, I explained.

"No, I don't think they knew about the bug," I said. "I just think it was a sincere gesture."

"Well here's to you," Magda said, raising her glass. "Congratulations on solving another murder."

"And to Keoni for giving you such a useful gift," Stacey said as she clinked glasses with Magda."

"Don't forget your friend Huw, for trying to rescue you," Maria added. "And did you ever get your weapon back? I'd love to see it. From the way you described it, it sounds really cool. I wonder if I could get a miniature one, sort of a souvenir of our investigation."

Stacey smirked. "Just the thing to fend off big ol' flies."

"You can get small ones as pendants," I said. "I'll ask Keoni to bring one back from Hawai'i. My gift to you for your help. Anyone else want one?"

Magda and Stacy shook their heads.

"The cops returned mine a couple days ago. Five of the teeth were loose but Keoni said he would fix them. Mom thinks he should go into business making pocket-sized *lei o manos* and market them as the ultimate self-defense gizmos. And of course, she can't thank Keoni enough."

"So what's next?" asked Magda.

"You could try to solve Wave Hog's murder," Stacey said.

Maria frowned. "What's a 'Wave Hog'?"

"The body Emma found last summer at the beach. We met a surfer dude who knew him and has some ideas of where Emma might start."

"No way," I said. "No more investigations."

"Not even to find out the truth about Janet?" Maria said.

I shook my head.

"Well, that's too bad, cuz I just happen to know an eensy-weensy secret about how she's earning extra income."

"How? I mean, how did you find out and how is she getting more money?"

Maria paused and took a long sip of her drink. "Ah, refreshicious. So, Janet. At the protest last month while Tino was checking out Justin, Janet brought me a coffee. She wanted to know if I'd have lunch with her. I couldn't, of course, because Tino and I were going to lunch. But then she asked when I might be free to talk. So I told her I was free then, but then she said she wanted to sit down some place so she could take some notes. And then I said ..."

"Where is this going?" I interrupted.

"I was getting to that." Maria pulled out her phone and began fiddling with it as she spoke. "Janet got my phone number and called me last week. We had lunch together on Saturday, so that's how I know."

"Know what?"

"How she's earning extra money."

"Enquiring minds would love to know. Feel like sharing?"

"She's a writer. She wanted to take notes on 'my distinct style of speaking.'"

"Janet? What does she write?"

She handed me her cell phone, her browser open to amazon.com featuring *Torrid Tartan: A Scottish Highlands Romance* by Aurora Bryce. With Stacey looking over my shoulder, I scanned the description of Cassandra, a young woman who travels to Scotland where she falls deeply in love with Padraig, a modern day pirate with raven hair and emerald eyes. Windswept hills, heaving bosoms and manly chests were all featured on the cover. I wasn't sure why a guy would wear a kilt and no shirt in the far north of Scotland.

"You're telling me Janet Rhoden is this Aurora Bryce person?" I asked.

"I don't believe it. Janet writes romance novels?" Stacey said.

"Uh-huh," Maria said. "*Torrid Tartan*, *Loch Lover* and *Bonnie and the Prince*. Janet was impressed when she heard that Emma had solved Laguna's murder and she wants to write a novel about it, with lots of romance, of course. Her working title is *Avenging Angel.* She wants a personal interview with you, Emma."

Dumbfounded, I could only stare at her. Magda and Stacey were laughing. Throwing them what I thought was an icy-cold stare only increased their amusement. Edson folded his paws carefully, narrowed his eyes, and hissed. Good kitty.

"Well? What should I tell Janet?" Maria asked.

Stacey was laughing so hard there were tears in her eyes. "Yes, Emma," she said, "what *should* Maria tell Janet?"

"Over my … no, over the *next* dead body."

GLOSSARY

(All words are Hawaiian unless otherwise noted)

ʻae – yes
a hui hou – until we meet again
aloha – hello, goodbye, love, compassion
ʻaʻohe, aʻole – none; no; not.
ʻaumakua – ancestor god
auē, auwē – oh dear, alas
ʻawapuhi – wild ginger
ʻāwīwī – to hurry
carpe diem (Latin) – seize the day
e ʻoluʻolu ʻoe – please
haole – white person
honu – green sea turtle
hoʻoponopono – to correct, put to right
hopena – result, conclusion, ending
huhū – angry
kaʻa – war chant or war cry
kau-kau – (Hawaiian pidgin) food
kino make – dead body
lei – flower garland
lei o mano – a Hawaiian weapon of wood and shark teeth
lūʻau – 1. taro tops 2. Hawaiian feast
mahele – division, portion
maikaʻi nō – good, indeed
make – death

makuahine - mother
mālama – to care for
mana – spiritual or divine power
nani – beauty
nei – 1. here, as in "Hawai'i nei." 2. darling, as in "ei nei."
nui – big
'ohana – family
'ōkole – rear end
'opihi – limpet
'ōpū – stomach, belly
pehea 'oe – how are you?
piko – genitals
pono – right, correct
post mortem (Latin) – occurring or done after death
pua – flower
pua lilia – lily flower
pupu – hors d'oeuvre
qui vive (French) – on the alert; vigilant
slippah (Hawaiian pidgin) – sandal, flip-flop
tiare (Tahitian) – *Gardenia taitensis* flower
'uhane – soul
'ukelele – ukulele
welina – greeting of affection, much like *aloha*

Made in the USA
Charleston, SC
03 December 2012